THE STRANGER BOOKSHOP

JOANNA O'NEILL

WOODEN HILL PRESS

ALSO BY JOANNA O'NEILL

THE STRANGER BOOKSHOP

For Gillian

Published by Wooden Hill Press

Second Edition 2021

ISBN: 978-1-9163476-7-0

PROLOGUE

Last year

PERHAPS YOU MIGHT PUT IT DOWN TO THE THUNDER.

Until three o'clock it had been a regular August Wednesday, hardly baking but sunny enough for sleeveless tops and dark glasses, and trade had ambled along in its pottering midweek way. But as the afternoon wore on, clouds gathered greeny-grey and big, splashing drops of rain fell. The arches under the bridge began to fill up.

Rain had been forecast but people don't pay attention – not an umbrella or mac to be seen. Nothing to stop pedestrians from taking refuge in the National Theatre, of course, or the Hayward, but Paul had long ago noticed that most people choose open shelter over anything with doors. Feels more neutral, probably; less of a commitment.

Besides, under the bridge there's entertainment, so long

1

as you like books.

As the rain poured down and the thunder crackled and grumbled and rolled ever closer, the spaces between the tables filled up and people began to jostle, shoulder to shoulder, back to back, bare skin pressing against other, unfamiliar, bare skin; bags squashed, toes trodden on, things dropped. Some people are afraid of thunder too, and before Paul's eyes the atmosphere altered.

Where before everyone in the market had been interested in the books (well, nearly everyone – there are always a few kids in tow), now most had no intention of buying and some weren't even bothering to look, standing instead with their backs to the stacked paperbacks and staring out across the darkened river. The core of punters who represented actual business braced themselves against the buffeting, trying to hold on to their bit of ground, and the thunder jitters spread.

People get ratty then. Paul had seen it often enough. He had been part of the Southbank Book Market for twenty years – Paul Bell Books, specialising in twentieth-century children's fiction but stocking pretty much anything else as well. Spend two decades face to face with the public and you're bound to pick up some basic psychology. Even so, the two women surprised him.

Although on second thoughts, not so much the young one. She was short and dark and something about her face – her jaw, was it? – gave her a look of assertiveness that bordered on the pugnacious. But the older woman, softer and graceful, he was surprised she was involved.

The moment he saw her he caught it: her fragility, the

sense that she was in some way vulnerable.

Mike at the next table drew his attention to her, elbowing him and pointing to the two women with a grin, and Paul was astonished to see them each grasping the same book and tugging. Squabbling over who was to have it! He had never seen that before, and as he squeezed a path through the browsers he had already made up his mind which of them he would sell the book to.

But he was mistaken. As he got near, a thunderclap overhead, like twenty metal doors slamming in unison, made everyone jump, even Paul. Several people squeaked, and the woman he had his eyes on started and loosened her hands.

'No! Wait–'

But as Paul thrust his way between two huge teenagers he knew he was too late. Having relinquished her stake, his customer, the woman he instinctively wanted to win, had escaped into the open, almost running, and all he could do for her was be glad the rain had suddenly stopped. Abruptly the clouds were shredding and watery sunlight slipped through, shining on the wet pavement.

The thunderstorm was over; people relaxed and the arches began to empty.

'This, please.'

The woman was gone. Paul swung his gaze back and met the stare of the victor as she held out her spoils. He looked at the cover. It was an Edith Waterfield – the novel, not one of the children's books – a second edition and fairly battered; it seemed an unlikely cause for a struggle.

Nothing else he could do.

'Four pound fifty,' he said.

...

ANGELS

CHAPTER 1

Now

BRYONY OPENED THE DOOR, STEPPED OVER THE THRESHOLD and saw all the books, spines outward on the shelves, faces forward on the displays, stacked on the tables and stools and on the floor, and her first thought, as always, was: *Mine.*

And then, as always, she cocked her head, listened and sniffed, and her second thought was: *Is he here?*

But there was nothing: no sound, no scent, no suggestion she might have company, so she closed the door behind her and locked it.

She didn't flip the sign. The side showing in the street was printed with the words *If the shop is closed please ring, because I might be in.* People often did, and beneath the print Bryony had added a handwritten PS: *But please wait a few minutes because there are three flights of stairs, you know!*

Three flights of stairs and no lift. Bryony, and Cedric before her, had got away with it because the house was Listed and because in Bryony's case at least she was prepared to shuttle up and down bringing stock to any wheel-chaired or becrutched or just plain ancient customer marooned on the ground floor.

Now Bryony climbed up through the storeys – she never tired of that pun – grocery bags in both hands, pausing briefly on each floor to sniff as had become her habit. When she reached the flat she put the food away first, Gabriel watching her coolly from the doorway, then snipped off the ends of the chrysanthemum stems and put them in the blue enamel jug ready to take downstairs. Chrysanthemums were boring but they were robust, like the potted geraniums, and that made them good.

Flowers were one of Bryony's hooks. Other hooks were the open fireplaces in each room, with clocks on the mantel-pieces and pictures hung above (an engraving of the book-shop; Gwen John's orange and white cat; a portrait in oils of a young man); at least two places to sit down on every floor (although not necessarily comfortable places – a stick-back wooden chair or a camping stool takes up a lot less space than an armchair); and something interesting near all the stairs (an early hand-drawn map of the county, the forests drawn as tiny trees; a patchwork coverlet of zillions of floral hexagons; the grandfather clock, which was the only clock in the bookshop showing the right time).

The shop itself was a hook, too, of course, with its rooms and passageways and staircases. There was also the head of a marble angel that she had found in the basement stockroom and managed to heave upstairs to wedge in a corner near the entrance because it was too quirky and delightful not to show off. Even the desk at the front door was notable: a mighty Victorian edifice reminiscent of Marble Arch.

Bryony was proud, too, of the Reading Room, once a bedroom on the second floor, where were squeezed two small sofas, a couple of floor cushions, a rickety table bearing mugs and a kettle, and a mini-fridge for milk. No sink, of course, so she had to factor in periodic washing-up trips when the shop was busy.

She really needed to replace Flossy, who had moved to Gateshead to be nearer her grandchildren and the airport and the shops. To be nearer the rest of the world, in fact.

Ravensburn wasn't near anything except the Northumberland moors and sheep. Its roots were in wool but its survival now was thanks mostly to being in the middle of the moors where the ramblers' routes criss-crossed to use the bridge, making the village a natural stopping point for hikers; and, yes, also because it was ruggedly lovely in a brusque sort of way. No thatch or whitewash like Devon, but lots of cobbles and slate and stone, and a certain take-me-as-I-am attitude.

You either liked it or you didn't. Bryony did from the moment she arrived last autumn, and within a day had executed a neat 180-turn so that instead of putting in hand the sale of this bookshop and moving its contents south, she returned to Surrey to sell *that* bookshop and bring *its* contents north.

When she discovered the Waterfield connection it only

reinforced her decision. Actually it explained it, but that wasn't something to share with others.

Today was the twenty-first of June – six months since she had re-opened the shop on the mid-winter solstice – and personally she felt comfortably bedded in, although she knew some people thought it odd to have someone so young running things in place of Cedric. Then again, Cedric had been pretty eccentric by all accounts so she might strike them as refreshingly straightforward.

Ha!

Bryony chucked together a watercress sandwich, cramming in the stalks that tried to escape, and ate with the door open so that she would hear if anyone rang. It wasn't restful, and tea would be like this too because it was late opening this evening.

She *really* needed to replace Flossy. Perhaps a student, for the summer at least? Except that she couldn't offer accommodation and the village was so remote…

I really ought to be able to do something about this.

Hmm. Maybe. When she had time she'd give it a go.

BRYONY LEFT her plate in the sink, dropped off the chrysanthemum jug on the second floor, stepped around something she *almost* saw at the top of the stairs (she would have an accident one day, she swore) and took her mug of coffee down to the front desk.

She was pretty sure the bell hadn't rung, but someone was sitting on the kerb outside the shop, facing the street.

Bryony unlocked the door and flipped the sign (*Open, so please come in and explore*).

The man looked round. 'Ah.'

'I'm so sorry,' Bryony said. 'Did you ring? I didn't hear the bell.'

'No, don't worry, I thought I'd let you have your lunch undisturbed.'

He stood up and smacked the dust off the seat of his jeans, extended his hand to shake, and then retracted it swiftly leaving Bryony's in mid-air.

'Sorry! Dusty now. I timed that wrong!' He swept his palms down his thighs. 'Aaron Eliot,' he said with a light but distinct Northumberland accent.

'Bryony Bower.'

He was very easy, Bryony thought, very at home in his surroundings. She made a guess.

'You're a local.'

'I am. But I've been away six months. Came back last week. Hello, Gabriel,' he added, as Himself arrived at his feet, and he bent and rubbed the cat's broad black head.

'Exact opposite,' Bryony said. 'Not a local, only been here six months.'

She stuck her hand out again, looking him deliberately in the eye, and he hesitated then brushed off his right hand one more time before shaking.

'Well, I'm open now,' Bryony said, 'so please come in!'

He waved her before him, but when she had slipped in behind her desk she watched him head for the stairs, ducking the low beam with the easy judgement of familiarity.

She had placed him now. He was the husband of Grace

Eliot, who lived at the Forge at the foot of the hill, the other side of the river. They had two children, old enough to come to the bookshop by themselves, and Bryony had vague recollections of having heard that their father was off somewhere, taking a sabbatical.

She wondered where he had spent the six months. He was quite tanned and rather nicely muscled in a lean kind of way. Dishy actually, for an old guy. Gabriel clearly liked him; he had followed him up the stairs, which was unusual.

Out of the blue came the thought: I wonder if he'll notice anyone up there.

Why wonder that?

The ceiling creaked as he moved about on the first floor. Bryony based her cataloguing on the Dewey decimal system but shuffled the categories a bit; she liked to surprise browsers by putting bird watching next to philosophy, astronomy next to architecture, although you could argue that no one thing was totally unrelated to any other and she sometimes thought her shelving policy was a parlour game waiting to happen.

Judging by the creaking floorboards he was in the corner directly over her head where botany and chemistry flanked the cookery books (a supposedly random triad it was easy to link). Was he a scientist or a gardener? Or both? And why was she interested?

Bryony took a sip of coffee and reached for the book from the stack on her desk, which might double as a counter but was never going to stop being a desk. Anyway, she spent more time working at it than taking money, the typewriter more active than the cash register. It had come with the shop, like the clocks and the art and the angel's head, quite possibly because no removal van suspension would be up to carting it away. It appealed to her and she felt important and historic when sitting behind it.

Right now she was in the process of typing up Thursday's acquisitions, which were heaped in unstable piles around her, those catalogued on the left, those yet to be dealt with on the right.

They had come from a house clearance, a woman in her sixties (too young, very sad) and were mostly novels – classics and sagas and historicals – but there was a fair amount of non-fiction amongst them, including several on the history of architecture and landscape. Good condition too.

Bryony worked slowly through the pile, examining the condition of each book. An elderly couple came in, smiled shyly, and drifted around the ground floor, and the ceiling creaked again as Aaron Eliot moved about.

The lavender in the glass vase in the front window gave its warm honey scent to the sunshine, and the ponderous tick of the grandfather clock on the stairs wafted in and out of conscious hearing, measuring away the afternoon.

Bryony was being sidetracked by very appealing pen-and-ink drawings illustrating the development of roof shapes (double-hipped, mansard, half-hip-and-gablet – she hadn't known there was something called a gablet) when the couple came to the desk.

'Just these, please.'

They were buying Edith's Calpurnia books, and as Bryony rang them up she became aware that someone else had joined them and there was now a queue. She glanced up. Aaron Eliot was twisting his head slightly to read upside down and said, 'Ah, Calpurnia, the queen of queens. Did you know Edith Waterfield lived here?'

Bryony opened her mouth and then shut it quickly; he wasn't addressing her. The elderly man said, 'In Ravensburn? No, no, I didn't. We're buying these for our granddaughter.'

'Not just Ravensburn. Edith lived in this very house. Her father saw his patients through that arch.' Aaron nodded in the direction of the two steps down to the lower floor where Bryony kept Classics, Biography and Travel. 'Where now there are maps and guidebooks to the great outdoors we see about us, once were treatises on pathology and disorders of the blood and diagrams of our inner worlds.'

Blimey. The customers were looking bemused, as well they might. Bryony handed them the bag of books ('Oh, cotton, how lovely!') and watched them sidestep towards the door.

When they had gone Bryony looked up to find the same gentle smile and amused eyes turned on her. She cleared her throat and glanced down at the book Aaron Eliot had placed on the desk. Neither botany nor chemistry, it was a dusty, cloth-bound edition from 1967: *The Girl's Book of Cakes and Biscuits.*

'I find I need to bake,' he said.

CHAPTER 2

Now

'YOU WILL, WON'T YOU, ROS? IT'S SUCH A BIG HOUSE. SAY yes.'

Rosalind struggled a moment longer, but through the line she could almost hear Octavia holding her breath. She sighed. 'All right. I mean, yes, of course.'

'Ros, you're an angel. Thanks. Honestly, you won't know we're there.'

Rosalind put down the phone and stared at it. In one sense Octavia was correct: Monks' Walk was a big house. But Octavia was also quite wrong: there was simply no way Rosalind would not know she was there.

Every minute.

Her summer was falling away from her, like flour

through a sieve; one good shake and it would be gone, lost in the great bowl of familial responsibility.

She had already agreed that Kerry could bring the twins for the whole of July, and while she loved the children dearly she did not relish two chunky toddlers crashing about the house for weeks on end. Also the prospect of her daughter-in-law's frozen ready-meals weighed heavily. She would feel obliged to partake ('We can share the cooking,' Kerry had enthused) and knew from experience that encouraging her to try preparing meals from basic ingredients was hopeless.

And now Octavia and her children too, with or without her eldest *('It all depends on whether the radio job comes through')*, which meant rock music and thumping floorboards from the bedrooms (why did teenagers tread so heavily?) and rolling television news and studio debate downstairs.

I could get rid of the television.

But she enjoyed David Attenborough, and Michael Palin. And anyway, since Andrew was a foreign correspondent it was only natural that Octavia should be interested in current affairs.

Hong Kong he was in, at the moment. Skyscrapers and junks, Rosalind thought, although aware that her knowledge of geography and politics jostled for bottom place in her list of talents. No doubt Octavia would put her straight. Octavia absorbed everything Andrew said and did in a way that made it seem she was all but living his life with him.

It wasn't how Rosalind had been with Matthew. Perhaps Hong Kong was more engrossing than personal financial services. In fact it certainly was, but even so Rosalind had tried, for a while, at the start, before it became clear what her half of the contract required.

Theirs had been a strange marriage and not at all what she had expected. But Matthew had wooed her well, and how could she have known? The family had been excited – an advantageous match, which sounded so very Jane Austen. But once the ceremonies were over Matthew was revealed to be a good provider of material matters only.

Well. It was a big house, of course, Octavia was right, and the lawns and the tennis court and the paddock – which had never been grazed by a pony but was useful when her sons wanted to kick a ball around or practice heroic cricket catches – were wasted now that the boys had grown up and she was left here alone.

The school holidays were only six weeks. They wouldn't be here forever.

It will just feel like forever.

Rosalind pushed her chair back and stood up. Octavia's call had interrupted her, and she needed to get on. It had been raining most of the afternoon and the shrubs would be dripping so she put on her gardening shoes and waterproof.

Monk's Walk had a stable yard as well as a paddock, tucked away behind the high brick wall that sheltered the flowering shrubs and ornamental trees of the main garden. There were three stables with half-doors and sturdy iron rings set into the walls for tying horses to, but neither of her boys had expressed any interest in riding. Instead the hay racks were cobwebbed and the stables housed only junk: a rusting lawnmower, the type you push, half-empty paint cans, boxes of surplus tiles, a tent. In one stable an assortment of wooden planks and beams leaned against the wall, left there by the workmen who had occasionally come to do repairs – Matthew's talents had lain in manipulating figures, not tools.

I ought to clear these out.

She could hire a skip, let people take anything they wanted and have the rest carted away. She could sweep out the stables and whitewash the walls and rent them out with the paddock.

Rosalind imagined a couple of cheerful, chatty girls grooming placid ponies in the cobbled yard or cleaning saddles in the sun. But it wouldn't be that simple, she knew. There would be alarms and emergencies, the ponies would escape or get colic, and the trough in the paddock would freeze over when the girls were at school so it would be she who had to trudge out with buckets of water for the ponies to drink.

More responsibilities.

Where is Yoda?

This was the third time the Watsons' tortoise had gone missing. After the second escape Rosalind had shown Pauline the arrangement of pens and tunnels where Sukie spent her days, solitary for the last six months, and suggested something similar might be helpful for a tortoise with wanderlust, but here they were again – a phone call in the evening asking her to *do that thing*. You had to seek out a licensed breeder and pay quite a bit for a tortoise these days; you might think they would take more care.

And she would *do that thing* if necessary but she would try plain old looking first.

Sukie was out of sight, either in the hutch or one of the plastic tunnels. She often came out when Rosalind called, but she was probably asleep. At fourteen she was a very elderly rabbit.

Rosalind walked the borders, parting branches and peering into the hearts of shrubs. Yoda was unhelpfully well camouflaged. Do tortoises know their names? Yoda was a silly thing to call him anyway. Rosalind felt uncomfortable when animals were given names from films, pop groups or television shows; it seemed demeaning, as if the animal were simply a way of exhibiting the owner's wit. She was not in a strong position to object, though, her own parents having christened their children as they had.

There was no tortoise in the shrubs, nor in the shed, nor amongst the hedges around the tennis court, nor loafing in the shadows of the water butts.

Rosalind went indoors, sat at the table and unfastened the chain around her neck. She laid the slender gold ring on the wood and sighed, but she was haunted by the image of a mild and innocent tortoise stumbling slowly but inexorably towards the road.

She lifted the chain, holding it lightly between forefinger and thumb. Resting her elbow on the table she settled herself, relaxed her shoulders, gazed at the dresser against the opposite wall, and said quietly, 'Is my name Rosalind?'

She glanced downward. Anticlockwise. That was usual, although she always checked. She stilled the swinging pendulum and asked, 'Do I know where Yoda is?'

Anticlockwise.

All right.

'Is he here at Monk's Walk?'

Anticlockwise. So far so good; now to narrow it down.

'Is he in the south border?'

Clockwise: *no.*

'Is he in the roses?'

Clockwise.

'Is he…'

The kitchen darkened as unseasonal cloud gathered outside, bringing dusk early; it had been a disappointing June so far. Rosalind asked variations of the question over and over.

Clockwise, always clockwise.

'Is he…' Running out of ideas, Rosalind rummaged in her mind for another possibility. 'Is he around the front?' she asked, and looked down to see the ring begin to swing in the opposite direction.

Oh dear.

Rosalind jammed her feet back into her shoes and ran through the house to the front door. The Watsons' tortoise was under the privet hedge, less than three feet from the ironwork gates with their deadly tortoise-height gap beneath the bottom rail. He waved his legs in slow-motion protest when she lifted him up even as an estate car whooshed past the gate.

'Bad tortoise!'

But a living tortoise still.

THE WATSONS HAD DONE nothing to make Yoda's home more secure. Rosalind, hiding her annoyance, offered half of

Sukie's complex as a temporary measure, and went over to the rabbit's pen to begin dismantling it.

But inside the hutch, curled in the shavings, her little black rabbit – who had lived longer than rabbits are generally supposed to and half a year longer than her sister, and who was the only creature left at Monks' Walk who really needed Rosalind – lay still and cold.

CHAPTER 3

Then

EDITH SWIVELLED THE CLOCK, PRISED OFF THE BACK PLATE and slid the key into place. Some of the back plates were sticky and liable to break your nails, and some keys needed subtlety and know-how – the mahogany mantle clock in her father's bedroom was particularly awkward and had to be approached at just the right angle, with a jiggle and a prayer – but this clock behaved beautifully. Painted bluebirds swooped between tendrils of painted ivy on the porcelain dial, and the key slipped in like a warm knife through butter.

Edith turned the key slowly, counting, conscious of her sister's irritation downstairs but ignoring it. Ruth would simply have to wait; clock winding was not to be hurried.

There was so much to enjoy about it. There was the intricacy and precision of the mechanisms for one thing –

the thought that metal had been extracted from its ore, refined, crafted, and finally fashioned into the exquisite complexities of wheels and screws and rods and shafts, all by the limitless ingenuity of man. Edith had no idea how any of it came about, but it did and she knew herself to be in awe.

There was the sound too: the light clicks of the mantle clocks, the darker scrape and clunk of the grandfather on the stairs, and the whispering fairies' footsteps of her father's fob watch, still kept running after all these years.

Knowing the idiosyncrasies of each timepiece was part of the appeal, especially as she was the only one now who did. Winding the clocks had been her job since she made double figures. On her tenth birthday her father had handed her the cigar box of keys, all the different shapes and patterns, and laid on her the responsibility of keeping the household's timepieces in order. *Your job now.*

Her mother had loved clocks and they must all stay in their places and count away the hours as if she were still here.

'Edith! It's on the table!'

Ruth's voice drifted up from below, more exasperated than angry.

'I know! Two minutes!'

She should have wound the clock earlier but she had been immersed in the affairs of the governess and wanted to settle her financial circumstances before finishing. She was anxious to find the right balance between so impecunious as to be pitied and rich enough to lose sympathy. She had to be just right for lovely John to fall in love with.

Edith counted. At nine she slowed down. At eleven she

met resistance; one more – twelve – and she stopped, withdrew the key, pressed the back plate into position and spun the clock round to face the world again.

'*Edith!*'

'Coming!'

But she turned left on the landing instead of right and climbed stairs instead of descending. Supper was cold – pork cheese, she had seen Primmy squashing it into the mould this morning – and the key needed to be put away. It would only take a minute and it was important. Hiding the clock keys was an integral part of the fun. Edith enjoyed thinking of places to conceal things and prided herself on being creative.

Not that this was one of her best. The key for the pink marble clock was hidden better, and the key to the padlock on her diary box was best of all; simple really, and yet so far no-one had come even close to discovering it. So much fun when anyone passed by the library.

Oh well; they couldn't all have genius hiding places. Edith burrowed to the back of her small linen drawer, popped the key into the empty tooth powder tin there, and cantered downstairs.

Cold but also hot; Primmy had cooked potatoes. Edith slid into her place and helped herself. There were tomatoes too, baked until their skins split and the soft flesh steamed.

'Sorry.'

'You could have wound it earlier.'

'I know. I was trying to sort out the governess.'

Ruth said, 'I hope she doesn't have red hair.'

She said it in the tone of voice one uses for a reprimand rather than a wish, and Edith sighed.

'It's all right, I haven't given her red hair.'

'And no mother living with her.'

'And no mother. Ruth, honestly, you do go on! And she's a governess anyway, not a schoolmistress.'

Actually, Edith would have preferred her to be a schoolmistress but that was the problem with setting a story in the past: one was bound by history, and unfortunately there simply were no village schools in the early nineteenth century.

Her sister chopped into her potato. 'I'm just reminding you.'

It was a recurring complaint of Ruth's that Edith was too candid in her stories, capturing their friends and neighbours in words that barely disguised their identities, from Tommy, who delivered their sausages, to Sarah Lynne, watching everyone's comings and goings from her window. Edith didn't think it mattered, but Ruth was adamant that it did so she had been more careful recently, especially in this proper novel that was intended for publication.

Lillian said, 'Has she got a name yet?'

She had been sewing: a snippet of black thread was clinging to her blouse next to the buttons. Something of Ruth's, then, which was typical, Lillian ever being one to help out. She had changed the subject now to smooth things, and Edith jumped in gratefully.

'No. It's awful. I keep trying different ones. I think she might be a flower.'

'Violet? Iris? Lily?'

'I'll think of one.' Edith didn't mind her sisters taking an interest, but she hated people making suggestions. 'Pass the pepper?'

'Buttercup?' Lillian continued. 'Tulip?'

She was trying to be funny now, like the boys, but not quite funny enough and it didn't sound right coming from Lillian. Too contrived. If Charlie had been at home he'd have taken over (*Sweet Pea? Foxglove?*).

Without warning, inside Edith's head, Eddie's voice said *Call her Thistle*. Edith squeezed her eyes shut.

Rose. That had a nice, classic feel – timeless grace and femininity yet with the dignity that comes from a single syllable.

Rose, with her dark gold hair centre-parted and her limpid eyes so watchful of her charges yet never seeing her own destiny as it lay before her…

'You don't intend to go back upstairs after dinner, do you, Edith?' Ruth asked.

'Have to,' Edith said, attending hard to her food. 'Going really well at the moment, bit of a risk not to keep at it.'

'It's just that Alfred may call on us later. He said so when he passed by this afternoon.'

'Oh really? Oh dear.' Edith spoke without looking up, keen not to see Ruth's controlled excitement, her efforts to conceal her hope. Edith had overheard the conversation being conducted directly below her window (why did Ruth never think about that?) and had her excuse prepared.

'Do you have to? You've been up there all afternoon. Lamp oil costs money, you know.' Ruth's voice was reproachful.

'I'll use a candle. It's going so well.' It wasn't, but Ruth wouldn't know. 'I'm sure Lillian…'

Lillian said, 'I'll keep you company, Ruth. I don't mind.'

'But–'

Ruth sighed. Edith knew she was foundering and braced herself for the words: *Edith, at this rate you will never*…but they didn't come, and she relaxed a little. 'Lovely potatoes,' she said brightly, hoping to change the subject; and they were: cooked just right, with floury edges but not too soft inside, the butter melting and sliding. There were some things poor Primmy did brilliantly.

'It's a wonder then. Half of them went on the floor. I don't know what's got into that girl.'

Ruth grumbled but she wasn't really angry with Primmy, Edith thought, just venting her general discontent. Nobody was ever angry with Primmy, who had a rare and childlike sweetness; it was herself that Ruth was cross with.

Well. She wasn't really being selfish. Alfred Wintersgill was not such terrible company; she simply didn't like him. Ruth did, though, and so far as Edith could tell Lillian was neutral, so let them entertain him – although it was more a case of them being entertained by him; Wintersgill's habit was to expound rather than to listen.

She'd have been able to put up with him better if it weren't for Ruth's persistent matchmaking. Over and over again: Do you *want* to end up like me? Don't you *want* a family? Can't you *see* how few men there are?

Yes, yes, I can see of course, but that doesn't mean I'm going to accept someone whose presence makes my stomach tighten and my skin prickle!

I want, Edith thought, a lovely man with steady eyes and quiet self-confidence, and a sense of humour but a *kind* one. A man who loves me for my ideas and opinions, not for my breeding potential, which is all Alfred Wintersgill is thinking about, I'm sure. And a man who…

…a man who is untouched by war. That, Edith knew, was where her dream fell apart. No man now, no young man, was untouched either by the dreadful experience of fighting or by the guilt of having not. The War, even three years on, even here in the Northumbrian moors, lingered in everyone's subconscious, infiltrating one's thoughts and plans and squeezing, crushing, turning to bitterness things that ought to be whole and sweet. Every day, every single day, Edith thought of Frank, far away in Belgium in somewhere they called Tyne Cot because so many English boys were buried there, and William, lost and never buried at all, and of Eddie, dear Eddie, whom she missed most wrenchingly of all.

I want a man whom the War has not touched.

Who simply did not exist any more.

Which was no doubt why she had made up John.

CHAPTER 4

Once

'LUCAS! LUCAS, LOOK HERE!'

As usual, Joseph Weatherstone began speaking from the passage, which at least allowed those in the workroom a few moments' notice. Lucas set down his graver gently and pushed up his eye shield as Weatherstone's presence burst upon them.

'Look! The Tower of Glass! What do you make of it? Very fine, I think, very fine, but I wish he'd given it pennants.'

Lucas took the drawing carefully, mindful of the paper, and ran his eye over the ink lines. Imaginative and beautiful, of course, but skilful too; the blocks that formed the tower were convincingly transparent, the expression on the young man's face at once both daunted and determined, the imprisoned maiden angelic in her beauty. The artist had managed to make the twisting tendrils of ivy at the foot of the tower seem sinister, and the brooding presence of two ravens almost out of the frame at the top left corner imbued a sense of darkness as well as providing counter-balance for the tower that filled the right-hand side. Lucas saw no reason to lament the lack of pennants, but Joseph Weatherstone had a taste for billowing cloth and liked it everywhere.

'What do you make of it?' Weatherstone asked again, his hand already hovering to take the paper back.

'I like it. It's very good. Well worth a two-month of any man's time.' Weatherstone's intention was as transparent as the tower and Lucas would have found something polite to say whatever the quality of the illustration, but it happened to be the truth. The commissioning of the book of fairy tales was bringing in outstanding work.

His employer straightened and beamed. 'Then you shall have it. The chapter piece is nearly ready, I think?'

'By tomorrow.'

The border that would frame each chapter heading was Lucas's own, only the third original asked of him and the largest and most prestigious by far. He had chosen ivy and bindweed to symbolise both the common currency of stories and how they can burrow into and entwine your heart, and then added a mouse partly hidden by one trumpet flower because he had read that as a child Petersen kept a pet mouse to whom he told stories. He hoped it was true but even if not, a mouse added charm, he thought.

'Thursday, then. Choose your block.'

Joseph Weatherstone patted Lucas's shoulder and trundled over to call on the other engravers in the workroom, each in turn: Samuel first, one week into his first solo job and bursting with the thrill.

Lucas lowered his eye shield to block out all but the detailed work before him. He picked up his graver and settled it in his right hand, his forefinger along the top, his thumb steadying the block; his left hand held the sand-filled cushion firm. He positioned the point of the cutter with care and pressed down to begin the quiet curve of the stem.

The point moved along the surface of the boxwood and the delicate thread of wood lifted in a curl above it in the manner that was so much more pleasing than merely making a mark with ink on paper. Not for the first time Lucas thought how blessed he was to spend his working life doing what he loved, alongside other men also doing what they loved. It was something that could not be said by many.

At what age had he chosen this? To be honest he couldn't recall. The register showed that he had been at the Weatherstones' workshop for ten years, first as apprentice then as man, but it felt like a lifetime and his memories of previous places were hazy. He must have learned his craft as an apprentice, like young William, who would be given the task tomorrow of chiselling the outer edges off this block, but the memory was lost.

The future, on the other hand, was clear. If the weather stayed fine then this evening he would take sketching paper to the churchyard and draw angels, who, unlike the passersby in the streets, remained motionless in their poses no matter how long he took.

The clock above the fireplace sounded the hour;

someone shifted feet and old Thomas – it sounded like Thomas – sighed and set down one tool to pick up another. From the back yard drifted muffled voices: too gentle to be Joseph: Daniel Weatherstone speaking with a tradesman, perhaps. Beyond his eye shield dust motes would be floating in the sunlight that flowed through the windows to pool around the engravers, warming the wood and lifting the scent from the stacks of prepared blocks, but all the men's attention was bent on their industry as each slowly and painstakingly turned an artist's vision into printable reality.

Lucas could have been here, in this moment, for ever.

He finished his stroke, pinched away the curl of wood, and repositioned his graver.

CHAPTER 5

Now

THE NEXT MORNING ROSALIND BURIED HER BLACK RABBIT behind the tennis court, chiselling up a thick slab of turf before she began to dig so that it could be laid back afterwards. She picked a plot eighteen inches along from where Sukie's sister had been laid to rest in the autumn, marked by a plastic plant-tie in the cotoneaster hedge. The tie was moved along each time a pet was buried: rather cold in its practicality but something softer, a ribbon say, would have perished.

The burial plots were a yard out from the hedge to avoid the worst of the roots. Nevertheless, digging a hole two feet deep was hard work.

Sukie was wrapped loosely in a shroud of cotton calico so that the earth would not fall on her soft rabbit face, and she went into the ground with her water feeder alongside because it was the last of her possessions; Yoda had the rest and was already the proud – can a tortoise be proud? – occupier; Rosalind had dismantled the sections and trundled them next door in the wheelbarrow yesterday evening; she did not wish to leave the tortoise at risk an hour longer than was necessary.

After backfilling the grave, Rosalind replaced the blanket of turf and trod it down. The grass would take again very quickly; it always did. Then she untied the plastic tag and refastened it alongside the new grave, less because there would be any more dead pets to be accommodated than from a feeling of completeness.

And that was that.

Or perhaps not quite.

The burial had made connections in Rosalind's mind. After she washed her hands and changed out of her gardening jeans she locked up and went for a walk to the cemetery. She wanted to visit her angels.

Rosalind had lived at Monk's Walk for a year before she discovered the cemetery, even though it was barely two miles away – twenty-five minutes at a brisk walk. Once, it had lined one side of the main road running south from the village centre, but a bypass built in the seventies had left that stretch a cul-de-sac, and now there was no reason to drive along it unless you wanted to visit the cemetery. Having just moved into the area and knowing no-one, neither Rosalind nor Matthew had any need to do that.

Eventually Rosalind found her way there by accident after taking a wrong turning, and thereafter it became a favourite destination when she had the time, although that was not often while the children were small. She had to wait until the boys reached school age before she could properly explore the place.

It wasn't Highgate but it was large enough – perhaps ten acres – and it had its share of interesting memorials. There were marble bibles and cherubs and obelisks and urns, and there were also angels of which two were memorable. My angels, Rosalind thought, having studied them for so long that their forms had taken root in her.

One was a little smaller than life size and knelt on her square plinth with her eyes cast upwards and her hands clasped in supplication. Her expression seemed to Rosalind more anxious than serene, as if she were not wholly certain the spirit she prayed for would be taken safely up, but it was not true desperation either, more…worry. The sculptor might almost have shown her biting her bottom lip – concerned she had spoiled the cake rather than fearing for a human soul.

The other angel was life size, or as close as made no difference, and ever so slightly portly; she had the soft hint of a double chin and that, with her deep-cut eyes and the fold of fabric veiling her head, suggested that she was older than is usual for memorial angels, more experienced and of a settled disposition. You could imagine this angel saying, 'Come along now, don't take on, we'll soon get you sorted.' No pleading or biting lips for her. She leaned on a column, her arm relaxed, her hand loose, and she almost, *almost*, looked bored.

Observing her from the foot of the grave, Rosalind

realised how much affection she felt for this lump of marble, which was ridiculous but perhaps no more ridiculous than loving a rabbit.

It was becoming hard to ignore the indications that something was wrong in her life.

Rosalind walked on along the gravel path to find her worried, kneeling angel. Other angels were sprinkled across the cemetery but none had the convincing faces of these two.

Statues were often used for life drawing practice, she believed, and there was a wide enough range of poses here, standing, reclining, kneeling or balanced on tiptoe, with arms bent or out-flung, wings extended or curving protectively around; not that wings counted as life drawing, of course.

Rosalind was not tempted. She had tried sketching but always gave up, dismayed at her ineptitude.

Edith Waterfield had drawn angels in a cemetery; it had said so in the short biography Rosalind had once read in one of the Sundays, and now, for no reason that she knew, Rosalind was reminded of her beloved children's author and her strange stories, so different from the usual run of junior fiction, so…alternate.

All those wicked cats.

Her kneeling angel was looking a little streaky from the recent rain. Rosalind paused, but her thoughts were on the clever, subtle cats and weirdly beautiful world of Edith Waterfield's stories. Rosalind's favourites had been those starring a bold, arrogant black cat named Mercutio, and remembered seeing a photograph of the real Mercutio sitting regally on a gate post in the Northumberland village that had been Edith's home.

The books had been illustrated by woodcuts laden with atmosphere: bare-floored cottages and creaking wagons, furrowed plough land, oak woods and crumbling stone walls, and secretive, knowing cats that were always just a little larger than cats ought to be. The first book, *Mercutio the Midnight Cat*, had come from the public library, a slim hard-backed volume with a grubby plastic cover and a brown stain spilled over the frontispiece. Later Rosalind had saved up for and bought the later stories, all now packed with other child-hood favourites in a box in the loft, but *Mercutio* lived on in her memory only.

It occurred to her now that if *The Holly and the Ivy* was available second-hand, so might *Mercutio the Midnight Cat.* She would check as soon as she got home.

And then, on her way out of the cemetery, as she passed between the great Victorian gateposts, Rosalind suddenly knew what she was going to do and how she would spend her summer. The knowledge sprang into her mind appar-ently from nowhere, fully formed and convincing, as if she had known for days and now all she had to do was set things in motion.

DECIDING that she would go was easy; deciding how to go was harder.

It was the car that was the problem. From her recollec-tion – admittedly hazy as she had been ten at the time – the village frowned upon the automobile as a disruptive and dangerous encumbrance, and while cars were permitted to drive through – it was not a coastal cul-de-sac, like Helford on the Lizard – parking was prohibited practically every-where. Even locals, if they had no private off-road parking, had to lodge their wheels in the tourists' car park at the top of the hill, before the village properly began.

Thirty-eight years was quite a while. Had the attitude changed? Rosalind went online to check tourist information for the Northumberland moors and found that no, it hadn't. The aim of the village was to serve hikers, cyclists and horse riders; there was a cycle repair shop and a saddler's as well as bed-and-breakfasts and, on the northern edge, a farm offering stables and a paddock.

The Handsome Jack Inn stated on its website that staff would collect and return guests to the railway station at Hexham, and that clinched it. Rosalind would arrive on foot, untainted by fossil fuels.

I could hire a bicycle if I decide to stay long.

Because she hadn't completely committed yet. She was excited, yes, but aware that her great idea had sprung out of nostalgia and a sense of time passing, with no consideration or planning behind it. She should be wary of it, she knew, even as she felt her spirits lift and her energy surge.

She rang the inn and received a bit of a blow when she was told they were fully booked throughout July. But all was not lost. 'Ben at Halfway House does pick-ups too. Lovely B and B. I'm sure you'll like it there.'

So Rosalind dialled again and five minutes later had a room and a date for arrival, and could set about organising her rail ticket.

The rest was straightforward, although she had to steel herself against the protestations and interrogation thrown at her.

'What do you mean?' Jonathan asked. 'Why won't you be there?'

'I'm taking a holiday. Kerry will be fine. I'll make sure the freezer is stocked up.'

That didn't come out right.

'I thought we could *talk*,' Octavia complained, with an unbecoming note of whine. 'I was looking forward to *talking*.'

'I'll have my phone, and I expect there'll be reception there.'

Fingers crossed not.

'Are you sure about leaving the car? Will you be all right without it?' Christopher asked, calling on hands-free as he negotiated the North Circular around Brent Cross.

'Absolutely sure. I'm not going to be touring,' Rosalind said, warming to the only one of her family apparently considering her welfare rather than their own.

'Well, have a good trip then, Mother, and look after yourself.'

'I will.'

On both counts.

WHAT TO TAKE?

Had she been driving Rosalind would probably have packed all her Edith Waterfield books, but by rail that was impossible. It seemed likely, in any case, that the bookshop would have them in stock since they had recently been reissued, although in paperback with nasty modern covers and, even more terrible, without the wood engravings. Rosalind, new to the possibilities of internet shopping, had searched for them on Amazon.

She did take *The Holly and the Ivy* though, which had not been reprinted recently and might not be in stock second-hand. Rosalind suspected very few aficionados of Calpurnia and Titus even knew of its existence. She hadn't until her eye alighted upon it at the South Bank, clearly a chunk of a book not at all like the slim children's volumes. The sight of its stained boards and battered corners had sparked a thrill within her that changed to a stab when she lost the purchase.

So much so in fact that the story had broken out of her when Christopher happened to call the next day.

'Go online, Mother,' he said. 'There's Amazon, AbeBooks, loads of 'em. Someone will have it.'

The idea that second-hand booksellers were putting their catalogues online had never occurred to Rosalind, and she was astonished and excited all over again to see the buying options for this extraordinary book that she had never guessed existed.

Three days later it arrived, wrapped in newspaper inside brown parcel paper, a clean copy in rather better condition than the one at the South Bank had been, and she read it in two days, absurdly happy, the bruises healed.

Rosalind decided she would read it again on the train.

Aside from that her packing was minimal: three dresses, and a pair of jeans for colder days; a lightweight cardigan that went with everything; and a pair of sandals as well as the comfortable shoes she would travel in. She wanted to keep to the smallest suitcase, so she would carry her jacket. That, along with underwear and her wash bag, meant the case was still light enough to lift rather than drag behind her.

Rosalind hated using the wheels, it made her feel she was consuming more floor than she ought, and she always feared she would trip someone up.

The house would be empty for a week before Kerry arrived, so she hid the car keys and put the plants outside under the shelter of the hedge until someone was in residence to water them again, although she feared neither Kerry nor Octavia were reliable in this respect.

'You must do your best,' she told them. 'I'm sorry.'

The taxi pulled onto the drive in good time, but she was ready, watching for its arrival from the kitchen window. A final glance round, although she knew the taps and switches were all turned off.

Her suitcase was in the hall, next to the socket where her mobile charger lived. Rosalind looked at the little white plug and for a moment she wondered whether she might forget to take it.

Tempting.

The driver's footsteps were crunching on the gravel as he approached the door. She should be sensible, shouldn't she? At forty-eight?

The bell rang and Rosalind slipped the charger into the zipped side pocket of her bag.

CHAPTER 6

Then

Edith leaned back and closed her eyes. It was a relief to shut out the glare and the sun warmed her eyelids.

After a few moments her spine told her the headstone it was pressed against was too hard, and she shifted a little. It didn't work – headstones are not designed to be comfortable. She could imagine what Ruth would say if she could see her.

Oh well, stuff. Ruth wasn't here and neither was anyone else, and the headstone was a crumbly, mossy one from so long ago she couldn't really be causing offence to anyone. And it was nice just to sit in the sunshine and not have to do anything.

Her back bone complained again. Edith sighed and sat up and looked at her drawing book, then up at the angel poised on her plinth across the gravel path, arms crossed serenely over her breasts, her face downcast.

She loved angels; she loved the idea of them: human beings with great big, beautiful wings springing from their shoulders, their roots always conveniently hidden from view, shrouded in falling cloth or simply out of sight, for who really wanted to how the mechanics worked? Even the word was beautiful: Angel, with the glottal stop of the A and the rasping harshness of the g. Edith had been delighted last summer when old Mr Ridley at the stonemason's had casually offered her the marble head from a piece that had been horribly shattered; she propped it up in the corner of the kitchen since Ruth refused to allow it upstairs.

She had tried to draw that too. According to Winifred Platt, a statue was the perfect motionless model for anyone learning to draw the human form. Now she tried to evaluate her afternoon's work.

Not good. She knew the principles – perspective, the value of shading, how to measure proportions and angles – but what appeared on the paper never matched the image in her mind and drawing was, ultimately, frustrating.

A few years ago she had tried wishing herself better at drawing, but to no avail. Perhaps she didn't care passionately enough; or perhaps she had lost her talent for fruitful wishing when she ceased to be a child. Months and months of desperate wishing had not helped her brothers...

Don't think about that.

Edith considered her angel again. It was probably not a good choice; the pose was too static, too symmetrical. A beseeching arm or a twist in the torso, although tricky to draw, could often distract the viewer from noticing mistakes.

Never mind…I'd rather be good at words anyway.

A comforting thought, but nevertheless she admired and was attracted to people who could draw, even when it was her own sister; even when it was poor, bent old Mr Turnbull, who had spent most of his life in London, engraving illustrations for the magazines. Mr Turnbull had been the source of all Edith's knowledge about the business of wood engraving, from line-blocks to halftones, and if he hadn't come back to the village after he retired, John would probably have been a boring old farmer or something. Thank goodness, then; it was much better that he was an artist.

Closing her eyes Edith sent her mind down a little pathway of imagination to where a man sat, head bent, quietly intent, learning to draw human anatomy from statues in a cemetery.

I suppose they did have angels in cemeteries a century ago?

Something she hadn't thought about; perhaps she should ask. It would be horribly inconvenient if they didn't.

Perhaps I'll just over-rule it: author's licence.

Anyway, his hair was dark but not too dark, oak-brown rather than black, and he was neither tall and gangly nor short and stocky but somewhere between – an inch or two taller than her beanpole self and neatly muscled in a quiet, workmanlike way.

Long eyelashes.

Edith sighed.

Lillian could draw, as well as sew, cook and arrange flowers, unlike herself, who loathed needlework, could never remember a recipe and always seemed to get flowers that flopped.

Edith thought about her sister's competency with water-colours – perhaps not professional but very good for an amateur. That was ostensibly the reason Billy Moffat came to call.

Edith leaned forward and covered her face with her hands. Imagination could be a curse as well as a blessing. She felt the nausea clutch, and struggled to turn her thoughts to something else, something clean and cheerful, but once Billy had got hold it was hard to shrug him off. Edith muttered a word that would have had Ruth throwing her hands in the air and scrambled to her feet. She shoved her drawing book under one arm and set off, marching fiercely between the graves, her fist clenched tight around her pencils, hoping for distraction in motion.

The motion helped, but there was better. The black cat was sitting on the wide gatepost at the entrance. He stood up and leaned towards her as she approached, and butted her palm with his round head. Edith stroked him, enjoying the feel of his fur, hot from sunbathing on the stone. He was a midnight cat with no white hairs at all, and a big, full-muscled lad too.

'You don't care about the war, do you?'

I'll give Rose a cat. A female, slim and aloof, who takes to John immediately. That will be one of the ways the readers will know he's lovely.

John would walk down the cobbled hill one morning, looking about him and wondering what lay in store for him in this sleepy village, and Rose would meet him there as she walked up from the baker's with her basket full of loaves and know, just know, that he was a man to revere and to cherish…

Hold on – wouldn't she be governessing at that time of day?

Evening, then. In which case, not bread but…oh, something or other; she'd think what was in the basket later. It wasn't easy, this novel-writing lark.

That time of day…Edith pulled out her pocket watch and grimaced. She had spent too long daydreaming.

'Bye-bye, midnight cat.'

She brushed her hand down her skirt and walked briskly, not looking behind in case she encouraged the cat to follow. As it was she would have to wash her hands the moment she entered the house if Ruth wasn't to start coughing and looking reproachful.

She grinned and broke into a canter down the hill, Billy Moffat's ravaged face forgotten and her head full of cats and angels and love-at-first-sight.

CHAPTER 7

Now

Rosalind's lift was waiting on the concourse, holding an A4 card with Halfway House printed in chocolate brown. It was a man, younger than Rosalind, tall and lanky in cement-coloured cotton trousers and a short-sleeved shirt. He was almost bald, the hair that remained clipped very close, and was wearing half-rimmed spectacles. Rosalind had the feeling he had guessed her identity even before she stopped.

He shook her hand with long, lean fingers. 'Ben Bradford,' he said, in a voice that bore not a trace of the north. 'Let me take your case.'

The car was a Land Rover Discovery, shiny black, and Ben drove smoothly and with respect for the sharp bends and steep gradients, which was a relief to Rosalind. She allowed herself to relax and look about.

She saw not green fields and hedgerows but dry-stone walls and moors purple with summer heather, dramatically unlike the Home Counties; she could have been in another country.

'Have you seen the Pennines before?'

Rosalind jumped very slightly. 'Yes, I have, but a long time ago. It is beautiful.'

'You've brought the sun with you. We've had four days of rain.'

Rosalind smiled politely. People often said that kind of thing and it was best to let it lie.

'Are you here for the walking?'

'Not really. Well, yes, a bit, I suppose. I haven't quite decided.'

'Just getting away for a while, then?'

'Yes,' Rosalind said. 'Just getting away.'

Ben Bradford didn't follow up with another question and she was able to turn to the window again. It was astonishing how little traffic there was, she thought. By the time they began the descent into Ravensburn they had seen no cars for three miles and only sheep shared the road with them, lying confidently on the verges and causing Ben to steer carefully around them.

The Land Rover zigzagged and passed a wooden farm gate bearing a sign with a horse's head looking through a horseshoe, then a pair of wrought iron gates, and then a car park marked with a tourist information board. After the next bend Rosalind saw at last the stone walls and cobbled street of the village she remembered. The sunlight was warm through the windscreen and the geraniums in the window boxes lining the street glowed with colour, and for a moment it was as if she had never married or been widowed, never had children and a household, or had even grown up at all.

It had taken thirty-eight years, but she had come back.

THE SUNSHINE ROSALIND had brought with her fingered its way through the airy, open-weave curtains to wake her before six, and she rolled onto her back and let the light fall on her closed eyelids.

Karen Bradford had warned her. 'Pull the blind down if you don't want the sun in the morning,' she had said. 'The curtains won't keep it out, I'm afraid.'

But Rosalind liked the light and had no objection to waking early. There was no house to be made ready for the day, no breakfast to be got, not even an elderly rabbit to be fed. She was responsibility-free and not only was the morning hers but the afternoon and evening too.

Nowhere to be, no-one to see, nothing to fill up her empty hours except whatever she chose to do.

The room had its own shower. Rosalind took her time and went down for breakfast at seven thirty to find two couples in their twenties at the long table, dressed in shorts and tee-shirts and talking weather prospects: *Good that it's cleared up! I thought they said it was going to rain all week.*

Karen appeared, her slight figure swaddled in a striped butcher's apron and bearing a Brown Betty teapot with coils of steam rising from the spout. When she had met Rosalind yesterday, her hair had been loose on her shoulders, but now it was put up in a twist with a claw clip.

'Good morning! Did you sleep well? Would you like a cooked breakfast?'

Rosalind eyed the eggs and sausages and tomatoes the walkers were demolishing. 'I slept very well, thank you. And no, just cereal and toast, please.'

'White, wholemeal or granary?'

'Wholemeal, please.'

'And tea or coffee?'

'Tea, please. Thank you.'

Rosalind helped herself to orange juice from the jug on the table. She smiled to the girl next to her as she reached across the tablecloth and thought, how lovely *not* to be setting off in walking boots and weighed down with a rucksack.

When it arrived the toast was thick-cut with the texture of home-made, the marmalade was dark and bitter, and the tea was subtly aromatic. Perfect.

By the time Rosalind had finished, the walkers had departed, replaced by a retired couple. The establishment was quite busy and the inn had been full so Ravensburn must have a fair tourist trade, but there was no sign of it when Rosalind stepped into the street just after nine.

The air – such a cliché, but it was true – smelled fresh and clean, full of interesting nuances that were absent from the air at Monk's Walk; there was stone in it, and distant heather, and the farmyard smell of manure where a horse had left a dropping in the road. There was a greengrocer's next door and Rosalind felt sure she could smell broccoli and cauliflowers as well as the oranges and plums and apples.

Halfway House was, as one might expect, about half way down the street, which stretched pearly grey in either direction. Confronted with the choice, Rosalind chose left and headed down the hill, fully aware of what drove her decision.

The bookshop lay behind her.

As a child, on Christmas morning, lying awake in the dark with the incomparable excitement of her Christmas stocking heavy against her feet, Rosalind had waited out the silent hours until Juliet, their eldest sister, opened the door and announced that it was time, and they could turn the light on and start.

Rosalind and Octavia were the youngest girls in the smallest room, and Octavia immediately dived in. But Rosalind would leave her sister and pad along the landing to the lavatory first, *in bare feet and without her dressing gown*, purely so that she would get cold and slipping back into bed would be all the more delicious. She used to take her time in the bathroom too, stretching out the moments of tantalising anticipation in a way her sisters thought insane.

Now, flutteringly aware of the Ravensburn bookshop behind her, Rosalind set off in the opposite direction purely for the pleasure of prolonging the wait.

More scents greeted her as she walked: leather seeping out through the open door of the saddler's; roses from the bucket of blooms outside a shop that sold cards and china ornaments as well as flowers; shoe polish and rabbit food from the hardware store. The place seemed alive with sensation, from the light breeze stroking her bare arms and the pressure of the pavement beneath her soles to the sounds of morning business: the scrape of an A-board being erected outside the narrow-fronted restaurant (*Lunchtime Special – Carrot and Coriander Soup!*), the jangle of a shop doorbell; a window opening above her head as she passed.

Rosalind walked easily, looking predominantly at the shops on her left as she descended, saving those on the right for later. There weren't many, and private houses broke up the row, with high steps and brass door furniture, and window boxes of geraniums red and salmon pink and white lodged precariously on stone windowsills.

At the foot of the hill a narrow stone-walled bridge arched over the burn, and beyond there was one more house, low and dark-stoned, with outbuildings, the moorland reaching right up to its walls. As Rosalind looked, a woman moved into view from behind the house, carrying a bucket. She paused and then waved. Rosalind glanced about but there was no-one looking her way so, shyly and discreetly, she waved back.

The woman smiled, Rosalind thought, although she was too far away to be certain, and went indoors.

There was nothing else, and Rosalind walked back up the hill, this time on the other side.

She was coming closer now. She passed Halfway House and then the pub she had first called, with the painted image of a round, well-muscled horse swinging above her, and ahead now she could see another swinging sign, with simple sage-green lettering on a cream background – clear enough if you were looking for it, scarcely noticeable if you were not: *The Stranger Bookshop*.

The Stranger Bookshop.

Aware that she was in the grip of childish excitement, Rosalind quickened her step at last and as she drew closer she strained to see into the bay window, peering past the handbills without reading them to stare through the small panes and into the shop.

The shock of what she saw was almost physical.

Rosalind faltered, her hands suddenly cold. Then she walked on past the window, past the door, past a young woman with peculiar hair and another woman bent double at her feet, past the wide entrance steps of the next building, whatever it was, and past a shop with bicycles outside, and all the while her lovely anticipation was collapsing about her like a house of cards deliberately tumbled by somebody cruel.

It seemed hardly possible.

And it was so *unfair*.

CHAPTER 8

Now

THE GIRL WITH THE CRIMSON HAIR DRIFTED BETWEEN THE books completely intent on what she held in her hand, like a geologist taking Geiger readings. Now and then she waved her arm from side to side or stuck it straight up in the air.

Bryony watched her balefully. Ordinarily she would have been helpful by now, but she had seen the way this girl barged into the shop and let the door fall back on the woman behind her with a pushchair. Heedless or selfish or possibly both. So she would let her waste a few minutes of her life.

The girl disappeared behind the Ordnance Survey maps, then re-emerged and headed for the stairs. Good. Bryony had a lot to get through and monitoring Miss Crimson Hair wasn't a sensible use of her time. Gabriel could do it, he didn't appear to be busy, unless you count staring into the sunlight through slitted eyes as work.

Already this morning she had invested a whole precious hour in worrying her problem about her staff shortage; not worrying *about* it, but just worrying it, like a Jack Russell terrier worries a rat. She had gripped the matter by the neck, shaken it from side to side and thrown it about a bit. She hoped very much that her efforts would pay off, although given Ravensburn's isolation in the middle of the moors it was hard to see how.

A few minutes later the girl had given up. Instead of climbing higher through the storeys as people sometimes did, she had clumped back down, loud on the wooden stairs, and this time as she passed the desk Bryony said, 'I'm afraid there's no signal in here'.

The girl stared at her and then went back out to the street, and within four strides of leaving the shop she had brushed shoulders with diminutive Mrs Goudge so roughly that Mrs Goudge actually staggered sideways.

Bryony's eyes narrowed and she stared at the girl's retreating back. After a few seconds the shoulder strap gave way and her bag upended, scattering its contents across the cobbles in a manner most satisfactory.

And then, in an exquisite counter-balance to the girl's bad manners, dear old Mrs Goudge actually walked back and *started to pick them up.*

Oh well.

Bryony sighed and returned to work, but as she reached for the next book to be catalogued she paused in mid-stretch and her eyes widened.

THERE WAS a bench at the top of the street, facing the road where it curved away and left the buildings behind. The bench was wooden, bleached pale by the weather, and there was a brass plaque screwed to the back rest to tell visitors that it had been paid for by Christie McLaughlin in memory of Dixon Blyth. Rosalind, sitting at one end and staring at the dark windows of the house opposite, concentrated on soothing her emotions and getting a grip on perspective, but it was a struggle.

She closed her eyes and tried to breathe from her diaphragm instead of high up in her chest.

Don't be childish. It doesn't matter. And she won't remember anyway.

But it did matter. Already her morning was spoiled and if she didn't get a grip on this her whole holiday would be ruined.

Don't do this. Just go in as if you hadn't seen her. And as if you don't remember.

Her inner voice was quite right and Rosalind knew it, but it didn't make the prospect easier. She sighed. Such a lovely morning too. The door across the street opened and a yellow duster flapped.

Housework: Rosalind didn't have any to do, nor cooking, nor gardening. She just had herself to please on a beautiful summer day in a charming Northumbrian village. To allow her plans to be derailed by an obstruction so flimsy was infantile and inexcusable.

Rosalind stood up, straightened her shoulders, and

walked down the hill with her eyes fixed on the projecting sign of the bookshop; she would not stop, she told herself, until she was inside.

THAT WAS NOT AT ALL what she was expecting.

Bryony was distracted, and had to come back to the present with a jolt when the woman crashed her pushchair into the carousel of postcards and bookmarks.

One could argue a case, Bryony thought, to require driving tests for buggy-pushing.

She straightened the stand, scooped up what had fallen out of it, and was returning to her desk when the woman who five minutes ago walked past the shop opened the door and came in.

Their eyes met.

Bryony smiled, slightly and briefly, and got a tight little smile in exchange, one formed by the mouth only, that did not involve the eyes.

She had been recognised then.

She busied herself with pen and ledger, not actually making any entries because her attention was on the woman's footsteps as she rounded the table of new releases and headed into the shelves.

Politics and Economics. Bryony stocked the driest subjects nearest to the door with the intention of luring people further in to find the fun stuff. Luring people in was an essential part of the business of running a bookshop, and Bryony had a number of little tricks in store for people who paid attention. Her shelving policy was not restricted to parlour games.

The woman reappeared briefly in the corner of the shop and climbed the stairs, her feet lighter than most on the uneven treads. Bryony relaxed a little, but paused from cataloguing. She stared at the rescued carousel, now slightly tipsy, and tapped her teeth with the pen.

She had been sorry, a bit, at the time, and she was sorry again now, which was not always the case when she had won by unfair means. Well. If the woman still wanted *The Holly and the Ivy* she had come to the right place, that was for sure.

Quite a coincidence, though.

Or was it?

Bryony opened the next book: *The Making of the English Landscape* by W G Hoskins – an early hardback, very clean, which would probably fetch a fair bit despite there being more recent editions available. It would fetch more than a fair bit if only she could list it online.

Bryony thought a rude word and pulled a face as she gave the flysheet a pencilled number and entered the details in the ledger.

A fly threw itself repeatedly at the bottom half of the window while sweet June air drifted in through the top half; sunlight stroked the wooden floor and the spines of the political memoirs and histories, and drew green and purple highlights out of Gabriel's coat as he jumped down from the windowsill and sauntered towards the stairs. Bryony's pencil point rasped on the page, and the ceiling above her creaked as the woman moved about.

The morning wore on.

ROSALIND FELT EASIER UPSTAIRS, separated from the young woman at the front desk by more than just shelves. What a good thing the fiction was up here.

On the first floor there was a narrow landing from which doors opened off to reveal room after room of books. No structural alterations had been made to turn the house into a shop; one simply wandered through what were once bedrooms, shoes audible on the bare floorboards, stirring the dust motes floating in the sunlight that filtered through the sash windows.

It was just as she had remembered. How could the staff know where a customer was? It was a shoplifter's paradise.

Rosalind found herself in the largest room on the floor and paused to take in the wood-panelled walls, the beamed ceiling and the high shelves. Appealingly, the fireplace had been left open and a framed watercolour hung on the chimneybreast above: a plump cat lying comfortably on its tummy, paws tucked away. It looked vaguely familiar to Rosalind, as if she had seen it reproduced in the past, perhaps in a book…

A black cat, a live one, had followed her up the stairs and now took up position on a kick stool in the corner, wrapping his tail neatly over his front paws, observing her.

Rosalind didn't mind.

The air was heavier than downstairs, despite the open window; it smelled of dry paper and dust, a back-of-the-throat smell instantly familiar to anyone who liked second-hand books, and mixed into it was a faint trace of gardens. A geranium sprawled from a chipped terracotta pot on the window sill, shedding coral pink petals on the floorboards.

The shelves were tall, the top shelves only just within Rosalind's reach at full stretch, and the passages between them were narrow; she was standing in a labyrinth of books.

There was a lot of stock here. It was very quiet, the only sound the steady ticking of a grandfather clock, which was rather surprisingly half way up the stairs, and Rosalind wondered whether she was the only customer here. Then she thought probably not; the room somehow did not feel like an empty room.

She ran her eyes along the ranks of spines, orienting herself. The fiction was in alphabetical order of author, of course, but paperbacks and hardbacks were all shelved together, and even more oddly, second-hand books were in amongst the new; spines that were broken and scuffed flanked by those that were pristine; sharp, crisp lettering adjacent to text almost too faded to read.

She was at the bottom of the alphabet when whoever had been behind the bookcases went upstairs and the ceiling above her creaked.

Good: alone.

Rosalind drew out a copy of Mary Webb's *Precious Bane* and then counted the remaining copies, checking the covers of the various editions. There was one with a landscape of a bank and a fence and a tree, another illustrated by a woodcut of Pru Sarn writing in the attic, and one cloth-bound edition with no dust jacket at all.

The woodcut reminded Rosalind of the Edith Waterfield illustrations. She replaced the book and ran her eye along the shelf. Weathers, Waugh, Watson…Waterfield. The tweedy spine of the same edition of *The Holly and the Ivy* that Rosalind now owned (not, she noticed, the black one she had lost at the South Bank) and one slim paperback of *Mercutio the Midnight Cat.*

Only one. Rosalind pulled it out anyway and was startled to find a sheet of paper pasted to the front cover. The paper bore a typed message:

Edith Waterfield's books are shelved separately, as befits the founder of this bookshop, opposite the sofas on the second floor (that's the next floor up). Most of her titles are in stock most of the time, but mostly in used editions because these 1990s reprints are horrible. I do have the 1990s editions too, because they are definitely better than nothing. Still, while the stories are stupendous and the words are wonderful, the pictures are perfect for them and it was a seriously crass decision of these publishers to leave them out: cheapskate bums.

And on this cover, which I have sensitively covered up for you but which you can see again in miniature on the back (how cheap is that?), Mercutio looks like some sort of catty ingénue and not at all like the fully grown-up, reckless and sarcastic guy he really is.

So find your way to the second floor (third story for you Americans), sit down and introduce yourself to the books that were written UNDER THIS VERY ROOF more than seventy years ago.

Bryony Bower

Proprietor

Goodness.

Rosalind pictured the jutting chin and narrowed eyes of the young woman sitting at the desk downstairs.

Bryony Bower.

She flipped the book and looked at the back cover, where

a lightweight and inconsequential black cat, painted rather inexpertly, tiptoed across a farmyard, which was a setting entirely absent from Mercutio's story.

Rosalind replaced the book on the shelf. It was time to get on top of Christmas Morning Syndrome; she climbed the stairs to the second floor.

Up here the scent of gardens was stronger: low, clipped greenery around beds in symmetrical patterns.

Box hedges. How peculiar.

She wandered along the corridor between the shelves and paused at the fireplace, where this time the picture over the mantelpiece was a portrait of a young man done in oils. His eyes were dark and steady, and for a moment it was like meeting a real person, there before her, in the flesh. A patch of sunlight fell on Rosalind where she stood and she felt suddenly warm and perfectly happy despite the uncomfortable young woman downstairs.

She smiled, and moved on.

As she turned the end of the bookshelf she just missed the other customer, the one who had come upstairs ahead of her. There was a whisk of something fleeting in the corner of her vision and footsteps thumped on the wooden staircase as once again he went up to the next floor.

The cat had followed her and she felt his shoulder against her calf. He was jet black with a white chest and spats, cool and elegant, and he pressed the breadth of his head appreciatively into her palm when she bent to stroke him.

The scent of gardens seemed to have faded.

CHAPTER 9

Now

THE SUDDEN CLAMOUR MADE BRYONY JUMP. SHE OPENED THE drawer and cancelled the alarm clock inside, and thought about what to do.

The problem was that it was a nuisance to have to close in order to eat; some people like to browse during their lunch break. On the other hand if she left her own lunch too late then she would frustrate customers who wanted the shop to be open in the afternoon. She had settled on eleven forty-five, which was way too early and meant she would be starving by mid-afternoon, but it allowed her to re-open at quarter past twelve and catch the lunchtime trade.

Mornings were usually quieter than afternoons, but the woman from last summer was still up there somewhere, apparently reading the entire stock. She had been silent for at least an hour and a half.

Bryony decided. She flipped the sign on the door and turned the key, then went upstairs. The customer – Bryony hoped she would turn out to be a customer – was seated on the scuffed leather pouffe under the window, leaning forward with her elbows on her knees and a book in her hands. It was a clothbound hardback, so second-hand, and open to about a third of the way through. She seemed quite engrossed, and when Bryony cleared her throat she startled.

'I'm just closing for twenty minutes,' Bryony said. 'For lunch.'

'Oh! Oh, right, I'll –'

'No, no, you don't need to leave. I'll be going up to the flat, though, so I've locked the door. You're welcome to stay, so long as you don't mind being on your own.'

The woman looked doubtful. 'Is that all right?'

'Sure. No problem. If a fire breaks out, the key's in the lock. Otherwise, if you need me just come to the stairs and bellow. Actually, it would be nice if you came to the stairs and bellowed if a fire does break out.'

Bryony left the woman looking slightly bemused and headed for the stairs, of which there were lots. Nothing sedentary about this job, where pounding up and down all day was like climbing Scafell Pike. But the woman called after her.

'Will you tell the other customer?'

'There isn't another customer, just you.'

'But someone went upstairs an hour ago or so. Oh I'm sorry, he was staff, I suppose.'

Bryony froze. Then, slowly, she turned around. Steadily, she said, 'Did you see him?'

The woman had crossed the floor to call after her. She stood now with the book in her hand and her expression embarrassed and reluctant. She said, 'Well, just briefly.'

Just briefly.

Only four people had been in this morning, five if you count the baby in the buggy, and none of them had been a man.

Bryony said, 'And he went upstairs?'

'Yes. I haven't heard him since, though.' The woman's voice faltered. She looked now as if she would really like to be somewhere else, almost shrinking inside her clothes as she evidently wished she had never started the conversation.

'Right. Thank you for letting me know. I'll…tell him I've closed.' Bryony smiled brightly. 'Great! See you in twenty minutes, then!'

On the next landing she paused. She listened and sniffed, concentrating hard, but there was no trace of what she hoped for, only the usual small, shadowy form crouching by the skirting board.

'You're no help,' she told it, and almost saw it turn to look at her.

Thoughtfully, she opened the door to her flat.

Rosalind returned to the footstool, but did not imme-diately resume reading. Instead she looked out of the window, where the dusty street baked and the shadows had shortened almost to non-existence under the high midday sun.

Her metaphorical shadow had shortened too, she thought. It was ridiculous to have been so upset. Clearly the young woman had not recognised her, so she could put the whole affair out of her mind and relax.

Odd about the books, though.

She had noticed quickly that the Stranger Bookshop's approach to categorising fiction was very free. There were no sub-sections for genres of fiction – romance, crime, fantasy and the like – and Ethel M Dell, Ian Rankin and Anne McCaffrey stood shoulder to shoulder with Martin Amis, Julian Barnes and Margaret Forster; and indeed with Dickens, Trollope and Scott, for the policy of mingling new with old meant that the classics were well represented too. Sharply cut current paperbacks stood flanked by the small, chunky volumes with Bible-thin pages that Rosalind remembered from school; glossy dust jackets wrapping just-published hardbacks jostled with the thick plastic covers of public library discards.

But the bookshop's idiosyncrasy went further. Here and there children's novels were inserted, still in alphabetical order, so that while browsing the Rs one's eye lit upon *The Teddy Robinson Omnibus*, or searching for Wilbur Smith one might come across *The One Hundred and One Dalmations*. Rosalind, who had once been horrified to find Angela Carter's *Book of Fairy Tales* shelved in the junior section of the public library, hoped very much Bryony Bower's policy of mixing things up did not extend that far.

And then there was *The Holly and the Ivy*.

The second volume Rosalind found was shelved under P. She retrieved it and put it with the other, next to the copy of *Mercutio the Midnight Cat* with its extraordinary typewritten label. Someone, she thought, had changed his mind and heedlessly abandoned the book in the wrong place.

But then she found another copy, a hardback, squashed between two Buchans, Elizabeth and John; and then yet another, this time a worn paperback with a very seventies Art Nouveau cover, in with the Fs. Eventually she counted thirteen copies, which seemed extraordinary for such an obscure book.

The misplacing had to be deliberate. Why?

Rosalind gazed into the cobbled street.

She wished she had not mentioned that man. How crass. Bryony Bower had looked at her very oddly indeed.

Rosalind sat down. Her book was a nineteen-fifties edition of Daphne du Maurier's *Jamaica Inn*, a favourite novel from her teens that she had not read for decades and was thoroughly enjoying.

Jem Merlyn was still gorgeous.

At one o'clock, beginning to feel empty, Rosalind took her books down to the desk. She was close to the end of *Jamaica Inn* and had copies of *The Scapegoat* and *The House on the Strand* too, all set for a blissful soak in nostalgia.

While she watched Bryony Bower check the prices, Rosalind surprised herself by saying, 'May I ask you, why have you scattered all those copies of *The Holly and the Ivy*?'

The girl – Rosalind thought she could not be much more

than twenty-two or -three – paused and looked up. 'Yes. Well. I have a lot of them and I thought I'd try to catch a few people unawares.'

'Unawares?'

'Well, if it's someone who's looking for a particular author and isn't ever going to reach the Ws, they might stumble across it and give it a look. You never know.'

'I see.' Sort of, at any rate, but it seemed a bizarre approach to selling books. Rosalind hesitated. 'But how is it that you have–'

'So many copies? Mm. Well. There is a reason.' Bryony Bower met Rosalind's gaze with unnerving steadiness. 'Sorry about the South Bank, by the way. I presume you managed to get yourself a copy later?'

Rosalind was taken aback. She said, 'Oh, well…yes, yes I did, thank you. I–'

'Do you have it here?'

'Well, yes, actually. It's–'

'Would you mind if I took a look at it? Could you bring it in?'

Rosalind drew breath. 'Of course you may. I'll bring it tomorrow, if you like.'

'Great. Thanks.'

Rosalind watched the girl operate the till, which was an old-fashioned manual kind, rather in keeping with the shop in many ways but not at all in keeping with its owner.

What a strange conversation. And she hadn't seemed at all embarrassed about last summer.

Rosalind, daringly, said, 'Could I just ask…why don't you try to sell the books on-line? That's how I found mine.'

'Mm.' The girl's mouth pulled into a wry shape. 'If only.' She handed Rosalind her change and pushed the charming cotton bag of books towards her. 'Enjoy.'

Something emboldened Rosalind, whether the relief of clearing the air or the lifting of her spirits by her impromptu holiday, or even simply the sunshine and the birdsong, and she said, 'It isn't difficult. If I can use the Internet, I'm sure you can.'

Perhaps she had gone too far. Bryony Bower looked at her again but with narrowed eyes.

'You're okay with computers and things, are you?'

'Well…my sons have taught me quite a bit.'

'And you're staying round here for a while, are you?'

'Yes, I am. I haven't decided how long, yet.'

Rosalind felt she was being considered. She was being looked at very directly – stared at, even. The young woman behind the gigantic desk was taking too much time to choose her next words, or perhaps to decide whether or not to launch them. Rosalind felt herself begin to shrink.

And then they came. Bryony Bower, proprietor of the Stranger Bookshop, idiosyncratic, opinionated and a bully, spoke.

'I suppose you wouldn't like a job?'

CHAPTER 10

Then

EDITH CLOSED THE DOOR TO SHUT OUT THE SOBS. IT DIDN'T work completely, but it helped. In any case, she had told them she was going to work so she had better make it the truth.

She sat on the edge of the bed, relieved just for the moment to be alone and unobserved…and quiet. Primmy cried so noisily, with lots of nose blowing. It was especially annoying because she refused to explain why. *I'm a good girl*, she kept saying, *I'm not bad*, but no-one had said she was, although Edith saw Ruth struggling.

To be honest, she wasn't likely to write much because Billy Moffat was on his way and she never could write when Billy was about. She could shut herself in a different room and even put her head under her pillow, but her cursed imagination squeezed in with all the images she was trying to hide from. It got hopelessly in the way of the affairs of John and Rose.

Or rather, Rose and John; the romance was supposed to be from Rose's point of view, although she was writing it in the third person. The problem was that she had become rather more interested in the hero than the heroine.

There was a knock on the door beneath her window and Edith shuddered. She waited, listening for the rasp of the front door opening and Lillian's bright, kind voice.

What with Billy Moffat in the evening and Alfred Wintersgill in the afternoon, was there any wonder she spent all her time dreaming about a man she had made up?

Well, even if she couldn't write, she could at least plan. As yet she hadn't worked out why John would go to Castle-hope in the first place, although she had come up with a few possible excuses. She tended to favour the idea of a deceased cousin, or better still a benefactor who was no relation at all, because she didn't want him to have close family who would get in the way. She was frightened of too many characters; she wasn't experienced enough yet to handle them without everything getting messy.

Edith plotted.

The benefactor could be someone for whom John had done a service and who had never forgotten him. It would be just like John to help a stranger with no thought of reward, and could be a useful character note for him. The bequest would come out of the blue, a complete surprise, and slowly he would realise that the best part was not the money at all but beautiful Rose…

Not utterly beautiful, though; not princess-beautiful.

Edith kicked off her shoes and sat back with her feet on the quilt, a habit Ruth deplored. She crossed her ankles and meshed her fingers comfortably behind her head.

Rose was beautiful in a certain way, but she wasn't *pretty*, which suggested a superficial attractiveness and an empty head. Primmy was pretty. Edith wanted Rose to be graceful and serene, with an inner beauty that would not alter with age. Like Margaret Eliot, she thought, who bore herself more like a noblewoman than like the wife of a blacksmith.

She liked Margaret, who was generous and wise. In the difficult weeks after the news came about Edward she had helped her more deeply than Edith had realised at the time. She had listened and baked, allowed Edith to unload her misery, and fed her with scones and malt bread, because whatever came out of Margaret's oven was wonderful no matter what the shortages.

'All the Eliot women are like that,' Ruth had said more than once. 'It isn't cooking that goes on in their kitchens, it's alchemy.'

Perhaps she could talk to Margaret about Billy Moffat, although how she'd get the words out she didn't know.

She sat up and covered her face with her hands as the memory of that first visit flooded back.

Vanity and self-deceit. She had fancied herself to be cool and competent, compassionate yet workmanlike, but when he had taken the mask off she had literally run from the parlour and vomited up the smoked haddock Primmy had cooked for lunch, because behind his mask Billy had nothing you could call a face at all any more, just a hole where his breath whistled and his slurred words emerged, and one blue eye that followed you.

Stop thinking about it!

How did Lillian manage it? Three times now Billy had come to the house and sat in the rocking chair while Lillian, at the table with her watercolours and her brushes, touched up the tin where the paint had flaked. And Edith knew they stayed in there for longer than the work could possibly take, while no-one dared open the door just in case.

We talk, Lillian said, *he's still Billy, you know.*

But in truth he wasn't, or not for Edith; he was a waste, a remnant of a man ruined by the horrible war, and despite her feelings of guilt she did not understand how Lillian could bear him.

Don't you know how few men there are now? Ruth kept saying, and Edith did know. One million Surplus Women, the newspapers said; some said two million. All those sweet boys murdered, and the junior officers, the first to go over the top, cut down the quickest. Practically the only young men left now were the maimed, like poor Billy behind his tin mask, and the shirkers, like Alfred Wintersgill, talking too loud and standing too close.

He was a horrible man; no wonder his housekeeper ran away home, poor girl. Edith intended to use him as inspiration for her novel's necessary villain, although she'd have to change his occupation: harness-making wasn't sufficiently brutal. A slaughterer perhaps? Or was too obvious? Herbert Douthwaite, he was going to be called.

She wouldn't allow Alfred Wintersgill to court her, no matter what Ruth said, no matter how thriving his business.

If they were very careful, if they lived frugally and counted the pennies, then Father's money would last them a good few years yet, and there must be something she could do to earn a little, at least.

But she envied John his benefactor and his unexpected inheritance.

CHAPTER 11

Once

LUCAS LEANED BACK AND CLOSED HIS EYES. IT WAS A RELIEF to shut out the glare and the sun warmed his eyelids. The headstone against his spine was crumbling and mossy, the name engraved upon it illegible. It was difficult to believe anyone would be offended by his using it as a back rest; and it was nice just to sit in the sunshine and not have to do anything.

The stone was hard, though. After a while Lucas sighed and sat up. He looked at the sheets of paper on the board across his lap, then at the angel poised on her plinth before him, her arms crossed serenely over her breasts, her face downcast. The grave she watched over must be as old as the headstone behind him, but she had not crumbled at all; she was pale and smooth, unmarked by the years. A different kind of stone, no doubt, one less susceptible to damage from rain and wind, but Lucas did not know what it was.

He was ignorant regarding stone; wood was what he knew.

He looked again at the drawing. There was an error in the angle of her right arm and he was less than pleased with the wings, which looked listless and unconvincing.

On the other hand, real people don't generally have wings.

There was an irony in life drawing from statues, but the graveyard was available and had taught him much. It was convenient too, devoid of people just after dawn in the summer, his favourite time; in the evening there were visitors and he had to draw on his feet, his board resting on his arm.

He wondered whether rural graveyards had statues. He might find a new pose to practise on if they did.

What kind of place was Castlehope?

Lucas had walked out of Camden on Sundays often enough, crossing the fields and stopping to draw cattle and sheep and the wild flowers and trees in the hedgerows, gradually building a store of knowledge of the natural forms with which he enriched his designs. If they were granted a holiday – the Weatherstone brothers were generous and holidays were not so rare – he would go farther, staying overnight in a hostelry or in summer sleeping under the open sky, and he was familiar and comfortable with cornfields and meadows.

The Northumberland of his childhood must be very different: hills and dales and wind-scoured moors; the humble flowers of heather and gorse underfoot, and in the skies above hawks, curlews and golden plovers.

He was looking forward to seeing moors.

The sun was gaining height. Lucas turned his drawings face down and scrambled to his feet. The Weatherstones had granted him leave to settle this affair, but now he must get himself to the workshop for *The Tower of Glass* must be finished first.

He quickened his step and began to whistle. Someone had placed roses on one of the graves near the west entrance, creamy yellow and white, and from nowhere a notion came to Lucas.

Rose, he thought; what a beautiful name for a woman.

CHAPTER 12

Now

BRYONY CHECKED HER REAR-VIEW MIRROR. THE STREET behind her was empty (when was it not?) so she pulled across and parked by the kerb to unload. There were three crates of mid-twentieth-century children's fiction: Noel Streatfield, Willard Price, Henry Treece and – yippee! – a whole stack of Tintins, which ought to zip out the door in no time.

She stacked the crates just inside and drove the Land Rover fifty yards further to the pub. The lack of parking at the shop was a pain but one she was used to now, and happily Dan, who was an angel and had sold her the Land Rover in the first place, allowed her to use his car park. *('Can't turn the old girl away. She knows where she lives.')*

The Land Rover wasn't a 'she' to Bryony, who thought

of it instead as a big, burly bloke ever ready with wellies and a shovel to dig her out of snowdrifts.

She parked in the far corner of the yard behind the pub and climbed out, the July sunshine warm on her bare arms.

As she turned onto the street she saw three hikers with bulging rucksacks and serious boots gathered at the door to the bookshop, but before her very eyes they turned and began to walk away up the hill. Blast. Bryony considered her options, but she'd never catch them running uphill and hollering would be embarrassing.

They were probably after maps, not books, but still… another sale lost. She *really* needed to replace Flossy. She would have to do some more worrying.

Bryony opened the door of the shop and listened.

She sniffed.

No.

She shut the door behind her and dragged the tower of crates round behind the desk; she'd start cataloguing them this afternoon, and then Rosalind could stick them up on the website.

Their arrangement was going very well, at least from Bryony's point of view. It was hard to tell how Rosalind felt about it because she was one of the most reticent people Bryony had ever met. She was insanely polite and her reserve was galactic. For all Bryony knew, Rosalind was sitting in front of the laptop right now absolutely loathing it and seething with injustice, but that was hardly Bryony's fault; she had asked, that was all, and if the woman couldn't say No…

It was getting the job done, though, and there had been

sales already. Two copies of *The Holly and the Ivy* had gone in the first twenty-four hours – two! She was now buoyantly optimistic about shifting the lot.

On the other hand, if the people who bought them were going to read them and resell, she'd end up buying the wretched things back again.

Tch!

Perhaps she could invent some kind of identification code…

It was a hot day and Bryony was gasping. She poked her head out of the door and checked each way, then locked up yet again and climbed through the storeys (so good!) to the flat, where she dumped her bag and filled a jug with apple juice and ice to take back down.

On the second floor now there was a scent of the outdoors and someone behind the book shelves was whistling softly. The temptation to look was very great, but it was never any good. Mindful of the top step, Bryony went on down.

An hour later she had logged and priced the contents of the first crate and was considering lunch when Rosalind arrived. To get some air into the shop Bryony had propped the door open with a shabby 1926 edition of Mrs Beeton's Household Management, which was exactly the right size for a doorstop and was never going to sell anyway, and her new employee hesitated on the threshold before stepping forward.

Bryony put on her bright face and said, 'Hello! Lovely day, isn't it!'

'It is.'

Rosalind had a shorthand notebook in her hand with a pencil clipped to the spiral binding. Bryony stood up. There was still a height difference but at least it was less extreme.

'How are you getting on?' she asked.

'Well, I'd like to talk to you, really.'

Rosalind opened her notebook but glanced around as if doubting this were truly the place for a business meeting. Bryony said, 'Hang on, I'll get another chair.'

There was a battered stick-back in the corner near political memoirs; she fetched it and plonked it next to the desk, but waved Rosalind towards her own more comfortable chair with its padded seat and wooden arms. 'No, honestly, I've been sitting in that for too long, I could do with a change.'

Tentatively Rosalind sat, and said again, 'I'd like to talk to you. About the internet.'

'Okay.'

Rosalind drew breath. 'Well, I have been listing your stock on-line, but last night I also did a little browsing.'

Browsing...one of those words that the computer thralls have so irritatingly hijacked, Bryony thought. 'Browsing' to her meant wandering through shelves stacked with books, not staring at an electronic screen. Although to be fair, goats had it first.

'Browsing?' she asked.

'Bookshop websites. Especially second-hand bookshops. Some of them seem to be quite quirky and have quite quirky websites. And I thought, well, your shop is...'

'Quite quirky?'

'Well, yes. In a nice way, of course.'

'A nice way. Oh good.'

Bryony saw the doubt flicker across her companion's face and thought, *Don't be sarcastic, she can't take it.* She quickly added, 'I mean, yes that is nice. I agree. Quirky and good.'

Rosalind looked relieved. 'Yes. And I'm sure a lot of people who buy books do also look at websites and might make a special trip if they thought this kind of…'

'Quirky.'

'…bookshop was here. Yes.'

'Hm.'

'And,' Rosalind continued, 'you could be selling on-line directly. Surely that would be helpful, especially in an out-of-the-way place like this?'

It was obvious what she was thinking: *Why on earth haven't you done this already? How on earth can you be so behind the times?* The whole world thought she was a Luddite; was this the moment to confess?

Bryony paused, considering. There was something about this Rosalind Cavanagh that disturbed her. For starters there was the fight she had put up at the South Bank last year. It had stunned Bryony, accustomed to having her own way against opponents much tougher than Mrs Cavanagh should have been, in her cabbage-rose shirtwaister and her slender gold necklace. The fact that she had turned up here gave food for thought too, not to mention the way she stirred her coffee and all those sisters.

Octavia…

And then there was that business with 'another-customer-oh-no-he-must-be-staff'.

Staff. Ha!

Yet here she sat, avoiding eye contact, full of unease at having spoken so bluntly.

Had Bryony brought her here? It was not what she had been expecting but that wouldn't be a first.

Should she tell her the truth, then? Bryony was tempted, but… perhaps not yet.

Instead, she said, 'The thing is, I really don't have time to put together a website. But if you think you might be interested…Look, would you mind hanging about here while I grab some lunch?'

CHAPTER 13

Now

As Rosalind walked down the hill, a woman wearing an artist's smock over her jeans was lugging a box of mounted prints into the gallery. She smiled at Rosalind and Rosalind smiled back, but her mind was barely there, fully occupied with the enormity of what she had apparently taken on barely two weeks since first setting foot in the Stranger Bookshop.

She wasn't at all sure how it had happened.

Rosalind avoided computers for the most part, although she had found email to be a wonderful way to keep in touch with her sons. She had never cared for shopping on-line, preferring to examine and handle washing machines or winter coats before she bought, and she shrank from the very idea of *blogs* and *forums* and *chat rooms*. But she was an anomaly even amongst women her own age, she knew, and she was astonished and even a little disturbed to learn that Bryony Bower, who could only be in her twenties, had chosen to shun the whole business.

She really dug her heels in, too. No email account, no mobile phone, and the typewriter on her desk was an ancient IBM Golfball from the nineteen-seventies, its housing grubby and the keys worn. There didn't seem to be any sense behind it. But then there was much about Bryony that didn't make sense.

Obediently Rosalind had taken her copy of *The Holly and the Ivy* to the bookshop and Bryony had seized it eagerly; but instead of checking the publication data at the front of the book, as Rosalind had expected of a second-hand book dealer, she had opened it in the middle, flipped the pages for a moment, and then snapped it shut and handed it back. *Okay*, she had said, and when Rosalind, confused, asked her if she had finished, Bryony said, *Yep, thanks*.

And she looked at Rosalind strangely sometimes; when she was making coffee, for instance. There was a very odd exchange last week when Bryony had said suddenly, 'You stir your coffee widdershins.'

'Pardon?'

'The direction you stir it in. It's called widdershins.'

Rosalind had frowned. 'It's called anticlockwise.'

'Yes. It's also called widdershins.'

Widdershins…It sounded like myths and fairy tales. 'Lots of people stir things anticlockwise.'

'They don't, actually.'

She visualised Bryony with a mug and a spoon. 'You do.'

'Yes, you're right, I do.' Bryony had looked at her hard and Rosalind had shaken her head and given up the fight.

There was all the interest in her sisters too, and even her aunts. Some people were strangely fascinated by large families, Rosalind knew, but when she had politely returned the question and asked whether Bryony had siblings it transpired she came from a family every bit as big.

It was all very odd, and one of the oddest aspects was that Bryony actually possessed a computer at all. Why had she bought one if she had no intention of using it? It was a Hewlett-Packard, a laptop, set up with the basic essentials: Microsoft Office, although an old version, and a web-browser. It was enough to allow Rosalind to put Bryony's catalogue on-line, but Rosalind doubted it had the capacity to design and maintain a website.

Rosalind doubted she had that capacity too. Okay, Bryony had said, breezily, I'll hire someone to set it up and he can teach you to run it.

Somewhere along the line Rosalind had gone from being casual, part-time and temporary to committed, practically full-time and, most alarming of all, permanent. She could hardly agree to this and then run away.

And where was she going to live? Karen and Ben were delightful and her room at Halfway House was as pleasant as she could have wished for a holiday. But if she was staying for longer she wanted autonomy; she needed a kitchen to cook in and a lounge to sit in, and privacy on the days when she did not want to talk to anyone; she needed the freedom on occasion not to be polite.

Three strides short of the door to the bed and breakfast Rosalind realised one of those occasions was upon her right now, and instead of mounting the steps she walked on past, although quite where to she did not know. This was one of the problems: having somewhere to go. She was missing her garden.

The village was closing business for the day. The buckets of chrysanthemums and roses had been taken indoors and the saddler's was shut; outside the hardware store two men stood in conversation, one of them elderly and stout with a tower of plastic buckets in his arms, the other younger and lean in a faded denim shirt and jeans. He glanced at her as she approached and smiled.

Rosalind smiled in return and passed them, aware that her anxiety was easing. It was the shock of realising what she had agreed to that had made her tense; she was becoming used to the idea now and perhaps it was not such a burden. After all, she had plenty of energy, she thought, suddenly feeling it; she might even enjoy herself.

At the bridge she paused, as she had on her first morning in Ravensburn. There was really no point in crossing unless to visit the one house on the far side or to explore the moors. Rosalind looked to see whether the woman was about, but there was no sign of her.

It was strange that the village had not spread across the river.

Rosalind felt herself relax. The sounds of the high street behind her seemed to have faded. A hawk was held by the sky above the heather, intent and silhouetted against the blue, and faintly Rosalind could smell bread baking.

'Hello.'

The voice should have startled her, but Rosalind wasn't startled at all. The younger of the men at the hardware shop had arrived at the ford and paused next to her.

Rosalind smiled slightly. 'Hello.'

She expected him to walk on by; why else would he come this far? But instead he stood, his thumbs hooked into the back pockets of his jeans, his weight on one leg and the other relaxed. There was a little distance between them, though, and he was not looking at her but across the burn. Rosalind knew because she was looking at him.

On realising this she swiftly turned her eyes away, hoping he hadn't noticed, and stared instead where he did, at the horizon beyond the house where the hills dissolved into the sky. A white van, some kind of logo painted on its side, was parked on the crest of the hill, marring the atmosphere of timelessness.

'Construction workers,' the man said, guessing her question. 'We're going to have a microwave tower.'

'Heavens! Do you mind?' Rosalind was oddly shocked.

'Not really. A village is only its people, and people need broadband. Ravensburn can't be frozen.' He turned his head to look at her. 'You're new, I think. Are you enjoying your visit?'

'Yes, and yes I am, thank you,' Rosalind said. Then she added, surprising herself, 'How did you know?'

'Population less than a thousand, you know when

someone new shows up.' He turned to face her and offered her his hand. 'Aaron Eliot. I live over there.'

'Oh – Rosalind Cavanagh.' She shook his hand, which was warm and dry and neither squeezed her fingers nor felt limp.

'Are you staying long?' he asked.

'I'm not sure…Possibly. I seem to have…'

Rosalind faltered, unnerved at talking so much and to so complete a stranger, but the sensation of unwinding, of being comfortable with herself, had seeped through her and she suddenly found that she wasn't embarrassed, or even very shy.

'Got involved?'

He was very attractive, Rosalind thought unexpectedly, although not exactly handsome. His eyes, especially. He seemed reassuring in some way, and…kind.

'Well, yes, I suppose.' She hesitated, then said, 'I've agreed to set up a website. I don't have the first idea how to do that. And I probably ought to find somewhere a bit more permanent to live. I'm in the Halfway House for now…'

His gaze had returned to the moors, for which she was grateful. It was more comfortable not to be looked at.

'Have a word with Dan at the Jack. His son Robby is on vacation from university and he's into that kind of thing. I'm sure he'd help you out.' Then he added, 'It's good to stretch your boundaries. It gives you energy.'

'Yes, I suppose it does.'

Aaron faced her again. 'Drop by any time. Do you like baking? Grace loves to bake with friends.'

'Oh – yes, I like to bake!'

'Any time, then.'

Aaron nodded and left her, striding over the bridge, and Rosalind turned and headed back up the hill.

As she walked she found a new vigour rising in her which made her strides strong and elastic and her spirits light.

Dan at The Handsome Jack, then. And perhaps he would know of some rooms for let too.

CHAPTER 14

Then

'WHAT WILL YOU DO FOR ROOMS?' RUTH DEMANDED. 'Where will you stay?'

'Oh Ruth.' Edith sighed. That her sister would protest was predictable; the only uncertainty was which specific aspect she would protest about first. Edith had guessed 'You can't go alone', but apparently it was to be accommodation.

'Two nights at the Station Hotel won't break the bank. I promise I won't eat much.'

She was being tactical; their father used to stay at the Station Hotel on the rare occasion that he travelled to Newcastle, and always maintained it to be genteel and good value for money. In fact it was the only hotel Edith knew of in Newcastle and the bald reality was that if it hadn't been for her father's endorsement of it for so many years she would not have dared to embark on this expedition at all.

The depressing truth was that she was not as bold as she pretended to be.

For doctor's daughters, their lives had been very secluded because their father disliked and distrusted urban society. Going alone to Newcastle now was an adventure, and there were little flutterings of nerves in her stomach at the prospect.

No need to admit it, though. Edith had explained that if she was to write this book at all then she needed to do her best to make it authentic. That required research, and just as she had been researching the craft and business of wood engraving by talking to old Mr Turnbull, and the history of it by talking to Winifred Platt, so now she needed to take a look at the city where John had stumbled into his calling.

Edith watched Ruth's lips: if she pressed them together it meant she disapproved but wouldn't argue any more.

'You can't go alone, Edith, and there's no-one to go with you.'

Ah, there it was.

'Ruth, I'm twenty-one. I don't need anyone to—'

'I'll go with her!'

'—Lillian will go with me. *Come* with me.'

That was unexpected. She'd find out what it was all about later. In the meantime she met her elder sister's frown with an expression, she hoped, of womanly resolve and quiet competence which was nevertheless respectably demure, while at the same time projecting her consciousness that

Ruth was the eldest and head of the household, with all the strain and difficulty that involved.

It was a lot to impart in one expression; she crossed her fingers behind her back.

Ruth's lips pressed together.

Yes!

'Two nights, then. But only two.'

LILLIAN HAD BROUGHT wool with her and crocheted on the train. There were times when she made Edith despair. How often did they do this? How often did the opportunity arise to look at different scenery, unfamiliar fields and farms and cottages? Edith couldn't tear her eyes away from the rain-spattered windows, and all her sister could do was stare at her own hands.

'Why don't you look where we're going?'

Lillian said, 'I want to get this finished. I looked on the way to the station.'

She hadn't been given much option, jolting sideways in Dixon Blyth's dog cart. The three sisters had wildly contrasting natures, Edith thought; it always amazed her when people commented how alike they were.

They mean our mannerisms, Lillian had once said, *the things we take for granted or don't notice.* No doubt she was right; at any rate Edith thought she had little of Ruth's dour respectability or Lillian's domesticity, and saw none of her own selfishness in her sisters. She doubted she would have put herself out to accompany Lillian on a daft jaunt, were their positions reversed.

'Lillian, why did you come with me? Really?'

'I told you. I need some new watercolours. I'm almost out of Payne's Grey.'

'But you could order those.'

Lillian rummaged in her bag for another skein. 'And I want to see a man about Billy's mask.'

'*What?*'

'Don't shout, Edith. It hurts him. Mr Barton told me about a shop where they make things fit better: wooden legs and so on. They stop the straps rubbing so much. I'm going to ask if they can help with the mask.'

Edith stared. She said, 'Mr Barton?'

'His nephew in Corbridge lost a leg.'

She was so calm. Edith found herself saying what she had wanted to say for weeks. 'Lillian, you and Billy, you can't really mean to–'

'I want a family.' Her sister's eyes stayed on her work but her voice hardened. 'I want children. It's only Billy's face that is ruined, there's nothing wrong with the rest of him.'

Edith had nothing to say. She swallowed, watching her sister jabbing the hook in and out of the yarn. She saw that her hands were trembling.

After a minute Edith turned back to the window and the rain and the fields where the bedraggled lambs, though destined for slaughter, at least knew nothing about it.

Dear God, how she longed for someone untouched by the war.

Don't think about it. Think about Newcastle.

'You've seen Newcastle already,' Ruth had protested, but the last time Edith visited the city she had been seventeen and without any idea she would ever need to know what it was like a century before. This time she would walk with an eye on the age of the architecture and try to imagine away the great bridges.

She especially wanted to see the site of Thomas Bewick's workshop. According to Winifred Platt, the original building was gone but one could stand in the corner where it had once been and look at the view as if from its vanished windows.

Because John, Edith had decided, was originally a local lad, perhaps even born in Ovingham like Bewick himself, and had been touched by the magic of wood engraving during a chance encounter as a child. Winifred assured her such happy accidents were not unknown even in the early nineteenth century.

It was difficult not to believe Winifred Platt knew everything. She was an exotic creature in Edith's eyes, having studied at Girton College and with sufficient financial independence to please herself without forever scraping and patching and making ends meet. 'Pleasing herself' included visiting the Northumberland moors twice a year to walk and paint, and Edith looked forward to her company tremendously. She didn't go with Winifred on her painting days, afraid to intrude, but sat in the back parlour of the Handsome Jack in the evenings while Winifred ate chunky vegetable soup or macaroni and cheese and talked about art and publishing and history and politics.

It was her talks with Winifred that had inspired her to begin *The Holly and the Ivy*. She couldn't wait to see her again in September and tell her that she'd thought of the title. She wondered whether Winifred would understand its significance without being told.

It was still drizzling when the train pulled in just before tea time. Lillian put her umbrella up for the few yards between the station entrance and the hotel but Edith made a dash for it. She only had one middling-sized bag. She clamped her hat down on her head and ran, jumping the puddles and leaping up the steps to tuck herself under the canopy of the porch, gasping and exhilarated.

'Good thing Ruth isn't here,' Lillian said when she caught up.

'Too true.' And not just because of the running.

Poor Ruth. She worked so hard and had very little thanks for her efforts from either of them, but there was no denying that the sense of holiday they were feeling was as much because of being away from Ruth as being away from Ravensburn.

They checked into their room, which felt grown-up and morale-boosting, and then indulged in the pure hedonism of tea in the hotel lounge, mutually agreeing that the bliss of delicate cucumber sandwiches (no crusts) and tiny iced cakes was worth forgoing lunch tomorrow. They'd stoke up with a good breakfast and then last out until dinner.

Tomorrow, Edith told herself, she would see where John had spent his youth, where he had discovered his talent, and where that talent had been discovered by the Master. She would walk the alleys and squares that he had walked, and would look at the same views that he had seen through the thick glass panes of Thomas Bewick's workshop.

Tomorrow John would become more real.

CHAPTER 15

Now

Dᴀɴ ᴀᴛ ᴛʜᴇ Hᴀɴᴅsᴏᴍᴇ Jᴀᴄᴋ ᴅɪᴅ ɪɴᴅᴇᴇᴅ ᴋɴᴏᴡ ᴏꜰ ʀᴏᴏᴍs in need of a tenant. 'Coachman's flat at the Law House,' he said, pulling a pint as he spoke. 'Been empty since Sally moved out at Easter. Went to Jedburgh to be near her sister, I believe.'

A woman who had moved to be closer to her sister. It takes all sorts.

The owners were called Soper. Rosalind obtained the number from Directory Enquiries and called from her mobile. There was a reasonable signal in the village, although none at all in the bookshop, which seemed odd. The Law House lay behind the wrought iron gates she had seen from Ben Bradford's Land Rover on her arrival, and

Rosalind walked there, leaving the village for the first time in a fortnight.

She had allowed plenty of time and arrived with ten minutes in hand, so she waited in the lane and watched the black-faced sheep over the stone wall. Already the lambs were almost as big as their mothers, but they were easy to tell apart: they hung about in gangs, looking alert and ready for mischief, like teenagers the world over, Rosalind thought.

When she stopped feeling too early, she approached the house and rang the bell.

The door was opened by a gentleman Rosalind guessed to be in his seventies, dressed rather formally in a shirt and tie. The hall behind him was carpeted with a Persian rug, soft blue and rose, and a polished console table stood against one wall bearing freesias in a cut-glass vase.

'Geoffrey Soper,' he said in a voice that was pure *Country Life*. 'Barbara is already over there.'

He shook Rosalind's hand rather too fiercely for comfort and conducted her across the gravelled drive and under an arch to a small courtyard.

'Here we are.'

There were stone buildings on three sides. The middle section consisted of three wide, arched doors beneath three gabled windows set into a deeply pitched slate roof. On either side much lower buildings projected a short way, their stable doors painted white and all of them closed; no horses lived there now, Rosalind thought.

An iron staircase was fixed to the wall and strains of orchestral music drifted through the open door at the top.

'My dear? Mrs Cavanagh is here!'

The music was cut off abruptly and a small, spare lady in a crisp, high-necked blouse and pleated skirt stepped into view.

'Mrs Cavanagh, how nice to meet you!' She shook hands, and this time Rosalind's fingers met no resistance at all, like shaking hands with string. 'I was just opening the windows and letting in some fresh air. May I show you round?'

AN HOUR later Rosalind had digs.

The flat had once been for the coachman, before the horses had all gone, and was compact: a living room, with a small kitchen and bathroom on one side and a bedroom on the other. The furnishings were not to Rosalind's taste – chocolate brown carpets and armchairs covered in toffee-coloured velour, the kitchen cupboards painted olive green – but it looked clean and smelled fresh, despite having been unoccupied for three months.

It had a telephone line and Rosalind was told she could use Wi-Fi to connect to broadband at the main house. 'Are you sure that's all right?' she asked doubtfully. 'I expect to be using it a great deal. Can I make a contribution?'

'No, no, and it's unlimited anyway.'

Unlimited what? Rosalind wondered; but the rent seemed reasonable and the Sopers pleasant enough in an old-fashioned sort of way, handshakes notwithstanding. She made up her mind quickly and found she was excited at the prospect of moving in. A bedroom and a sitting room all for herself, and a kitchen of her own too! She could cook again, albeit on a rather small hob, and she could even bake if she chose!

And that reminded her of Aaron Eliot and his wife.

Normally she hated open invitations. How could one possibly guess when would be a good time? It always seemed to Rosalind that the person doing the inviting left all the anxiety of planning and fixing to the poor guest.

Like 'bring a dish' parties, Rosalind thought, disliking those too. If she hosted a gathering, she provided the food herself.

Yet for some reason this particular open invitation had not set her hackles rising. Perhaps it was the feeling of being on holiday with only herself to please, although she did seem to have committed quite a lot of time to the bookshop; or perhaps it was Aaron Eliot's easy warmth that reassured her and left her believing that perhaps any time really would be fine.

Rosalind had never cooked alongside anyone before. She wondered what it would be like.

By the time she reached Halfway House she had made up her mind. She would walk across the bridge tomorrow morning and ask when would be a good time, and if Grace Eliot was baking right then, she'd join her, and if she was going to bake later, Rosalind would come back. There. Decided.

Rosalind realised she was smiling. For the first time in many months she looked inward and thought she detected a difference.

I'm changing, she thought. *I wonder why.*

CHAPTER 16

Now

'AND,' ROSALIND CAVANAGH SAID, LEANING ACROSS THE slatted table in the pub garden, 'we need to make much more of the Waterfield connection.'

Bryony said, 'Mm,' mostly to play for time while she processed the change in her companion's attitude. She had come on board with an alacrity that was almost shocking.

Did Rosalind herself realise how she had altered? It was hard to believe she could not.

It was just over a week since Bryony had asked her to put a website together and in that time a web designer had been engaged (albeit an amateur one), a wizzy new software package had been bought, and Bryony had shelled out for some horrendously expensive ink cartridges to replace the ones in the printer borrowed from the Bradfords, which had been drained dry by printing out sheet upon sheet of web pages belonging to other bookshops with an interesting On-Line Presence.

Honestly, this terminology…

Rosalind had clearly been startled when she discovered that she needed to print out any pages at all: 'I'll call them up and show you on the screen,' she had said, followed a little later by, 'I don't understand why it keeps crashing'.

Bryony was going to have to tell her at some point, but for the time being Rosalind was so absorbed by what she was learning that she seemed oblivious of the weird stuff around the edges, so Bryony let things ride.

Now she said, 'Mm,' again and stood up. 'Do you want another?'

'Oh! Yes, please. But let me –'

'No way. You're doing all this work.'

Bryony headed indoors to the bar. She had found it was easy to interrupt Rosalind's flow if you needed some thinking time; you just had to do something for her. That invariably flicked a switch and turned her back into the reti-cent, please-don't-do-me-any-favours-I'm-not-worth-it woman who had once walked straight past the shop because she recognised a former adversary.

Oh well. Not adversaries any more. Bryony was surprised at how quickly they had become friends, sort of, as if she had been working on bringing forth a companion as well as an assistant.

She was surprised, too, at how readily she had confided in Rosalind, happily telling her about almost anything save the strange stuff. Perhaps she was responding to Rosalind's eagerness; everything about the bookshop seemed to interest her.

'Who was Bernard?' Rosalind had asked one day after Mrs Bobble-hat had been chuntering on about the old days.

'Cedric's cat. Before Gabriel. A tabby, I believe.'

'And Cedric?'

'Cedric Stranger was the guy here before me,' Bryony said. 'Before him it was just The Ravensburn Bookshop,' and she explained how she came to be the owner of a business at an age when most people are just emerging from university.

'You didn't go to university?'

'No. Got a place at Kent but when it came to it I decided to stay on at Circe's. Enough people coming out with degrees and going into retail, I thought I might as well cut out the preamble and jump straight in.'

Circe Stranger had a twisty, labyrinthine bookshop on a narrow alley in a village outside Haslemere, and having been intrigued by the place since the age of ten, Bryony inveigled her way into a Saturday job when she was sixteen. The job quickly expanded to school holidays, and when she left the sixth form and started at the shop full time she had expected to get a good grounding in book-selling from someone who had done the job on a one-woman basis for decades. And she did; but she got a whole lot more.

Circe had been an old-school eccentric – a bit of a nutter according to most people – and was alone in the world apart from her estranged brother Cedric. The two of them once run the bookshop together, but they had some kind of bust-up in the nineteen-seventies, after which Cedric decamped up north and did his own thing. The two of them had not been on speaking terms since.

There appeared to be no other family, and Bryony had certainly never enquired about Circe's love life. Despite having been named after a renowned temptress, her employer was aloof and a little severe, although Bryony became fond of the old harridan and was perfectly satisfied with her career choice.

Then Circe died, startlingly, from a single massive coronary between bites of her egg-and-cress sandwich one Tuesday lunchtime, and a week later Bryony was astonished to learn she was the sole beneficiary of Circe's will. She had been left everything.

'Goodness!' Rosalind said.

'Yes, goodness. But.'

Her inheritance was a mixed blessing. On the one hand, even after death duties, if she sold up she would have a lot of money; property prices around Haslemere were enormous and the hard assets were worth a bundle.

On the other hand, after death duties, she would have nothing like enough money to keep the business going. Bryony realised she would be forced to sell the twisty, labyrinthine bookshop, and by now she had fallen irrevocably in love with twisty, labyrinthine bookshops.

Then came the second call from Circe's solicitor, only a day after the first, and Bryony learned that Cedric Stranger, having struggled with a wonky heart for years, had finally given up and breathed his last within twenty-four hours of Circe breathing hers.

And crucially, Cedric died first.

'The thing is, despite their thirty-year quarrel, he had made Circe the sole beneficiary of *his* will.'

'Oh Bryony!'

'I know! You couldn't make it up, could you?'

So having inherited two bookshops in the space of forty-eight hours, Bryony set off for Northumberland in order to sell Cedric's business and thereby raise the necessary funds to pay the death duties on Circe's without destroying the bookshop.

'And you can see how that turned out.'

She had felt the first worms of doubt even as she climbed down from Dan's Land Rover after he picked her up from Hexham, and by the time she had reached the third floor of the bookshop she had made up her mind to reverse her plan; she would sell Circe's shop and settle here instead.

'Just like that?' Rosalind said.

'Hm, well, I wobbled a bit when I saw the state of the flat. You know the stereotype of the fussy, house-proud old bachelor? Well, Cedric wasn't that. Do you know what I found in the airing cupboard?'

'No, and don't tell me, Bryony, please. I mean it.'

Bryony reluctantly shut up. It was a pity because the story was a good one, although preposterous. Maybe she could sneak it in another time.

And it was scarcely any more preposterous than the bookshop lingering on in so remote a village.

She knew the business looked shaky when she took it on, but somehow Cedric Stranger had managed to make enough income to survive and so far Bryony was doing the same. It didn't make sense and practically every sale surprised her, but she was able to keep herself in tee-shirts and stand a round at the pub once in a while.

She paid and took the drinks outside. They had come to the pub straight after closing the shop; Dan wasn't serving dinner yet and theirs was the only table in use. Web printouts were strewn across the slats weighted down with coasters Bryony had pinched from indoors: rather nice ones with Bewick's bird engravings on them. Bryony especially liked the Redstart, probably because of the ruined castle behind it. You can't beat a ruined castle.

She set the drinks down and climbed back over the bench. 'Okay, the Waterfield connection. Let's get the Society involved then.'

'The society?'

'The Edith Waterfield Society. Did you not know about them?'

Rosalind shook her head.

'You can look forward to finding out, then. They're Edith Waterfield groupies – meet up twice a year to read the books aloud to one another and argue about their favourite cat. They have a newsletter – I mean honestly, how can it be news? – and they write fan-fiction about Calpurnia and Mercutio, and Rose and John.'

Bryony felt herself getting into a rant. 'Really, Rosalind, they're all bats. They descend on this place every May and September, and they also hit on Cawton because someone worked out from the position of the pub that Edith used it as a model for Castlehope. They're quite keen on the Bewick bits and pieces in Newcastle too, because of John Day of course. But they are seriously rose-tinted-spectacles. They don't like to talk about the scandal.'

'Scandal?'

'No, not at all. Cats, cottages, cats, True Love and more cats is what they're about, basically. The scandal doesn't fit with how they see their golden girl.'

Bryony took a sip of her Coke and added, 'So you can imagine how they feel about the murder.'

CHAPTER 17

Once

Lucas stepped out of the station and paused, disoriented. He needed to find his bearings. So much would have changed.

When he left twelve years ago it had been clinging to the rail on top of a coach, while old Mr Weatherstone sat snoring inside. He had been thrilled and terrified, and almost overcome by gratitude to the old man who had such faith in him; he would have been full of determination to prove his worth and pay his employer back for his fare, in service if not in cash.

And now the railway had arrived, crossing the Tyne on a brand new bridge that symbolised the promise of the modern industrial age, and he had made the journey in just one day. It was almost a miracle.

He felt stiff though. He was accustomed to stand at his work and all those hours sitting down made him long to walk. He didn't recognise the street, and the sun was hidden by the day's dark clouds, but in Newcastle up is always up and down always down, and using this rule of thumb Lucas set off towards the river to find the lodgings Jack from the King's Head had recommended. The house was near the quayside and likely to be rough, but Lucas believed he could look after himself and wanted to be thrifty.

In truth, he didn't yet really believe in this news. He certainly would not be hiring the dog cart Joseph Weatherstone had suggested.

An hour later he had found the boarding house and taken a bite – day-old bread and sharp cheese, not the best he had eaten – and was walking into the town. He headed first for the spire of St Nicholas, and skirted the church walls to the south-east corner of the yard where the narrow fronted workshop belied the magic that lay within.

The Master's workshop. Lucas had, he somehow knew, set foot inside this wondrous place at the age of only nine, although he had little recollection of the event. He had been patted on the head by the great man himself, and given a leaf of spare paper and a stick of charcoal with which to amuse himself.

His life's career had been forged in that warm afternoon while his father measured the frame for a new door, lying on his stomach on the flagstones and making marks with the tool in his hand.

Who would have thought pictures could be created so easily? First cows and sheep and cats and dogs, and trees and carts and houses, then his friends Will and Johnny and John-ny's brother George, and his father, with chisel in hand, and his mother, whom he did not remember but thought might have looked like Will's mother, whom he called Aunty Meg. All these flowed across the pages as if by themselves, as if the burnt wood in his hand had life of its own and he had only to think of a thing for it to appear before him.

He didn't want to stop, and when his father had finished his business, the child Lucas had to be removed from the workshop physically, the hand that had been busy making miracles now heartlessly caged by his father's calloused fingers.

Lucas had heard the story from Joseph Weatherstone, who had been in the workshop that day, himself a young apprentice. *So eager to draw were you*, Joseph said, *it was as if you had come alive at last.*

As if he had come alive at last. And yet he could not remember.

How could that be?

NEXT DAY, the train deposited him at Hexham just after midday, in good time for his meeting with Mr Stratford's attorney. An hour after that, Lucas stepped into the street bewildered and still not entirely convinced, but willing to tread this amazing path and see where it led.

While he had been closeted in the attorney's office the sun had shaken itself free of the clouds and now the morn-ing's rainwater sparkled on the pavement. Lucas asked his way and quickly left the market town behind, striding out at last, invigorated by the sunshine and the clean air. Rooks cawed and distant sheep bleated, and once a horse and wagon clumped and rolled past him. Lucas began to whistle. He found his spirits were high.

Three miles from Hexham the road forked and Lucas turned left as instructed. This route was less travelled, and grass grew thickly between and around the ruts made by cart wheels. When Lucas halted to eat the sausage and bread he had bought in town, the quiet was profound: silence but for the faintest, most distant murmur of air moving through grasses, and the sound inside his head of his own chewing. He might have been the last man left on the earth.

Lucas tucked the water bottle into his bag and walked on.

The miles passed and afternoon turned gradually to evening. Then the ground began to fall, twisting around hummocks and dells, and small stones slid under his soles.

A curlew cried.

And suddenly, below him, Lucas saw the thread of smoke that spoke of human habitation, and shortly after heard the distant ring of hammer on anvil; he was nearly there.

He quickened his pace. The first building was a low, stone cottage with chickens in the yard, followed by a wide barn and then an inn, and as he rounded the corner of the inn Lucas saw the street fall away before him, wide enough for ease, narrow enough for comfort, and filling now with the long shadows of evening. The village was quiet and the street empty of people, only a black cat was stretched sunning itself on the wall of the churchyard.

Lucas hesitated, and suddenly it seemed to him that what he saw before him was momentous, pregnant with possibility, unguessable, and unguessably important. He was stranded, marooned between his past and his future. It was, he thought, as if he stood not at the top of a hill but in the wings of a theatre, and the next steps he took would bring him onto the stage.

He did not want to go. He felt he did not know his part.

And then, ahead, a woman came out of a door and began to climb the hill towards him. She was slender, and carried a basket, and the sun struck her hair and turned it to gold.

Lucas felt his heart miss its beat.

Standing stock still like a fool, unwilling to stare but unable to drag his gaze away, he watched the woman draw nearer and saw her smile as her eyes met his.

Somehow that enabled him to take a fresh grip on himself and smile in return.

He bowed. He could even speak.

'Forgive me, but I am newly come to Castlehope and am looking for the house of Mr Stratford. Can you direct me?'

'Of course. Mr Stratford's house is next but one to the baker's shop, with clematis around the door. But I am afraid…' She hesitated, then said, 'Are you a member of his family?'

'No, not family, but in a way…' Lucas collected his thoughts and bowed again. 'I seem to be Mr Stratford's heir. Allow me to introduce myself.

'My name is John Lucas.'

CHAPTER 18

Then

Edith and Lillian split up after breakfast, Lillian walking purposefully north-west with her umbrella in one hand and a map hand-drawn by the concierge in the other. Edith watched her sister's back recede. She seemed so sure.

Oh Lillian. And all for Billy Moffat. It wasn't as if they were sweethearts before the war, and the Moffats were hardly, well…

Edith paused, reluctant to follow the thought to its conclusion: *not really like us.* It was so ungenerous, when Billy's brother had been lost and Billy left…the way he was…but snobbish or not, it was how Edith felt. What did they talk about, he and Lillian, alone in the parlour after the paint-brushes were put away and before Ruth reappeared with tea and toast? What could they possibly have in common?

Edith sighed. She was supposed to be a writer, with insight, yet there was so much about human relationships she could only guess at. Nothing was straightforward. Lillian was courting a farmer's boy; Ruth had clearly given up on her own prospects and was dedicating herself to matchmaking for her sisters; and as for herself, in love with someone she had made up…

The thought made her grin. She settled her umbrella more comfortably and crossed the road, avoiding the puddles. The cathedral of St Nicholas, that was what she wanted, and she didn't need a sketch map to find it either. St Nicholas might be small as cathedrals go, having been built as an ordinary, every-day church and only come to glory decades later, but it was still a large chunk of stone with a spire that soared above the humble buildings surrounding it.

One of those humble buildings, now sadly demolished, was where Lovely John had discovered his calling, or rather where his calling had been discovered. He had been a little boy accompanying his father on a job because his mother was dead. She had to be dead because living parents would only complicate the plot, and she had to have died a while ago or John would have had siblings. At the same time, it could not be so long ago that his father had recovered from his grief and married again.

Authors had to do an awful lot of background planning, Edith thought grumpily.

John's father had been the victim of a tragic accident soon after his son was apprenticed, which got him safely out of the way. Oh, and his joinery business was failing so that there was nothing left for John to inherit once the debts were paid off.

One really had to think of everything.

While his father, still alive at that point, measured up for a new door, the kindly, bluff old man known by his craftsmen and apprentices as The Master gave the child John paper and pencil to pass the time.

Perhaps not a pencil, perhaps charcoal. She would have to ask Winifred. Thank heavens for Winifred.

The Master, of course, was the great Thomas Bewick, but Edith had yet to decide whether to use his real name or to invent a fictional figure and imply heavily on whom he was based. She was new to writing for publication and didn't know the rules.

In her father's library was a natural history of Northumberland illustrated with wood engravings, which had captured Edith's imagination before she could comfortably read the stodgy text. There was something so deliciously confident about the crisp black-and-white images, so decidedly *there*, finished and unalterable – quite unlike her own hesitant, feathery pencil sketches or Lillian's soft-edged watercolours.

Her father told her about Thomas Bewick, the artist-craftsman who drew with an engraving tool and who had shunned the commercial opportunities of London to remain steadfastly a Newcastle man. How her father knew all this Edith had never thought to ask. Perhaps it was common knowledge.

In any case, wood engravings remained her absolute favourite art form, and when the first inklings twinkled into existence of the story that would become *The Holly and the Ivy*, it was immediately clear to her what her hero's profession would be.

A gentle man but robust; sensitive but strong; clever, quick, neat and wise. Edith loved the mixture of artist and craftsman, the intellectual and the practical. Her father had read voraciously – practically everything ever written, she once thought – and spoke eloquently on a wide range of subjects, but he had to call in Dixon Blyth if he needed so much as a nail hammered into something. Billy Moffat could cut and lay a hedge in a day – well, once upon a time – but had never in his life read a book through to the end. Surely somewhere there was a man who could do both?

Edith stood with her back to the site of Bewick's workshop, trying to rid her head of these distractions. She looked around and scribbled notes about what she could see (rain on the cathedral) and hear (rain) and smell (rain).

Perhaps she would make John arrive in Newcastle on a wet day.

After that she walked up Grey Street, identifying the age of the city landmarks and making notes about John's reactions to what he saw a century earlier. It was all guesswork; she had no idea how much of this was here a hundred years ago; thank *heavens* for Winifred.

Mind you, she should probably include a preface: *Historical inaccuracies are entirely the fault of the Author*. Surely people wouldn't mind? It was fiction after all.

The rain had ceased while she was in the Laing Art Gallery, which definitely post-dated John, and the sun, emerging startlingly from the clouds, set the puddles sparkling. Edith liked the idea and made another note: *The morning's rainwater sparkled on the pavements.*

The air smelled of warm, wet stone. Ruth was twenty-six miles away and a dainty tea would be waiting at the hotel in an hour; life, Edith thought, could hardly be better.

BUT IT COULD BE MUCH WORSE.

As Edith drew near to the hotel Lillian ran down the steps towards her, and her sister's face made Edith's stomach contract.

'Lillian, what–?'

'There's been a telegram!'

A telegram.

In an instant Edith's skin turned icy and her hands and feet began to numb. Her jaw was stuck. But it couldn't be a telegram, could it? The boys were already dead, almost all of them…

Her throat would not work. 'Charlie,' she tried to say, but Lillian was ahead of her.

'No, not Charlie. It's Primmy.'

Lillian reached for her hands and clutched them.

'Edith, Primmy is dead.'

...

GHOSTS

CHAPTER 19

Now

Bryony sat, feet flat on the floor, hands folded in her lap, ignoring the rain on the window behind her, trying to be still.

It wasn't easy.

She spent her life cramming jobs into the hours she was awake, of which there were never quite enough. People might think a bookshop was a sleepy backwater of a place but being in sole control of one was far from soporific, and that was before you factored in the three flights of stairs. Since Rosalind Cavanagh had become involved life had definitely got easier.

At least a bit.

Bryony waited for her muscles to relax. She breathed

deep, using her diaphragm, and willed her shoulders to soften.

How long was Rosalind going to stay? If she had indeed answered Bryony's summons in July then one would think she would be here for several months at least, a year even. Rosalind was not what Bryony had expected to come forth, but no-one else had popped up on the scene despite her heavy-duty, concentrated worrying.

And there was that other matter, as well.

The smell of warm books seeped into Bryony's consciousness, and a trace of something sweeter, like black-currants, probably from the children who had been up here earlier. Neither was the scent she was hoping for.

Bryony closed her eyes, but her thoughts remained on Rosalind Cavanagh.

Did she know what she was? Unlikely, Bryony thought. *I suppose I ought to tell her.* But she'd have to time it carefully. She suspected Rosalind's reaction might not be the same as her own.

She grinned, still with her eyes shut, aware she must look like a mad thing and relieved nobody could see her.

Discovering the truth about herself had been amazing – wild and ridiculous – and she loved being who she was, even if it did mean she would be forever excluded from the heady delights of texting and Facebook.

Shh. Relax.

Yes, relax. Open your mind, Bryony Bower, and free your senses. He's around here somewhere, I bet.

Come out, John Day, and reveal yourself.

She had positioned herself where the portrait could see her. She thought it might help.

Was it John Day? Bryony had searched the picture front and back for a hint but it remained stubbornly anonymous apart from a scrawly signature she couldn't decipher. It was twentieth-century, she was sure; the paint had been laid in thick slabs and the brushwork was choppy (a layman's description), slavish realism taking second place to the capture of character, the expression of expression.

He was definitely attractive: dark hair softly curling, dark eyes with a hint of something other. He looked, Bryony thought, as if he still believed in fairyland. Long nose, grave mouth…If he was indeed John Day then Bryony could understand Edith falling for him.

Was he haunting the bookshop where they had lived and loved?

She was pretty certain the ghost was John Day because of the atmosphere of ease and familiarity that accompanied it. You wouldn't get that from a visitor, would you? He had to be someone who had called this home. To begin with she had thought the ghost might be any age and from any age, but then she had stumbled across the article on Edith Water-field in *The Northumbrian Gazette*, stashed in a metal trunk with a load of other local periodicals from the 1950s, and read Edith's response to the journalist's question.

Ghost? she was reported to have replied. *Do you really believe in such things?*

That was after she had got the bookshop up and running, so post-1952.

She could have been lying, of course, but Bryony trusted

her personal, in-built lie detector, which had proved very reliable in the past, and reckoned Edith had been telling the truth. So far as Edith Waterfield was aware at that time, the bookshop had no resident ghost.

So that was another reason to think it was John Day who still trod the passages and staircases.

On the other hand, if the ghost *was* around in Edith's time and she was lying about it, then the obvious candidate was Albert Winter-thing.

Wintersgill. Albert Wintersgill.

Al*fred* Wintersgill.

Because it is the victim of violent death who haunts the living, isn't it? And it seemed at least possible that poor old Alfred Wintersgill had indeed met a sticky end at the bookshop one way or another.

Her internal lie detector had wriggled a bit at that though; not a flat-out denial, more a sense of uncertainty. Odd. It was a pity there were no descendants to offer an opinion about what had happened that night.

Although…

'Oh, *stuff!*'

Bryony opened her eyes. It was no good; meditation did not suit her. She might have been able to summon flesh and blood to her aid in the form of Rosalind Cavanagh but it seemed spirit and dream were less compliant, and in the meantime there were the day's cheques to enter and Greedy Gabriel to feed.

As she stood up it occurred to Bryony that 'spirit and memory' would have been more apt, and she wondered where that word 'dream' had come from.

CHAPTER 20

Now

ROSALIND DROVE HER FINGERS INTO THE BOWL AND LIFTED them, drove and lifted, over and over, stroking her thumbs against her finger tips, searching for the soft clumps of margarine and lard yet to be dispersed into the flour. She enjoyed rubbing-in and much preferred to do it with her hands than with the food processor at Monk's Walk, which sat in the corner of the kitchen next to the bread-making machine: two sparkling appliances scarcely ever used. That Matthew had bought them for her was as good an indication as any that he had not understood her.

Across the table, whisking eggs, Grace Eliot was petite but curvy in her husband's denim shirt with the sleeves rolled up. It would never have occurred to Rosalind to wear any of Matthew's clothes. Aaron's shirt was too big for Grace, of course, and the shoulder seams were half-way to her elbows, the shirt tails over her thighs, but she managed to make it a beguiling look.

Grace's fork clattered inside the glass bowl. She was making a Dundee cake, the currants and sultanas and almonds weighed out and lined up waiting to join the mixture. Rosalind was making short-crust pastry for an apple pie, using thinly sliced Bramleys from the Eliots' orchard.

'We're about to enter a glut', Grace had assured her. 'You'll be doing us a favour.'

When the pie was baked and still steaming in its tin, Rosalind would place it carefully into the open basket strapped to her handlebars, with a clean linen cloth to protect it, and push her new bicycle up the hill to the book-shop. She would deliver slices to Megan at the gallery and Jo at the flower shop too.

Rosalind had been in Ravensburn for nine – no, ten weeks, and had made friends.

It was the third of September and the glorious weather that had just managed to linger over the August Bank Holiday had given way to gunmetal skies and steely rain. Beyond the kitchen window, drips from the gutter beat a rhythmic tattoo on something metal ('That loose drain cover', Grace said) and from time to time a flurry of wind threw the drops against the window panes like bird-shot.

'Awful day,' Grace said, pushing back a strand of hair with her wrist. 'I do wonder sometimes about that tower. I hope they've done their sums right.'

On the hill above the Forge the microwave tower was taking shape as a high, spindly affair of struts and cross-pieces like steel lace. Rosalind wondered how Grace could bear to have it there, so aggressively industrial in the midst of the heather, but Grace simply shrugged: 'It's a cliché, but you really can't hold back time.' Although she was anxious about water run-off from the foundations.

Now she glanced at the window and said, 'You'll need an umbrella to get up the hill.'

Rosalind thought she probably would not, but in any case she had a small folding one in her bag; it seemed to her profoundly arrogant to assume she could rely on the weather. One day, she was sure, she would be caught out.

Baking alongside another had turned out to be utterly delightful, and after the first anxious minutes back in July when she had been welcomed into Grace's comfortable farmhouse kitchen, Rosalind had relaxed into the restorative business of combining flour and butter and sugar to make food that she felt was good for the soul as well as the flesh.

Grace's kitchen was less shiny than Rosalind's at Monk's Walk but the essentials were all present: a deep Belfast sink to take even the largest pans; a Welsh dresser laden with china; shelves holding every size and shape of dish and baking tin; a solid table at the right height for working; and presiding over all, a wide, multi-oven range cooker that allowed plenty of elbow room.

The cooker at the Forge was solid fuel and the furniture was all free-standing, and some of it not what one might expect: a rocking chair, a bookcase, and a heavy oak blanket chest.

'All hand-me-downs,' Grace explained. 'Been in the house forever.'

The Forge had been lived in by generations of Eliots.

'The girls go but the boys stay. Aaron was the only son, as were his father and his grandfather.'

'Why do you have a blanket chest in the kitchen?' Rosalind had asked, and Grace had shrugged and said, 'I think it has always been here: the Eliot family history's in there, along with I don't know what. We've never tried to move it.'

The work surfaces were wood, and met pots and utensils with a thump rather than the high-pitched chink of the Monk's Walk granite.

There were rag rugs over the stone flags and family ephemera in odd places: snapshots propped between cups on the dresser, a plaited friendship bracelet dangling from a drawer knob, Aertex shirts stacked on the chest, topped by a bundle of name tapes to be sewn in.

'A bit last-minute,' Grace admitted, 'but I'll finish them this evening.'

Her eldest, Polly, started secondary school on Monday. It was she that Rosalind had assumed owned *The Girl's Book of Cakes and Biscuits* she was surprised to find amongst Grace's collection of cookery books; it didn't fit well with Elizabeth David and Jane Grigson. But Grace had laughed.

'No, that was Aaron. I went to stay with my sister for a week and he had withdrawal symptoms.'

Rosalind smiled. It was understandable, and none of the other books were what one might call primers. Like herself, Grace bought cookery books for inspiration rather than as instruction manuals.

Grace was an easy, comfortable friend, and each

Wednesday now Rosalind stood at the wide table and mixed her ingredients in a beautiful, aged Mason Cash bowl while Grace did the same. Grace used measuring cups, though, rather than weighing by eye as Rosalind did, and her bread too rose beautifully, her pastry crumbled meltingly, and her cakes never cracked or sank.

Rosalind said once, 'Karen told me that alchemy happens in this kitchen; that all the Eliot women bake like magicians.'

'Alchemists, possibly. We grow like our husbands, don't we? But not magicians. You, though, Rosalind – the way you measure everything by instinct, that's proper magic.'

Aaron Eliot was not exactly an alchemist. He inhabited the Forge where his ancestors had served the village as black-smiths, and he had mastered the art of iron and fire, but spent only a couple of days a week at the anvil; from Monday to Thursday he taught geology in Newcastle.

'You can't survive on the bits and pieces that come in,' Grace explained. 'The odd tool to mend, door hinges or a weathercock to make, occasional exhibition work. And he's not a farrier, of course.'

Farriery, the incredibly skilful task of nailing a shoe onto the foot of a living horse, required years of specialised training and practice.

Grace's children, Polly and Aidan ('just the one son again!'), had two ponies that grazed under the apple trees and hoovered up the windfalls, but they were ridden straight onto the grassy moor and did not need to wear shoes at all.

'Right. That's done.'

Grace slid the cake tin into the warm oven and closed the door tight. 'Coffee when you're ready?'

Fifteen minutes later Rosalind's pie was in the hot oven, the bowls and spoons washed up, and the two women were sitting on mismatched chairs at the table, cuddling mugs of fresh coffee.

'So tell me about the Society,' Grace said.

'Ah yes, the Society.'

Rosalind paused, recollecting Bryony Bower's acerbic words: *Average age ninety-three, and nine out of ten of them women. They have cream teas and hold séances and someone wins a china plaque for the best-dressed cat.*

Rosalind could never be entirely sure when Bryony was joking.

'I gather they're a bit eccentric,' she said now, 'and quite elderly.'

'Eccentricity goes hand in hand with enthusiasm, don't you think?' Grace said. 'Which doesn't say much for the non-eccentrics among us, does it? When are they coming?'

'Saturday week.'

The Edith Waterfield Society scheduled their autumn visit to Ravensburn after the schools had gone back but before the cold weather set in. *It would be nice if it was sunny*, Bryony had said with a rather odd emphasis, and Rosalind certainly hoped that it would be.

This year Bryony had invited them to hold an open session in the bookshop, reading aloud in the children's area and spreading the word about Edith's books to anyone who strayed too close. She was also sponsoring the Best-Dressed Cat competition.

'Is it really the best-dressed though?' Rosalind asked Bryony. 'Surely it's just the nicest cat?'

'Nicest cat in a right ridiculous set up. Just you wait until you see those photos.'

The prize would be a small, framed print of John Day's wood engraving of the bookshop's street façade and £50 credit to be spent on books at Ravensburn. *('I'm not giving them Book Tokens and watching them skip off to Waterstones.')*

'I'm looking forward to it,' Rosalind admitted, and Grace said, 'I would be too. I'm sure they'll be charming.'

Rosalind wasn't sure how charming they would be, but she expected the members of the Society to be *interesting*, and she had plans.

Not everything was published on the internet. Rosalind had been researching Edith Waterfield and discovered more than one dead end. What she was hoping for most of all when the Society descended on Ravensburn were some answers.

CHAPTER 21

Now

THE DOOR BELL JINGLED AND BRYONY GLANCED UP FROM THE papers she was reading. Two elderly women she recognised as regulars from Hexham stood in the doorway and carefully shook their umbrellas outside. (*Take mine, Jean, and give me yours – I'm here now so I might as well.*)

'Still raining, then?' Bryony asked unnecessarily, to be friendly.

'Yes, still raining, but it's getting lighter. There are chinks in the cloud to the south.'

'Really?'

Bryony glanced at the clock that stood on the mantel-piece above the hearth: yup, Rosalind would be walking up from the Forge soon.

Time to put the kettle on, then. Bryony stretched,

wondering happily what delectable deliciousness would arrive this week. She flipped the door sign and turned the key, then ran upstairs. Jean and Marjorie were in the fiction stacks on the first floor.

'Just popping up for a coffee,' Bryony told them as she breezed past. 'Back in a sec. The key's in the door.' They knew the score.

No-one had used the kettle in the Reading Room so she didn't need to refill it, but the asters on the window sill were past their best. She'd ask Rosalind to change their water later; that would do it.

She grinned. Since Rosalind had arrived her flower bills had been halved.

On the other hand, that particular saving was wiped out several times over by the expense of starting the website. Robby assured her that once it was up and running, actually maintaining it would cost next to nothing, but the software and Robby's services had not come cheap even if Rosalind's did.

Bryony might have felt guilty about Rosalind, but she had decided not to.

From the window of her tiny kitchen she squinted down the street and saw that the cloud was indeed breaking up and there was a patch of clear, bright blue floating above the Forge. Already the rain outside the shop had reduced to just spitting.

She'd timed it just right.

Back at her desk, Bryony shuffled through the papers for the sheet she wanted. It was a page printed from something called Wikipedia, a free on-line encyclopaedia apparently created by anyone and everyone, and while for that reason it was wise to approach it with caution, it did seem very useful.

The entry for Edith Waterfield was not long, though.

After a brief introduction, which basically just gave her dates and the fact that she was an author, there were two paragraphs on her life (born in Ravensburn, family more or less wiped out by the First World War) and a list of her books. That was it, apart from a note about *The Holly and the Ivy* having been dramatised on radio in the early nineteen-seventies; a one-off, not a serial, so brutally abridged.

Exposed to Wikipedia for the first time in her life, Bryony was not impressed. What did they mean by saying Edith's father was a doctor and 'an occasional poet'? Ridiculous way to describe someone! And what was all that about 'most' of the cats being named after Shakespeare's characters? Which, pray tell, were not?

When Rosalind arrived, bone dry and lit by sunshine, Bryony growled, 'So which names did this idiot think were not from Shakespeare?' Then she stopped growling and said, 'Ooh, is that apple pie?' as Rosalind finished wiping her shoes on the doormat – she might not get rained on but there were always puddles – and whisked the cloth from the top of the dish to reveal a pie crust the colour of honey, simply but expertly decorated with hand-cut pastry leaves and bejewelled with crystals of sugar. A good-sized segment had already gone, the soft, pale apples spilling across the base of the dish. It smelled heavenly.

Rosalind cut into the pastry and lifted a generous wedge onto Bryony's plate. 'What names?'

'Edith's cats. This Wikipedia thing says only some of them come from Shakespeare.'

'Well, Jessica perhaps. It's quite a common name now and someone might not realise.'

Bryony grunted, but the deliciousness of the apple pie was erasing her irritation. 'Rosalind, you bake like an angel.'

'Oh…not really.'

Rosalind did not like compliments. Bryony didn't believe that should prevent her from giving them when they were called for though, and the treats that emerged every Wednesday afternoon definitely called for them.

Someone came in for a map while Bryony was eating so Rosalind took the money, fiddling the dockets into the track of the old card reader and trundling the top back and forth over the raised numbers as Bryony had taught her. She smiled gently so that the customer also smiled and doubtless departed thinking that the Stranger Bookshop was a gem and he would return as soon as possible.

It was a pity Rosalind wasn't on the till full time. She wouldn't be on the till at all for the rest of this week, because she was going home to that big old house of hers to collect winter clothes. She had been waiting for the schools to go back, for some reason. It was a pity she wouldn't be around for the weekend trade, but winter clothes was a really good sign.

Bryony hid the plate and spoon on the floor under the desk, wiped her hands on a tissue and said, 'Okay then, what about the locals? She was here until 1978; that's less than forty years ago. Loads of people round here must remember her. Mrs Pigg can't be the only one.'

They were piecing together what was known about Edith Waterfield in order to hold their own against the Society. When the members had descended on the bookshop in May, Bryony had been woefully unprepared and ended up having to sit with her mouth shut while she was Told Things. It wasn't enjoyable. This time she wanted some Things of her own to Tell. In any case, adding a biography of Edith to the bookshop's cool new website would be another way to register its existence and attract surfers.

It was all about Attracting Surfers, Robby said. There were now so many zillions of internet pages that the chance of someone stumbling across yours was so remote as to be nearly impossible. That meant you had to work hard to make your website feature high up with the Search Engines. Bryony had a beguiling image of a cheeky blue steam engine with a smiling, painted face looking under table cloths and behind wardrobes.

'How do we do that?' she had asked.

'Oh, there are ways,' Robby told her. 'Don't worry, I'm on it.'

Bryony didn't worry. He was a nice bloke, cheerful and full of ideas, and was clearly competent with this stuff. The number of hits they were getting was increasing day by day, according to Rosalind. Robby had put a counter in; you just clicked on it to see the number of visitors.

She'd get used to the jargon in the end.

Now Rosalind said, 'Mrs Pig?'

'What? Oh, yes, Mrs Pigg.' Bryony paused to think. 'If you have to ask then you haven't met her. She's unmistake-able even apart from the name, which has two Gs, by the way. A hundred and twelve and a foot shorter than even me. Wears black, although she has a woolly hat in the winter that is sort of chartreuse: quite bilious. And wellies, you never see her out of wellies spring, summer or winter.'

'Goodness.'

'Yes. She shuffles about staring up at people. Dead creepy. And she lives in that cottage just past the stables, with the wooden shutters.'

'You make her sound like a witch.'

'Oh no,' Bryony said, 'she's not a witch. But she's been here all her life and knew Edith well, and yet she never, ever, comes in here. Why should that be, do you suppose?' She leaned back in her chair. 'Actually a hundred and twelve is a lie. She told me her twenty-first birthday was the same day as the Coronation so she pretended the street party was for her. So when was that? Nineteen fifty-what?'

'Fifty-two, I think, or perhaps fifty-three.'

'Mm. So she's in her eighties. She looks ancient though.'

'So she might have some information about Edith,' Rosalind said.

'Oh, she has information all right,' Bryony said. 'The problem is she won't impart it. Not a word. She absolutely knows they weren't married, you can tell because she gets very shifty, and she gets even shiftier if you ask her why.'

Bryony recalled how the old woman had wriggled in her wellies when cornered at the spring fair, and then cut Bryony off and stomped away towards the handicrafts tent. Bryony had asked her again in the Post Office, queuing for stamps, only for the old girl to snap that she believed in keeping faith with family secrets and shuffle off, boots clumping, to crash straight into Aaron Eliot coming in.

'People who have lived so long deserve our respect, don't you think?' Aaron said mildly to Bryony afterwards, and she felt reprimanded and hadn't raised the subject again with Mrs Pigg. But it was tantalising.

Why was it a family secret? The Piggs weren't related to the Waterfields, were they?

'I think you can get quite a lot of information about family trees on-line these days,' Rosalind said, her elegant brows drawn into a frown. 'I'll see what I can find.'

'Yes, do.'

Prodding Rosalind into internet-land, Bryony thought, had been like releasing the genie from the bottle; she was an altered woman; who knew where it might all lead?

CHAPTER 22

Now

By the time Rosalind reached home the apple pie had cooled and she could safely put it in the fridge. She made herself a cup of tea and settled down at the table.

She opened the laptop and checked that the power lead was connected. The poor thing was spending so much time searching the internet these days she generally left it permanently charging, the cable snaking across the carpet as if her lounge were a teenager's bedroom.

Well, it couldn't be helped. And she was not expecting visitors.

Rosalind had begun to bookmark web pages she thought might be useful, and now she called up the two Wikipedia entries she had printed yesterday for Bryony. The first was on Edith Waterfield, whom it called Edith Susan Waterfield.

The entry began by giving her dates as 1st April 1899 to 14th September 1978, and then went on to say that she was an English author best known for her fantasy stories written for children about cats, 'most of whom are named after characters from Shakespeare's plays'.

That was what had sparked Bryony's ire. Bryony was a rather spiky person in some ways.

Under *Life*, the entry read:

Edith Waterfield was born in the Northumberland village of Ravensburn, near Hexham, which, along with Cawton, is believed to be the model for her fictional village of Castlehope. Her father was a doctor and also an occasional poet, who encouraged his daughter to write imaginatively as a child. Her early life was filled with tragedy, as her mother died in 1910, followed by her father in 1917; her four elder brothers were all lost in the Great War, and Edith was brought up by her elder sisters. Despite achieving recognition for her children's fiction, she never left Ravensburn and died in 1978 after a brief illness.

Edith had a long-standing association with the wood engraver John Day, who illustrated all her children's books. Contemporary authors Carolyn Hodge[1], Stephen Godwin[2] and Joan Jefferson[3] have said they enjoyed and were influenced by Waterfield's books.

'…a long-standing association…' That was one way of putting it.

'Of course they were lovers you know,' Jo at the flower shop said, wrapping six lilies in a cone of tissue paper. 'My mum said it was obvious when you saw them together, but why they never married is anyone's guess. Mrs Pigg probably knows. Do you mind coins? I'm out of fivers.'

'My Dad said *his* Dad said they were no better than they should be,' said Dan at the Handsome Jack. 'Used to seem quite upset about it, but Dad reckoned he fancied her himself. Why don't you ask Mrs Pigg?'

'You know, my Auntie Ethel always thought there was something a bit You Know about them,' said the little old lady sitting on the bench at the top of the street, to whom Rosalind found herself chatting after she stopped to say 'Good afternoon'. Her name was Mrs Goudge, she said, and she had been born and raised in Ravensburn. 'They had eyes only for each other, you see, and yet they never married. Perhaps he wasn't suitable. No-one knew anything about him, he just arrived in the village one day out of nowhere. And she said they never, ever left the village, you know, not even for a few days, and I think that's queer. But there. Anyway, that's what my Auntie Ethel said.'

Then she added, 'I'll tell you who knows a thing or two. Mrs Pigg, that's who. But she'll never tell.'

No, apparently not, if Bryony was to be believed.

Rosalind ran her eye over the rest of the entry, which listed Edith's books in order of publication – *The Holly and the Ivy* was the first, a few years before *Mercutio the Midnight Cat* – and offered a link to the Edith Waterfield Society.

Rosalind had already visited the Society's website and been disappointed to find the biography there a direct lift from the Wikipedia version.

She had printed out a second Wikipedia entry, which was about *The Holly and the Ivy*:

The only full length adult novel written by Edith Waterfield, The Holly and the Ivy *has been consistently reviewed as a 'problem' book and is often described as 'a novel of two halves'.*

Despite a strong story line, the characterisation is inconsistent, with the character of John Lucas drawn powerfully in the first half of the book but thin and unconvincing in the second half, and that of Herbert Douthwaite seeming a cardboard, stock villain in the first half but all too credible and menacing in the second. No reason has been put forward for this anomaly.

This anomaly had not occurred to Rosalind, neither on first reading the book nor when re-reading it on the train, but it was true she was not a critical reader. On reflection, she could see what the writer of this article meant.

Finally there was the explanation of the title:

The title of the story refers to the medieval poem The Contest of the Holly and the Ivy[1] *concerning the battle between these two woodland plants, most commonly read as an allegory for the battle between the sexes, the holly being masculine and the ivy feminine. (See also* Ivy, Chief of Trees, It Is.[2])

Rosalind had followed both links and read the poems, and now wondered why she had never thought before about the ivy's place in the popular Christmas carol, appearing over and over in the chorus but with no part to play in any of the verses.

What a lot slips by without us noticing.

On a whim, Rosalind searched for both Edith Waterfield and the title of the book together, and found a list of websites belonging to booksellers and reading communities where reviews were posted.

She started to read.

As she had begun to realise, *The Holly and the Ivy* was something of a cult book, and most of the reviews were given four or five stars. Some of them positively gushed:

An enchanting book full of a truly magical sense of period and place by an author who clearly lived and breathed her characters. That was one.

Another read: *The history and dialect of rural Northumberland come alive in this beautiful, passionate story of a village governess torn between the two men who love her*.

One, very upfront, said: *If you like Precious Bane you'll love this, and John Lucas knocks Kester Woodseaves into a cocked hat!*

I discovered this book when I was fourteen and have been in love with John Lucas ever since was a fairly typical response and one Rosalind thought might well have been hers had she known about the book at that age. Where had all these girls found it?

This was lurking in a bookcase in our rented holiday cottage, said one reader; *my Nan gave it to me* said another; and one proclaimed: *I first found this in Edith Waterfield's VERY OWN HOUSE in Ravensburn village! It's called the Stranger Bookshop and it's STILL THERE! Go and see, it's FANTASTIC! – lol*

Rosalind made a note to share this with Bryony… although perhaps she would omit the 'lol'…

One or two reviews were more measured: *A good read if you can overlook the shift in emphasis in the second half,* said one, and another: *The clumsy leap between chapters 23 and 24 raises the question of whether Waterfield changed her mind while writing the book.*

Was it clumsy? Rosalind had assumed you were meant to think of chapter 24 as beginning a new period. It seemed she lacked any kind of critical eye.

She closed the laptop and pondered.

Why had Edith Waterfield not married John Day? It had been much gossiped about and disapproved of in the village at the time. *Living in sin* it would have been called, and Edith must have suffered socially from cohabiting with a man yet not marrying him.

So why had she?

And why would Mrs Pigg never tell?

And would the members of the Edith Waterfield Society know any more when they descended next week?

CHAPTER 23

Now

'WHAT IS THE MATTER WITH YOUR CAT?'

Bryony almost said, 'He's sulking because I beat him this morning', but she shouldn't tease customers. She looked up at the sharp profile of the woman staring out of the window and answered instead, 'He's defending his territory.'

The woman must know that. She was very spare, her shirt hanging straight from her shoulders as if from a clothes hanger and her linen trousers loose; she looked both outdoorsy and creative, bohemian but practical, and Bryony wondered what she could be: a weaver, raising her own rare-breed sheep? No, not quite, she thought.

'But there's no other cat there.'

'Already snuck away.'

'In that case your cat would not still be in defence.'

'Just out of sight, then,' Bryony said. 'Behind the flower pots, probably.' She did not look because there was no need. Gabriel, she knew, would be crouched, thrumming with tension, tight as the strings on a violin, staring out his rival in that obsessive feline way. That the rival was not visible was impossible to explain.

It's a ghost cat would not be a good thing to say, however true. How would the Edith Waterfield Society react if told there were any number of little catty wraiths inhabiting the bookshop, curled cutely in corners, waiting watchfully on windowsills, scampering up and down staircases, trying to trip her up? They'd run for the hills and never return.

Although actually they might come more often; they were a very cat-focused bunch. Photographs spread out on the first floor landing showed cats in artfully arranged situations from the classic – a white Persian sitting beside a vase of lilies (how long before she was covered in pollen?) – to the frankly embarrassing – a kitten in a tea cup, a kitten in a slipper, even a kitten in a saucepan, which struck Bryony as pretty sinister.

She'd be judging them later. Happy days.

The tall woman did not look convinced but that was her problem; Bryony couldn't help it if along with the bookshop she had inherited a psychic cat. She said, 'Excuse me,' and squirmed past with the tea tray. Where was Rosalind? She had been hoping to offload at least some of this catering lark onto her, but she seemed to have vanished.

~

BY THE HEARTH on the second floor, overlooked by the young man in the portrait, Rosalind said for the third time, 'I see,' and this time she meant it. What she had been politely listening to for the last ten minutes had been more or less unintelligible – black-line, white-line, rhythms and cross-hatching – but this even she could understand.

'Yes, I see…Oh, and these deer as well, in the meadow…'

'Exactly.'

Her eyes on the page, Rosalind realised she had moved from looking to peering and tried to stop, drawing back a little and raising her eyebrows, but the urge to find more examples was irresistible and she took the book from the elderly gentleman's hands and turned the pages herself.

Edith Waterfield's cat stories had been given a table of their own, every title represented; and such wonderful, evocative titles they were, Rosalind thought: *Mercutio the Midnight Cat*, the first book Edith wrote after *The Holly and the Ivy*, then *Mercutio by Moonlight*, followed by *Calpurnia by Starlight* and *Titus by Twilight*.

After that came the couples: *Calpurnia and Claudio*, *Julius and Jessica* and *Viola and Valentine*, and then *Romeo the Rainbow Cat* and Rosalind's personal favourite, *Rosencrantz the Wanderer*. What a delicious title for a story – it sounded like poetry!

After *Rosencrantz* Edith produced three shorter, simpler stories aimed at younger readers: *The Thunderstorm Cat, Cobweb's Kittens* and *Mustardseed and Moth*. And then: nothing. *Mustardseed and Moth* was published in 1951 and was the last book Edith ever wrote.

The books were illustrated lavishly; almost every chapter had its full-page drawing and the chapters were not long.

Not drawings: engravings.

She had known that, of course. On the title sheet, where normally one would see the words *Illustrated by*, in Edith Waterfield's books were *Wood engravings by*, followed by the name, according to Bryony and half of Ravensburn, of Edith's life-long lover, John Day.

They were still illustrations, of course. How odd that publishers were so anxious to tell you when the pictures in their books were engravings or colour plates, as if mere drawings were in some way inferior. To Rosalind all drawing was magical. She was never able to produce anything that was recognisable – her sons had thought her sketch of a cow was a dog: 'But look at the horns,' she would say, and 'I thought that was his sticky-up hair,' they replied.

Now she gazed at the picture of the cat Rosencrantz cadging a ride on a hay wagon. The strong, stocky horses raised a foreleg each in a stately walk but the deer in the meadow behind galloped like George Stubbs' racehorses, with front legs reaching forward and back feet anchored to the turf. The illustration for the following chapter showed Rosencrantz watching with disdain from a tree while a string of dogs streamed past chasing a rabbit, and there it was again: all of them at full stretch, like rocking horses. Now that it had been pointed out to her, Rosalind could not think why she hadn't noticed it before.

'How odd.'

'Well, it is and it isn't.' The gentleman laid one hand on the book. 'May I?'

'Oh, of course; I'm sorry.' Rosalind relinquished the book, wondering how she could have forgotten her manners.

'You see, I think he was deliberately emulating the style of a previous age. Pre-Muybridge. It isn't just the way the animals move; the whole image has a mid-nineteenth-century feel to it.'

'Does it?' Rosalind was ready to believe him; he exuded erudition, although clothed in kindness so that she wasn't embarrassed by her ignorance. It seemed his major interest in Edith Waterfield's work was in its being the inspiration for John Day's; he was an engraving aficionado and expert. *Fascinated since childhood*, he had said, *potato printing*. He had progressed to lino cuts and finally boxwood, apparently the perfect material for engraving: *very dense, you see; close-grained*.

He himself, he said, was a mere plodding draughtsman, but he had found a niche illustrating privately printed books – memoires or poetry – and designing greetings cards.

'Do you use the internet?' he asked now. 'Well then, if you are interested, search for Wood Engraving Twentieth Century and then for Nineteenth Century, and I'll tell you what to look for.'

I wish I had a notebook, Rosalind thought, but she listened carefully and tried to remember, and by the time Bryony tapped her on the shoulder she was fired up and ready to embark on the next bit of research.

'Cake?' Bryony said.

· · ·

BRYONY SHUT the door and locked it. She turned around, saw the balled-up tissue on the floor and considered unlocking again and tossing it into the street.

Then she heard footsteps on the stairs and quickly changed her mind. She picked it up, gingerly by one corner, and chucked it in the bin.

'All clear upstairs,' Rosalind said.

'Yep, all clear here too.'

'Coffee? I'll make it.'

'No,' Bryony said. 'Pub.'

The September sunshine the Society had been enjoying all day had hung around until the last member reached the car park. Now rain threatened, but Bryony was confident they'd reach the pub before it fell, and get home again later; no need for a jacket.

'Learn anything interesting?' she asked as they walked.

'Well, not about Edith. But lots about wood engraving!'

Bryony shot a sideways glance at her companion. Rosalind looked very buoyant for someone who had spent all day in the company of lunatics. 'Wood engraving?'

'Yes. Mr Peters was very knowledgeable. Did you know that John Day emulated a style of wood engraving that was prominent in the middle of the nineteenth century? I wonder why.'

Bryony got the drinks since she was, technically, the boss, and slipped into the place Rosalind was saving for her. The pub was surprisingly busy; the Edith Waterfield Society's coach was not the only one parked at the top of the hill. Ravensburn was a popular stop-off for general tourists as well as those hung up on literary cats. And thank goodness: every bit of trade helped.

Bryony listened – ish – while Rosalind talked about sequences of legs and rocking horses and George Stubbs, whom Bryony had heard of, and someone called My Bridge, of whom she had not, and then said, 'Yes, well, anyway, I've found out about Mrs Pigg. Or at least, how she's involved, although I don't understand why she's so touchy.'

The outdoorsy woman had told her. She turned out to be a spinner and knitter, not a weaver, and raised alpaca, not sheep, which explained why Bryony had not been able to place her, ignorant as she was of the burgeoning alpaca industry. *The perfect fibre if you have a sensitivity to wool – no lanolin, you see!*

Her name was Jocelyn, and she had skipped off at lunch time to visit an old friend of the family who lived in the village.

'Guess who.'

Rosalind raised her eyebrows. 'Mrs Pigg?'

'The same.'

Bryony had enquired about the friend out of politeness and then listened amazed as Jocelyn-the-alpaca-breeder described how her mother had been evacuated to a farm near Ravensburn during the Blitz and had been taken in by Mrs Pigg's parents. *My mother and Mrs Pigg were almost the same age and got along tremendously; neither of them had a sister, only brothers who were quite a lot older, and so they both thought it wonderful fun to have a sort of foster-sister.*

Jocelyn's mother had recently died but Jocelyn was still in contact with the family who, bizarrely, also now raised alpaca. Her interest in Edith Waterfield stemmed partly from her memories of the children's books, partly from her enthusiasm for cats, and partly from this rather loose personal connection.

Bryony found herself becoming excited all over again, now that she was telling it to Rosalind.

'The thing is,' she said, 'Mr Pigg was only Mrs Pigg's second husband! Before that she was married to Augustus Heron, and Augustus Heron was the actual Son of none other than Heron and Son!'

Rosalind was looking blank.

'Heron and Son?'

'Oh, of course, you don't know.' Bryony gathered herself. 'Right, well…Heron and Son were the local printers. They lived and worked in Ravensburn from the nineteenth century and only moved to Hexham in the nineteen-sixties. They're still there now, I think. But the point is, they were Edith Waterfield's first publishers.'

She looked at Rosalind, willing her to understand the significance.

'Heron and Son published the first edition of *The Holly and the Ivy*.'

THE COACH TRIPPERS were a noisy bunch. Bryony waited until Rosalind had finished her Chardonnay and then said, 'Shall we make a move?'

They wove their way to the door, where an old boy in the porch commented, 'Lucky for you the rain's just stopped.'

'Yes,' Rosalind said. 'Lucky for us.'

She hadn't even glanced out of the window. Bryony led the way into the street and then said, 'Lucky, Rosalind?'

'I beg your pardon?'

For a fraction of time Bryony hesitated, on the verge of disclosure; but she decided not to open the can, not right then. She feared it would take a while to do it tidily and she needed a plan for rounding up the worms afterwards. At the moment she was more interested in Edith Waterfield and the first edition of *The Holly and the Ivy*. It was not yet time to explain to Rosalind about Rosalind, but it was time to explain to Rosalind about the book.

'Come back to the shop with me,' Bryony said. 'I've got something to show you.'

CHAPTER 24

Then

PRIMMY HAD DROWNED. HER SOFT, SOAKED BODY HAD BEEN discovered early in the day, by Armstrong's sheepdog, where it had become jammed against the stepping stones half a mile east of the bridge. No one seemed to know when it had happened.

'She made tea,' Ruth said, over and over, her usual sharpness stolen by shock. 'She made tea, but she didn't make supper.'

Her sister's voice was light and fluttery. Edith gripped her thoughts and dragged them away from memories of previous telegrams, previous bereavements.

Primmy had vanished from the kitchen some time between half past four, when she delivered the tray to the parlour, and six o'clock, when Ruth gave up ringing the bell and went downstairs to look for her. She found the kitchen and scullery deserted, the water in the saucepans cold and the potatoes half-peeled, the paring knife lying on the chopping board next to the King Edwards.

Like the Marie Celeste, Edith thought. *Poor Primmy*.

'I told her off,' Ruth said, her voice trembling. 'For crying.' Edith watched the water gather in her sister's eyes.

'Why was she crying?' Lillian asked.

Ruth flapped the question aside with her hand as if dealing with a fly. 'When do we ever know why Primmy's crying?'

That was true. For the past month or six weeks the poor girl had been all over the place, trilling away like a songbird one moment and sobbing the next, and never offering a reason.

'I should have made the tea myself.'

Lillian said, 'Oh Ruth, Primmy didn't go off and drown because of overwork. You often make the tea anyway.'

'I told her to do it because Alfred came. I wanted…well, you know.'

Yes, we know, Edith thought. Ruth liked to maintain standards. How horrible to think that these days Ruth considered Alfred Wintersgill someone to be impressed.

'He didn't know you were away,' Ruth added. 'He came to see you really, Edith. Like he always does.'

'Ruth—'

'That's all neither here nor there,' Lillian said quickly. 'It has nothing to do with poor Primmy. We don't know why she took it into her head to go out, but it isn't because of making the tea. Or the supper. Didn't anybody see her after that?'

But nobody had. Primmy's progress from the scullery to the stepping stones was a mystery, and Edith was relieved that at least the girl had no close family to grieve. One advantage to being an orphan: your death doesn't cause suffering to anyone.

John is an orphan.

She wanted to get back to her story, where it was comfortable and safe and nobody ever died for the simple reason that nobody there was real.

THE CORONER RETURNED AN OPEN VERDICT.

'What does he mean, open?' Ruth protested. 'It was an accident. She must have fallen in.'

'Hardly *must*,' Edith said, 'only *probably*.' She had woken up with a headache and stomach cramps, as the calendar promised, and was feeling spiky and unkind.

Lillian shot her a warning look and said, 'Yes, Ruth, but there isn't any proof, so he has to leave it open. He has to follow the rules.'

'Open,' Ruth said, disgust packed into the syllables. 'As if she could have meant to do away with herself.'

She wouldn't say the word *suicide*.

Edith said, 'Or as if she was murdered.'

But she said that to be unkind too. The aggravation of her monthly was compounded by the three of them having to share the chores until they found a new maid-of-all-work, and she knew she was being selfish but didn't care. There were carrots to scrub and apples to peel when she wanted to be planning Rose and John's courtship, and to cap it all Billy Moffat would be calling later.

Well, she would get the wretched vegetables done but after that she'd be shutting herself away to write. And what's more, she'd be writing what she wanted to write, too, no matter what Ruth said.

Edith, do not put this affair into your story, do you hear me?

Yes, yes, she heard. Ruth had always hated the little bits and snippets of their lives that appeared – cloaked, always cloaked – in the stories she made up, even the silly, childish stories she wrote as a girl, which no-one outside the family would ever read. Edith wondered whether her sister would recognise how much of Lillian there was in Rose…

But poor Primmy was unlikely to find a place in Castle-hope. The plot had no call for tragic house maids. Rose, hardly wealthy, was a quiet, capable soul and took care of herself, and John Lucas would not be hiring staff.

The one bright chink in the clouds was that Alfred Wintersgill seemed to have given up; they hadn't seen a whisker of him since she and Lillian returned from Newcastle, not even walking past on his way to the Handsome Jack. So that at least was a relief.

CHAPTER 25

Now

THE BELL JANGLED AS THEY WENT IN. IT MUST BE STRANGE, Rosalind thought, to enter and exit your home through a shop. Bryony had a metal stairway outside for a fire escape, of course, and a rear door from the stock room, but she always went in and out through the books.

'It's easier to enter from the street', she said. There was a narrow alley alongside the house that allowed you into the back yard where Gabriel reigned amongst the bins for rubbish and recycling and the abandoned, upturned terra-cotta pots. 'I'll stick some more geraniums in those', Bryony was apt to say, always followed by, 'Some time.'

Perhaps she could plant them up for her. *I'll ask.*

Rosalind immediately had a mental image of Bryony's

face displaying a mixture of tolerance and exasperation. Bryony did not share her appreciation of flowers, she thought. Rosalind suspected they were in the shop only as a marketing ploy.

She followed Bryony to the stairs and nearly collided with her when she halted abruptly half way up the first flight.

'Can you smell that?'

Rosalind sniffed. 'That? It reminds me of box, although I don't think it can be.'

'Mm. Me too. Makes me think of my granddad's garden.' Bryony resumed climbing and spoke casually without turning round. 'Hear those floorboards?'

'Yes, of course.'

'Sound so much more like footsteps than just expansion and contraction, don't they?'

She could be very odd sometimes. As they reached the second floor she said, 'You don't think there's anyone here, do you?'

Rosalind had never been much concerned about intruders. Octavia had remarked upon it more than once – *that big house full of stuff, aren't you ever afraid of burglars?* – but then Octavia was always anxious about one thing or another. The truth was that Rosalind felt she knew whether a house was empty or not without thinking about it. She had never been startled when the boys jumped out at her. She hadn't wanted to spoil their fun, so she squeaked and laughed, but it was all pretend.

She hadn't thought Bryony was at all like Octavia

though, and the question took her by surprise. They were the only people in the shop, she was perfectly sure, and she said at once, 'Of course not, but would you like me to take a look?'

'No. No need. I'm sure you're right. Cup of coffee?' She clumped on up the wooden stairs, the matter apparently dropped, and then sidestepped rather elaborately and uttered a loud *Tch!* for no reason Rosalind could see.

Yes, distinctly odd.

The final flight of stairs was just like those below apart from being less worn; the treads were not so scuffed and the hand rail less polished. Rosalind had never climbed it before. She waited while Bryony unlocked the door, which bore a sign, *Private*, Times Roman engraved on slate like the name on the gatepost at the Law House, and then the door swung inwards and for the first time Rosalind stepped into Bryony's home.

'Coffee? I suppose you wouldn't…' Bryony tailed off. 'No, it's okay, I'll get it.'

Rosalind would have preferred tea but Bryony was a coffee girl through and through. Sounds of the kettle and coffee jar and mugs and teaspoons rattled off stage and Rosalind put her bag down on the sofa and looked about.

The room was not what she had expected.

Not that she had prepared a picture of Bryony's flat; she wasn't aware of having spent time considering it at all. But she realised now that she had assumed Bryony, in her early twenties, sharp, critical, and dressing as she did predominantly in jeans and the sort of tops that go with jeans, would have similarly casual, pared-down furnishings: bare floor-boards or fitted carpet in a neutral shade, blinds in place of curtains, white walls with contemporary prints on canvases. The sort of style her sons favoured.

She was taken aback by the mustard-coloured upholstery, the square of maroon carpet with swirling patterns laid over grey linoleum, the red Formica table against the wall. The window frames had been painted carelessly, and above her head the loft cover had never been painted at all. Shabby, yes; chic it most certainly was not.

Bryony emerged bearing mugs. 'Sit down, Rosalind. Anywhere you like.'

Rosalind lowered herself onto one end of the sofa and took her mug. 'It's very nice.'

'No, it's not,' Bryony said cheerfully. 'It's hideous. All this was Cedric's and I haven't got the money to redo it yet, but one day. I did buy a new bed; didn't fancy carrying on with his old wreck. And a wardrobe; his smelled of mothballs.'

She took the chair opposite Rosalind and set her mug down on the carousel bookcase beside her. She didn't use coasters, Rosalind noticed, and the top of the bookcase was marked by overlapping mug rings. Not just the bookcase either; there was a rickety, narrow-legged coffee table between them similarly disfigured.

Not dirty, though; just spoiled by the heat. The flat was clean, it just wasn't cared for. On the other hand, it would be difficult to care much about these bits and pieces.

'Sixties tat,' Bryony said. 'I reckon Cedric bought every-thing second-hand when he moved in and never thought about it again. I wonder what Edith's furniture was like.'

'Did Cedric Stranger buy the business from Edith, then?' Rosalind had not thought about this before. There must be all kinds of questions she could have been asking that would have given her a more complete picture, a more rounded whole, of the context for Edith Waterfield and her magical books.

Bryony waved a hand dismissively. 'There are enough people in the village whose families have been here forever and grew up knowing all this stuff. Local lore…like the Eliots and Handsome Jack and whatever.'

Rosalind said, 'The Eliots and the Handsome Jack…?'

'Sorry, two separate stories. Apparently the pub used to be called The Black Horse. Before the first world war, the landlord had a black horse that used to haul carts up the hill – probably a Fell pony, Dan says – which became so famous he was challenged to a pulling competition. Some local farmer who reckoned his horse could do better. So they had the competition, and bets were taken, and the landlord's horse – called Jack – won. Big pay-off. Honour and glory. So they renamed the pub after him.'

'What a lovely story.' Rosalind thought of the painted pub sign, and the round hindquarters and proud neck of the stocky horse. 'And the Eliots?'

'Blacksmiths for centuries. Unbroken line through the men, so the Forge has been inhabited by Eliots at least since the sixteenth century, apparently. Amazing.'

It was amazing. Such continuity. Matthew had sold his city flat and bought Monk's Walk after they were married, and his parents hadn't been in Sussex much longer than that. Rosalind's own parents had moved about more than was usual, her father a nomad at heart, everyone changing schools periodically. All over the country there must be people in their forties who remembered a herd of girls descending upon the classroom, all of them blonde and all of them named after Shakespeare's ladies. No identifiable ties to the land at all.

Not really any identifiable ties to people either. One way and another Rosalind had lost contact with all her old school friends. She was, she began to realise, rather lonely, despite her sisters, from whom she had always felt somewhat detached. They were so unlike her, so rowdy and sociable and quarrelsome. Sometimes it seemed to Rosalind she must have come from some different set of people, quieter and more introspective, and had been thrown in amongst her sisters by mistake. A changeling.

Bryony had lots of sisters too. Whereas her own parents had turned to Shakespeare to name their children, Bryony's had chosen a horticultural theme, with Clover, Sorrel, Holly, Hazel, Rosemary, Rowan and, of course, Bryony.

Or rather sisters and brother, because one was a boy. 'Rowan,' Bryony had said, 'and they'd already used that, so Rosemary had to stop being called Rowan and start answering to Rosemary. She didn't like it much but she was only two so she had to lump it.'

'Your parents changed their daughter's name so that they could use it for their son?' How extraordinary!

'Well, just to keep the theme going. It was that or christen him Basil. Or Good King Henry. Anyway, we ended up calling them both Ro, so it didn't really matter.'

Other people's families.

According to Wikipedia, Edith had come from a large family too; more common in those days of course, and she had lost so many of her brothers to the War. It didn't bear thinking about.

They would have been younger than my boys. Rosalind shuddered inwardly. Then she thought, Where did her sisters live? Also in Ravensburn? Did any outlive her? Where did they go when the family home became a bookshop?

If Bryony was right then there would be local residents able to answer at least some of these questions; and if they couldn't, then she would ask the internet. She was confident there would be a way to find out on-line. Did people not use the internet for researching family history? That's all it was, after all – just somebody else's family.

'I'm sure I can find out about Edith's family,' Rosalind said, aware the conversation had taken a bit of a jump.

'Okay. Good. How?'

'I'm not sure, but I'll Google it.'

Rosalind had discovered that if she typed a question, any question, into the search field then someone somewhere would have asked a similar question and the miraculous power of the internet would have found answers to it. *Who wrote the music for 'The English Patient'?* she had asked. *What should I do if my mobile phone is frozen? What causes stitch?* It was wonderful, like magic.

'Bryony, why don't you try it?'

It was the question she kept coming back to, unable to imagine what stopped her friend – surely she was that, by now? – from using computers herself. If Rosalind could do it, then anyone could.

But Bryony had twisted around and was rotating the carousel bookcase, carefully and with one eye on the mug on top, and seemed not to have heard. Rosalind could have repeated herself but she was already regretting having asked and did not press the point.

Another time, perhaps.

Bryony had drawn out a book, clothbound in faded green, and now she leaned forward, elbows on knees, as she flipped through the pages.

'Here.'

She turned the book to face Rosalind, holding it open somewhere near the middle.

'What do you notice?'

'Well…'

Rosalind took the book. It was *The Holly and the Ivy* of course, but an edition she had not yet seen downstairs. She began to read the page, but Bryony said, 'You don't need to read it. Just look at it.'

Just look at it.

Rosalind looked. The pages were yellowed with age but thick and almost spongy, the print rather large. What else? She was conscious of Bryony's attention on her, eager and hungry.

'Um…'

There was no text above the story either on the left page or the right, no book title or chapter heading; the pages were numbered at the bottom. The sentences marched across the pages just as they should, with indented paragraphs and full stops and old-fashioned double inverted commas for speech. What was it she was supposed to be noticing?

'Well?' Bryony asked, impatient.

'I don't–'

And then, all of a sudden, she did.

CHAPTER 26

Then

Edith stared out of the window and tapped her diary against her chin: tap-tap-tap – flapping the book with a repetitive flick of her wrist so that the soft leather of its cover stroked her skin.

She had been writing for three and a half hours, and now she was thinking.

The writing had gone well; well-ish. John was getting to know Rose now and beginning to fall in love with her, but slowly, slowly, careful, level-headed fellow that he was. Rose, of course, had fallen for him hook, line and sinker the moment she set eyes on him in the evening sunshine. Edith's intention was that the reader would not be absolutely sure until a lot later in the story that the two of them would come together, or at least not sure how they'd do it. She wanted to make Rose steady and calm and restrained on the surface, and certainly very self-disciplined, while secretly battling with tempestuous emotions which nobody guessed except John, naturally, who would see through the tight-laced exterior to the passionate spirit that was contained therein.

Easier said than done. Edith wasn't sure she was managing it. It was fairly straightforward writing Rose – she was more or less herself although more responsible and less selfish (one had to be honest). But John Lucas, the wood engraver who had come from London to accept his inheritance, was causing problems.

Edith had never been a man, so perhaps it was that. On the other hand, the early chapters about John in Camden had gone well enough; she was pleased with those. It was now, after he had found the village and met Rose, and even had his first, brief encounter with the dastardly Herbert Douthwaite, that he was getting sticky. She had spent all this morning working on dialogue for his visit to Rose with the eggs (which was a bit thin as devices went and she would try to improve on it later), but although bits here and there were all right, it was hardly scintillating. It was almost, Edith thought, as if John was getting distracted – a ridiculous and self-indulgent excuse if ever there was one.

And Douthwaite was awkward too. Edith had thought she would find him quite easy, modelling him as she was on ghastly Alfred Wintersgill (she was keeping that from Ruth, for sure). But it wasn't. She suspected her characterisation was clumsy, and didn't think she was getting down in words the mixture of local bully and something more sinister.

All very difficult.

Tap-tap-tap went her diary against her chin.

The street was empty apart from Smiler, Billy Moffat's whiskery terrier, sniffing his way along the wall opposite with great concentration. Ruth didn't allow dogs indoors and there was laundry on the line in the back yard, so while Billy sat with Lillian in the parlour, Smiler had to wait in the road.

I'm sure he'd prefer it anyway. Better having a good old sniff at what's been going on out here than minding his manners on our hearth rug.

Lillian thought Billy might propose. *I think he's near to the tipping point*, she had said. But if he didn't, which Lillian said was perfectly possible because he was so appalled by his injuries, then she was going to propose instead. Edith expected Ruth to throw her hands up in horror at this and was taken aback when her eldest sister said simply, 'Be careful how you do it, then, Lillian. Don't scare him away.'

It was the spectre of the Surplus Woman; it was why Ruth ploughed on with Alfred Wintersgill.

Who had come back.

Three weeks after Primmy's funeral, paid for out of their meagre coffers and attended by more people than expected because she had been so well liked, Alfred had knocked on the door and been given tea and muffins by Ruth, albeit rather sourly. She was disgruntled over his absence.

'You'd have thought he'd come to pay his respects. It isn't as if he'd never spoken to her.'

No, Edith thought, he had spoken to Primmy often enough, always with that leering look and slippery tone that made his words seem more pointed, less innocent than they should. Ruth said it was rubbish but Edith hadn't liked it and neither, she knew, had Primmy, who always did her level best to get out of the room as quickly as possible.

Tap-tap-tap.

Why *had* Primmy cried so much?

Ruth said Edith mustn't make any mention of Primmy's fate in her novel, but Edith had an idea and was going to write it down somewhere. It was what she did. Usually her imagination twisted her odd notions into stories but if that wasn't to be allowed she had to find another outlet. Writing was just plain vital, even if so far today it had been unsatisfactory.

Billy's Smiler finished investigating, lifted his leg to leave his own calling card, and flopped down with his back to the water trough and his little legs outstretched. Dogs were so untidy compared with cats.

If Ruth found out she was writing a journal there would be hell to pay. But there was no reason for Ruth to read her diary, was there?

Despite the beautiful leather bindings, Edith's diaries were sparse, boring things only used for dates and appointments. Even if Ruth broke her personal code of honour – and she never would – the diaries offered no interesting insight into Edith's thoughts. And that made them the obvious place to hide precisely that.

All right, she'd do it. Not at her desk, though; that was for the novel.

She reached for the atlas she used as a lap desk and made herself comfortable on the bed, the pillow pulled up behind to cushion the bed frame. She opened the diary, flipped quickly to today's date, and began to write:

I have had an idea about Alfred Wintersgill which I hope is groundless but I just don't know. Perhaps it's my imagination, but why was Primmy always so upset on the days he called?

The thing is, I didn't make a note of it at the time. But now, looking back, I'm sure there's a link between the dates of his visits and the days Primmy cried. That time Primmy was serving when Ruth told us she had met him at the Post Office and invited him over, and Primmy dropped the soup ladle. Mulligatawny everywhere and Ruth exasperated.

And the way his eyes used to slide about. He was watching her all the time, I'm sure of it.

And the thing is, what I'm thinking, the thing I keep coming back to, is: what was stopping him from going out the front door and straight round the back?

Edith bit her bottom lip. She stared at the wall opposite and visualised the alley that ran into the back yard and the door into the scullery. Then she bent her head and wrote again.

Absolutely nothing at all.

CHAPTER 27

Now

Rosalind thought for a few moments and then typed *How can I find out about somebody's family history?*

She pressed the carriage return and scanned the results. Beneath the advertisements at the head of the page were several American sites, a lot of them concerned with Mormon genealogy, so she added *in England* before the question mark and tried again, and this time the first website below the adverts had a *.co.uk* address. Rosalind clicked on it, and began to read.

Wonderful! Not only helpful notes and FAQ but even video tutorials! Twenty minutes later, she had a fair idea of what to do and reasonably high hopes of being able to do it.

An hour and a half after that, she surfaced from a veritable binge of researching with a stiff back, an empty stomach, and a sheaf of papers waiting in the tray of the lovely printer Bryony had bought, which unfortunately had to sit on the floor under the table because there was no space for it on top. It looked huge to Rosalind, but it could photocopy things as well as print them from the computer, and even did colour, so she couldn't reasonably complain.

It was past nine o'clock and she hadn't eaten. Going online simply gobbled time.

An omelette and salad seemed the quickest meal to throw together. After that she returned to the sitting room with a cup of coffee and her notepad and pen. The printouts she straightened and left on the table with Bryony's copy of *The Holly and the Ivy* on top as a paper weight.

Bryony had lent it to her but with a caveat: 'For God's sake don't leave it behind if there's a fire at yours tonight!' She was aware Rosalind's flat was above a garage.

'Don't worry, they assured me the conversion was done properly, with a fire-resistant floor and so on. I'm sure I'm perfectly safe.'

Safer, to be honest, than the bookshop, with its rickety staircases and even ricketier fire escape, not to mention all that wood panelling. She had mentioned it once, only for Bryony to laugh. 'Wood panelling's the least of it – think of all the paper!'

Her next assignment was to see what she could dig up about Heron and Son, the publishers of this green, cloth-bound first edition. But before that, she needed a break from the screen and a chance to think about what she had learned.

The Census of 1911 had been the most exciting part. The website had allowed her to see the actual form that related to the Waterfield household in Ravensburn. It was awful to read the names of the boys and know that in the next few years all but one would be dead.

And another large family! Lots of offspring was much more common back then but still, it was very strange that Edith, Bryony and Rosalind herself shared exactly the same number of siblings: seven; they each came from a family of eight children. It is in the nature of coincidences to startle, but it did make Rosalind feel as if some force was at work bringing them all together here in Ravensburn. Which was nonsense, of course.

After that, Rosalind had searched for the names of the Waterfield sisters hoping to find marriage records, and she discovered that Lillian had married a William George Moffat in 1921. Of a marriage for Edith there was no trace, so the popular gossip was probably true; nor was there anything for the eldest sister, Ruth.

There were several William Moffats in Northumberland but only one William George. He had been born only eighteen months after Lillian and on the 1911 Census he popped up, aged thirteen, living with his parents and three sisters at somewhere called Hare Rigg Farm near Ravensburn.

Farms rarely change their name and they often stay in families.

Rosalind experienced again the small shiver she put down to the thrill of the chase. It was like being a detective, or a treasure hunter. Could Edith Waterfield's personal history be called treasure?

Perhaps not. But those missing pages certainly were.

Rosalind reached for the book and opened it again to the place near the centre that Bryony had shown her earlier that evening, leaning forward eagerly as she watched Rosalind discover the truth.

You had to open the book wide to see it. But if you bent the covers back and pressed the pages apart you could see that paper had been cut, very neatly, close to the stitching. It was difficult to count how many pages had been removed because what was left was so narrow and so tightly packed, but you didn't need to count because the page numbers told you.

At the foot of the left hand page was the number 132. Facing it, on the right hand page, was 141.

Bryony had then turned to the same place in a later copy, the black bound edition they had squabbled over in London no less (how unseemly; how she regretted it now) and shown her that the page numbers ran on correctly and no paper had been removed. That edition was exactly eight pages shorter, the final page numbering 255 instead of 263.

The text was almost unchanged, but not quite. The bottom line on page 132 of the damaged book read:

be all that Rose wanted. But the swifts were in flight and

In the later edition the chapter ended with the full stop – the swifts were not mentioned.

Both books then began a new chapter on the following page, but in Bryony's first edition the chapter numbers were out of synch too.

The implication was unavoidable. Between the original publication of *The Holly and the Ivy* by Heron and Son and the book being taken up by mainstream publishing house Maxwell Harvey, a whole chapter had been removed.

CHAPTER 28

Now

'HARE RIGG?'

Bryony felt the syllables roll around in her mouth. She liked them; they sounded wild, slightly uncanny (that would be the hare) and deeply Northumbrian. 'Right.' She reached for the telephone directory.

Moffat…

She found the number and dialled. When she glanced up she saw that Rosalind, sitting across the desk from her, was looking a little shocked.

'What? What's wrong?'

Rosalind said, 'No, nothing really…it's just…you make decisions very quickly, Bryony.'

Bryony shrugged but heard the ring tone in her ear interrupted as someone at Hare Rigg Farm picked up.

'Hi,' she said. 'My name's Bryony Bower, I own the Stranger Bookshop in Ravensburn. I wonder if you could spare a few moments?'

THE FEW MOMENTS took up four minutes but were highly satisfactory. She put the phone down.

'Done. We're going there on Saturday after I shut up shop.'

'To Hare Rigg Farm?'

'Of course. They're related. There'll probably be nieces and nephews and stuff. They must have tons of information.'

'Well, yes, but–'

Sometimes she drove Bryony wild. What must it be like to be so hesitant, so concerned about weighing everything up and taking everyone into consideration before ever actually doing anything?

'Rosalind. You can't only research things remotely, on a computer. Sometimes you have to get out there and talk to people.'

Almost instantly she felt mean. She tried again.

'Look. Think how much you learned about wood engraving from that Society guy. And you didn't have to drag it out of him, did you? He was longing to talk about it to anyone.'

That came out wrong; hurry on: 'So for all we know, the Moffats are dying to talk about Edith Waterfield but haven't got anyone to listen. Well. We'll go and listen.'

Rosalind sighed. 'You're probably right.'

177

'Of course I'm right. And I've been thinking. It's all fine for Dan and everyone to keep telling us what their parents thought, but there must be people in the village that actually knew Edith. She was alive less than forty years ago. Loads of people must remember her.'

'But how do we find them? We absolutely cannot knock on doors, Bryony.' Rosalind's voice was as near to concrete as Bryony had ever heard it, but that didn't matter. Knocking on doors was not what she had in mind: far too tiresome.

'No. So we'll advertise.'

She had planned it overnight, waking suddenly with the idea fully formed and jotting it down on the notepad she kept by the phone lest useful thoughts vanished into the murky recesses of her brain before dawn. She would place a notice in the local paper requesting reminiscences of Ravensburn in the first half of the twentieth century, and in particular those concerning Edith Waterfield.

'It isn't as if she was just anyone. She was an author, she must have been famous in the village. They probably boasted about her.'

It took a little while to convince Rosalind, during which it occurred to Bryony to wonder why she was trying so hard, given that she owned the business and could do whatever she liked, with or without the approval of Rosalind Cavanagh, part-time, casual, unpaid assistant. But she knew she did want Rosalind's approval, and was pleased when she got it, even if she had to modify her plans.

'Oh all right. The parish newsletter then, not the Chronicle.'

It seemed a bit tame. On the plus side, though, it wouldn't cost anything like as much. It might even be free – news rather than advertising.

'You'll have to make a donation,' Rosalind said. 'Parish newsletters struggle to survive these days.'

'Of course.' *Rats.* 'So…shall I pick you up at six or will you be helping in the shop on Saturday?'

Beneath the desk Bryony's fingers were crossed, an important element when dealing with Rosalind but by no means reliable.

'Oh, I'll come in if you like.'

Bryony let out her breath and uncrossed her fingers.

Rosalind was lovely with customers and Bryony could prove that more books went out the door on the days she was at the shop. Especially if she was actually on the till. Bryony had watched her, surreptitiously from behind the shelves, and the effect she had on people was every bit as remarkable as Bryony's own. When Rosalind engaged them in conversation, people glowed.

When Bryony did, they merely caved.

And, glowing, they bought more, not just books but bookmarks, cards and even the heavy-duty cotton shopping bags Bryony had bought in, printed like the cheap freebies with John Day's engraving of the shop front. They had seemed a good, eco-worthy promotional idea at the time but precious few people had seemed to want them.

Until Rosalind arrived anyway. Now she'd need to order more. Not printed with the engraving this time though, which had been a mistake because the lines were too fine for the coarse weave, but a new logo she had been playing with:

Stranger Books in an interesting font and with an ivy tendril winding through the capital letters. The ivy suggested fairy stories or the countryside, depending on your susceptibilities, but was really, of course, a reference to Edith Waterfield. It needed more tweaking before it was ready, and Bryony intended to run it past big sister Hazel, who painted a bit and did calligraphy as a hobby. It already had Rosalind's approval.

It was another of those coincidences-that-probably-weren't that Rosalind shared her appreciation of illustration. Their tastes were remarkably similar, both of them attracted to the flowing lines and clear pen-and-ink of artists such as Pauline Baynes, Jan Pienkowski and Rebecca Mulligan, the illustrator whose landscapes reminded Bryony so much of childhood holidays in Skye, and who had apparently dropped off the face of the planet.

'Why do you say that?' Rosalind had asked when Bryony mentioned it.

'Well, she used to be pretty prolific – won the Kate Greenaway Medal and all that – and now, nothing. There hasn't been a new book illustrated by her for ages.'

'Has she retired?'

'Hardly. She was really young, the reviews all called her a prodigy.'

'Well then, perhaps she's taking a break to start a family,' Rosalind said.

'Mm. Maybe.'

What a boring explanation. Bryony preferred to think Rebecca Mulligan had been whisked away by fairies, her pen abandoned in mid-stroke and her publisher furious;

vastly more interesting than buying cot mobiles and baby-grows.

Anyway, Rosalind's newly gained knowledge of wood engraving was interesting. It seemed the species of wood with the closest, hardest grain, and therefore the commercial choice throughout the industry, was box.

That was very interesting. So interesting that Bryony had felt the need to clarify it.

'*Box?*'

'Yes, box.' Rosalind clearly realised something was amiss. 'You know, Bryony – the plant box. Boxwood. Buxus.'

'Yes, yes, I know what you mean. Mm. Well.'

It was also clear Rosalind had yet to make the connection.

Anyway, the broad sweep of chronology was that medieval wood cuts – engravings made on the plank, which were bound to be coarse and fuzzy because of the longitudinal wood fibres – gave way around the late eighteenth century to incredibly detailed wood engravings which used the hard end-grain of the cross-section. Thomas Bewick, he of the Handsome Jack coasters, had been a prominent artist-craftsman of the time.

'He used the white-line technique,' Rosalind had said, buzzing with the excitement of newly acquired knowledge. 'He drew with his graver.'

'Graver?'

'The tool they used to make the cuts. If you look closely you can see that the white lines compose the picture. So skilful. But later people just cut away everything that wasn't a black line, which isn't the same thing at all.'

Bryony struggled with this concept.

'I know, so did I at first,' Rosalind said kindly. 'But if you keep looking at lots of examples you find you get your eye in and it starts making sense.'

She had been researching again. Was there no stopping the woman?

The point was that as wood engravings became ever more popular as a means to illustrate the periodicals and books and broadsheets of the day, it became common for illustrators to produce the original artwork in pen and ink which journeymen engravers then copied. Some engravers designed their own work as well, though, and the best work-shops encouraged their craftsmen to study draughtsmanship.

Rosalind painted a picture of benevolent employers and passionate workmen. Could it really have been like that in the nineteenth century?

'Then new processes involving photography came in which were vastly quicker and cheaper, and wood engraving became an intellectual choice. Lots of twentieth-century artists made wood engravings too: Walter Crane, Eric Ravilious…and John Day, of course.'

What was intriguing about John Day was that he imitated the style of the previous century. Instead of the stark lines and stylised character of most twentieth-century engravings, John Day's work bore a close resemblance to those of the eighteen-forties and 'fifties, right down to the fact that he depicted animals running like rocking horses, front legs and back legs outstretched and neatly paired.

It seemed a bit pointless to Bryony. Fine, George Stubbs had done it but he hadn't known any better. Why carry on drawing unrealistically after it was understood how animals organised their legs when they ran?

'What were you thinking of?' Bryony asked the portrait over the mantelpiece that evening, on her way up to bed. And she sniffed, but there was no scent of boxwood.

CHAPTER 29

Once

THE COTTAGE WAS TIDY, PRETTY, AND CLAUSTROPHOBIC.

Lucas felt too large. He did not stretch his legs out but sat with knees bent. The parlour was not smart but it was decorative, with its chintz upholstery polished with wear, the gay rag rug before the hearth, the mirror above the mantelpiece speckled and cloudy in its gilded frame, the rose-patterned china.

He felt too masculine also.

Rose had taken the other chair after handing him his cup, and they faced one another across the floor, awkward now that the practicalities had been concluded.

This was not how he had imagined it. This was probably a mistake.

The basket of eggs rested on the deep windowsill and Rose had made no move to unpack it. The basket belonged to Mrs Fogarty, Lucas had watched her rummaging for it amongst the pots and trugs, so should he not take it back when he left? Or was that not how it was done? Perhaps one simply kept the basket and returned it later with a gift of equal value – bread or conserves or flowers. He did not know how women arranged such things; he was just a go-between, glad to be given the opportunity to call at the cottage.

Where he now sat, ill at ease, his tea too hot yet to drink and unable to think of anything to say. Poor fool.

Rose bent as she sipped from her cup and Lucas noticed the oval crown of her head, and the way her hair sprang from its centre parting and resisted the pins. An angel might have hair like that, he thought; fierce and alive, fighting to fly free. It was amber-gold, an extraordinary colour, and that was angel-like too, but Lucas did not think about colour so much as line and tone.

He wanted to draw her. In many ways she was the perfect model – slender but womanly, her face heart-shaped and symmetrical, the angles of neck to shoulder and chin to throat clean and correct. She could indeed provide the figure for an angel, or a princess, or even a demi-goddess, a naiad or dryad. She was straight and graceful like a young tree – a silver birch, he thought, and smiled momentarily at the image.

Rose smiled back. 'And how are you finding the village, Mr Lucas?' she asked.

'Very well.' So inadequate a reply. 'Very different from Camden,' he added, but it would be hopeless to try to encapsulate what he really thought in a few polite sentences.

The truth was that Castlehope had knocked him down, then picked him up by the scruff of his neck, shaken him properly, and stood back to laugh. The whole of Northumberland had done that, to be honest; he would never forget the shock of the wide moors, the ancient stone walls and the shaggy, disgruntled sheep. And the skies…islands of mounded white, floating in archipelagos; dark, rolling bastions of cloud like the foothills of mountains; peach and coral still streaking the soft indigo blue far into the night, when it should have been dark…How to capture that in black and white? How to describe the colours in line and hatching?

He had bought paper in Hexham and filled it with sketches of clouds and rocks and streams, trees and hedgerows, grasses, wild flowers, and sheep, cattle, ponies and still more sheep. People too: farmers and housewives and shepherds and the blacksmith, and bright, canny children who knew a different way of living from those in the city and proved it in the way they ran and laughed and stared.

His work would be changed. He hoped the Weatherstone brothers would approve; little he could do if they did not.

He should return. He had sent a letter: *The financial affairs are confused and I would beg an extension*, and had been relieved although not surprised when Joseph Weatherstone replied with a kindly *Take what time you need*, although he had added above his signature: *We are missing you.*

The letter had caused him some guilt. It was true Stratford had left his estate in disarray and it was taking longer than Lucas had expected to sort matters, not helped by the solicitor's relaxed attitude. Lucas suspected his business was not considered the highest priority. But he had not disclosed to the Weatherstones the size of his inheritance.

He did not have to return. He could, if he wished, remain in Castlehope, living comfortably, if carefully, on the income from Stratford's bequest. He had become independent: a man of property. All he had to do was decide how he wanted to live his life.

All he had to do.

The ramifications of this decision, when made, were huge; he had never dreamed of being faced with such. Now his dreams were of little else and he fretted through the dark hours, playing out hypothetical versions of his future – the owner of the tall house opposite the church, patting children on the head and sketching them at play; a freelance artist serving the printers in Hexham; engraver John Lucas at the Weatherstones' bench working only the hours he chose.

And there was the rub. How could he choose his hours and yet fulfil his duties for the workshop? How could he continue to work for the Weatherstone brothers when it was known he could walk away if he pleased? Lucas was realist enough to know that even with his own commitment and the goodwill of the brothers, the relationship would inevitably break down. His position would be untenable; it couldn't be done.

But to abandon wood engraving? That could not be done either.

He woke more often than not uneasy and dissatisfied, and conscious of the irony that his great good fortune was causing him so much unrest. It should not be so. In some way he could not describe, he felt he was failing destiny, except that to say so sounded presumptuous.

And so he said instead that he found the inhabitants welcoming and the countryside beautiful, the weather refreshing and the cats, chickens and children all quite charming, and it was easy enough to smile because Rose, with her grave face and amber hair, was a beautiful woman and a pleasure to look at.

It was just that he had somehow expected there to be more: a flicker or a spark that would catch his breath and cause his pulse to race – something to which mere beauty would take second place.

And Rose did not have it.

IN THE END it was a disappointing visit, for all that he had volunteered so eagerly to carry the eggs. But as he rose from his chair to leave, his attention was caught.

Above the mantelpiece, shadowy and difficult to make out, he thought he saw a woman in the mirror. But Rose had moved to the door and there was nobody else in the room.

Lucas was transfixed by the faint profile and dark dress of a woman who seemed to be *behind* the clouded glass. She was seated at a table, her head bent as if she were working, and he spun round to search for a picture of such a woman on the wall behind him. But there was only a small, dark oil painting of bluebells in a wood, and he turned back, his breath held, to stare.

And then, suddenly, she was gone. The mirror showed him only the chintz armchair and the bluebells, and Rose was waiting at the door with curiosity in her eyes.

Lucas took his leave.

CHAPTER 30

Now

THE WOMAN WHO OPENED THE DOOR HAD A SOFT, ROUND face and soft, curling hair, but there the softness stopped.

'Oh yes, the book lady. Well, you can talk to Mum but I've got a meal to cook.'

How ungracious, Rosalind thought. Perhaps not *absolutely* dying to talk about Edith, then.

By that time Jacqui Moffat was already walking away down the hall and Bryony was following her, or rather chasing her because she had set off at a very sharp pace, so Rosalind brought up the rear.

The book lady. How rude.

There were wellington boots and walking sticks by the door and a row of waterproofs on pegs. A whiskery pepper-and-salt terrier trotted busily up to sniff their shoes before losing interest and sauntering away. Mrs Moffat opened a door and waved them through.

'Here's the book lady, Mum!'

'Thank you,' Rosalind said.

They were standing on a sage green carpet in a sage green room: wallpaper, curtains and lampshades. The armchairs were upholstered with sage green leaves on a beige ground. But there were books on shelves built into the alcoves either side of the chimney breast and the small, thin woman struggling to rise from her chair held a paperback open in one hand: a very early Penguin, the green spine faded to dusty blue.

'How lovely to meet you. I'm Dorrie Moffat.'

She was like a bundle of sticks, Rosalind thought: frail-looking and somehow diminished in her loose shirt and trousers. But her voice, though creaky, was deep and she looked surprisingly like a man. Her hair was very short and her wire-framed spectacles very plain, and really her clothes could easily have been men's clothes.

Bryony shook hands with her and said, 'I'm Bryony Bower. I own the bookshop in Ravensburn. This is my friend Rosalind Cavanagh.'

Rosalind shook hands too. 'Thank you for inviting us.'

Dorrie Moffat folded back into her chair and the Penguin slid to the floor. Rosalind retrieved it, smoothing the pages. It was a Dorothy L Sayers.

'Thank you. Just some old murder. Poor woman had the same name as me. I've read it before. I've read them all.' The old woman tucked the paperback between her thigh and the chair arm and leaned forward. 'Now, tell me what it is you do. A bookshop, did you say? In Ravensburn?'

'That's right.' Bryony was plunging in. 'Edith Water-field's old house, that was Lillian Moffat's sister. Lillian that was your–' (Rosalind watched, knowing that Bryony was trying to guess the old woman's age) '–your mother-in-law. No, grandmother. No, mother-in-law. Wasn't she?'

'That's right, Lillian was my Bob's mother. This was the family farm, so even though he took it over when he was very young she was living here all the time we were courting and stayed on after we were married. A bit of an old biddy I thought her, Mum Moffat, but she wasn't so bad really. And now I'm the old biddy! Ha-ha!'

Her laugh was a bark of real amusement; no embarrass-ment there, Rosalind thought. What an uncomfortable woman.

'Oh, I'm sure–' she began, but was cut off.

'Are you Cedric Stranger's girl then? I didn't know he ever married.'

'No. I inherited the business from him through his sister.'

'Cedric had a sister?'

'Yes. I–'

'What was her name?'

'Circe. When–'

'I don't remember a Circe. Where did she live?'

'In Surrey. Haslemere. She never came up this way. I–'

'Well well, Cedric had a sister. I never knew that. How is Cedric these days?'

'Well, I've inherited the bookshop, so obviously he's de–'

'Sadly he passed away last year,' Rosalind said quickly and gently. 'Did you know him well?'

But it seemed there was no cause for concern; Dorrie Moffat took the news in her stride. 'Oh yes, you said, didn't you? No, not what you'd call well, only to chat to when I was in the shop. Funny old bird. I always thought he was one of those. That's why I was surprised he had a daughter.'

'I'm not his daughter.'

'Oh no, that's right, that's what you said. But I wouldn't worry dear, you don't look much like him.'

Rosalind suppressed a smile. She watched Bryony take a breath and start again.

'Mrs Moffat–'

'Dorrie.'

'Dorrie. Rosalind and I are very interested in Edith Waterfield because of her connection with Ravensburn and the bookshop. We were wondering whether you might share some of your memories of Edith. Did you meet her?'

'Oh yes, of course. Mum Moffat did most of the visiting but Aunty Edith came out here sometimes. To see Aunt Ruth.'

Dorrie was of a generation who called their husband's relatives 'Mum' and 'Dad' and 'Aunty' as if they were their own. It was a comfortable habit, Rosalind thought, and one she was sad had gone. Now Dorrie's voice took on a more reflective tone, as voices often do when they speak of the past. Rosalind watched the old lady dip into her memories.

'Aunt Ruth wouldn't go to Ravensburn, not if she could help it,' she said, her eyes focused far away. 'That was one of the secrets for a start.'

THE LOW EVENING sunshine warmed the room, brightening the carpet and bleaching yet more colour from the book spines. It fell across Rosalind's lap, and glinted on the wire frames of the old woman's spectacles as she talked.

And talk she did. Bryony had been right after all; it was as if a switch had been thrown, and while Dorrie Moffat's grasp of the present might be a little shaky (*'Never thought Cedric could be such a dark horse; who was your mother, then?'*) her recollection of the past was in crisp focus.

They listened as the old lady took them back to her arrival at Hare Rigg as a newly-wed, homesick and baffled by the business of a farm. 'Bob was a good man but he was always busy. Lily, now, she was the one that cheered me up.'

Lily was Robert Moffat's younger sister, the same age as Dorrie. 'She had always wanted a sister and we were close from the start. Thanks to Lily I found out a lot more about the family than Bob ever gave away. But even so, she didn't tell me everything.'

Secrets abounded: why Ruth refused to visit Edith at home in Ravensburn; why Edith had never married John Day; why Lillian and straight-laced, church-going Ruth defended their wayward life style; why Edith was so reluctant to leave John Day even for an afternoon's visit (*'You'd have thought she was afraid he wouldn't be there when she got back'*); and what had really become of Alfred Wintersgill.

'And why the police suspected Edith and John of having murdered him,' Bryony prompted, repeating the nugget of well-known scandal.

'Oh, that was no secret. Theirs was the last place he was seen, of course they were suspected. And Uncle John popping up in the village that very same night always struck me as peculiar.'

Bryony, Rosalind could see, was concentrating on the woman's words like a hound on the scent and was in no mood to pause and consider the numbers. So she said, gently interrupting, 'This all took place in 1921, didn't it?'

'1921, that's right.'

'Were you a *very* little girl at the time?' Rosalind asked, a touch ashamed of her disingenuousness.

Again that bark of a laugh. 'Oh, I wasn't even born. I had to do no end of ferreting about to find out anything at all. I never did work out whether Bob knew, but I didn't think he'd let on even if he did. Lily spilled little bits here and there, and enough was known in the village.' Dorrie Moffat paused. 'After all, if you were going to marry the nephew of a suspected murderer, wouldn't you want to know the facts?'

Well, put that way…

'Would you like to see some snaps?'

Rosalind felt her heart leap and Bryony sat up suddenly straight. 'Yes please!'

'Well, the thing is, the albums are all in boxes in the attic and Jacqui will have to fetch them out. She'll be in the kitchen now and won't want to. I suppose you wouldn't care to ask her?'

CHAPTER 31

Then

'THE REGISTRY OFFICE,' LILLIAN SAID. 'AND JUST FAMILY. Immediate family. We don't want a fuss.'

Well…no. The idea of a church wedding was uncomfortable for all sorts of reasons: Lillian processing up the aisle with only Ruth to give her away; Edith a solitary, overgrown bridesmaid trailing behind; Mrs Moffat sobbing in the front pew, not, like other mothers, because her boy was growing up but for the reason she was always crying: because her boy had lost his face. And the groom brushed and scrubbed and topped by that ghastly tin mask.

Much better the Registry Office. Although Mrs Moffat would still cry.

Edith sighed, and Lillian gave her a warning look.

'Don't. It's what I want, and it's what Billy wants. That's all that matters.'

'Yes. Sorry. Of course.'

She just hoped the babies would come. How terrible if, after all this, they didn't.

The sigh hadn't been solely for the sad wedding, though. Life in general was so unsatisfactory. She missed Primmy's voice chirping away in the kitchen more than she had expected, and she thought the others did too – even Ruth, who was being very common-sense and no-matter about it. Edith had found her more than once stalled at the kitchen table staring into space.

Lizzy, the new maid, was a much quieter girl; pleasant enough, and a very good cook, but she lacked Primmy's sunny disposition.

Perhaps she just needed to get used to the family. She had come from Corbridge and might be missing home. Families were funny things and it must be horrible to find yourself in the middle of someone else's. They were all being very kind to her.

And the novel had ground to a halt. John Lucas wasn't behaving. Why couldn't she get him to fall properly for Rose? She had heard of novelists claiming their characters were disobedient and chose their own destinies, but had always put it down to artistic temperament and exaggeration. It had knocked her back a bit to find it happening to herself. She kept writing different versions of a scene in which John saw Rose in a mirror and realised how much he loved her and wanted to spend the rest of his life with her. The idea had come to her while brushing her hair one night and she thought it quite promising, but writing it – writing it convincingly – was proving a nightmare.

Poor old Rose. Perhaps she had made her a bit insipid.

At least Ruth had finally abandoned the Alfred Wintersgill project. Her elder sister was single-minded and determined but even she couldn't carry on against Edith's absolute refusal to co-operate. *I won't talk to him, I won't sit in the same room as him, and I won't ever agree to marry him.* And at last, hallelujah, Ruth had given in.

About the other matter Edith had as yet said nothing, neither to Ruth nor to Lillian. She wasn't sure why. Perhaps because it seemed so…melodramatic? It was in books that people drove other people to their deaths, wasn't it?

'Murders happen,' Winifred Platt said, sipping her beer (beer!) in the snug at the Handsome Jack. She was passing through on her autumn tour of the moors and Edith had found it possible to reveal her fears to her, probably because she was so transient. Perhaps also because she was one of the few people Edith thought might not say she was being silly.

And Winifred didn't, which then seemed rather alarming.

'What do you think I should do?'

'Go to the police. Tell them what you've told me. Let them take it from there.'

She made it sound so easy.

'But what if…' *What if what?* 'What if I'm wrong? What if I'm imagining it all?'

Winifred sniffed. 'Then when they investigate him they won't find anything and that will be the end of the matter.'

Except that it wouldn't be. Winifred was from the city;

she had no conception of what it was like to live in a village the size of Ravensburn. Bring a charge against a man such that the police investigated him and expect it to be forgotten inside a week? Inside a year, even? Madness.

Winifred shrugged. 'Well then don't. Leave it. But in that case you'll have to live with the possibility that he murdered your maid and got off scot-free. Although to be honest, Edith, it doesn't sound very convincing.'

No, Edith supposed it didn't. But she hadn't told Winifred the other part of her suspicions, because then her worldly friend really would think she was hysterical.

CHAPTER 32

Now

'Do you know what you should do?'

Bryony knew without looking that Rosalind was staring straight ahead through the windscreen and had spoken without turning to face her. Understandable: the twisting, swooping roads were killers and could hijack your stomach in an instant if you didn't keep an eye on them.

She braked for the right-angle bend where the road crossed a stream. 'What's that?'

'You should take the bookshop out to other villages. There must be lots of people like Dorrie, who can't get into Ravensburn or Hexham but are longing for new books.'

'The mobile library's supposed to look after that.'

'New books, Bryony. Not everyone wants heavy old hard-backs with sticky covers.'

'Mm.' The Land Rover grunted as she changed gear and powered up the hill. 'Diesel costs a bit.'

'Sales would cover it, I'm sure. And anyway, it's a service. You'd be doing the community good.'

Driving, or rather passengering, had an effect on Rosalind, Bryony noticed. It made her more assertive. It had been the same when they went to the piano recital at the Queen's Hall in Hexham: *Do you think you might have been just a little brusque with that young woman?* No, actually, and Rosalind hadn't heard the woman in question explaining to her friend that she should browse in the bookshop but buy the books from Amazon, where they were cheaper.

It was probably down to the absence of eye contact when they were in the car. Was Rosalind aware? Did she deliberately save up topics to berate her with? Unlikely, Bryony thought; it was the sort of thing she might do herself, but not Rosalind.

Take the bookshop to the customers. It was a thought. She'd need–

'You'd need someone to do it for you, of course. I'm not suggesting you close the shop. But if you found an assistant...'

'You?' Bryony asked, taking her eyes off the road for a moment. 'Would you do it?'

'Well...I suppose so. Possibly.'

Still reluctant to commit. Bryony guessed what her companion was thinking: occasional days helping in the shop was one thing, even handling the website. Taking on a regular mobile service would be less easy to abandon.

Bryony said musingly, 'It is a bit sad to think of old

Dorrie reading the same murders over and over. I mean, you can do that with Jane Austen or Dickens, but if you like mysteries, surely you want new ones all the time?'

'Exactly.'

That would do for now. She'd let Rosalind settle into the idea.

'Anyway, we'll take some who-dunnits for her when we go with the painting. What do you think she'd like? Who's a modern take on Lord Peter Wimsey?'

She hoped Rosalind was more up on contemporary murders; she herself hadn't a clue. But Rosalind surprised her by saying reproachfully, 'Oh Bryony, we can't do that!'

'What? Why? I thought that's what you–'

'We can't take the picture to Hare Rigg. How rude!'

'Then how–'

'We'll bring Mrs Moffat to the shop. She'd love an outing, I'm sure. I got the impression nobody spends much time with her, didn't you? And she can choose her own books at the same time.'

Crumbs, so now she had become a pensioners' bus service, had she? Oh well…

The photos had been marvellous.

After Dorrie Moffat's warning about the likely obstruction of her daughter-in-law, Bryony had set off towards the kitchen in high hopes of a battle. In fact there was none; the farmer's wife scarcely resisted at all. Bryony had to hang around in the doorway while the woman put lids on pots and adjusted cooker knobs and wiped her hands on a tea towel, but then she led Bryony along the passage, round a corner, through a small stone-flagged scullery that smelled strongly of sour milk, and up a narrow staircase that rivalled the bookshop's for creakiness. On the next floor they went along further corridors and turned a couple more corners to arrive at a dingy velvet curtain behind which was a plain, unpainted door. Jacqui Moffat unlocked it with a key she scooped up from the lintel, and it opened to reveal yet more stairs, this time between unplastered walls.

By now Bryony was prepared for anything from mad wives to magic wardrobes, but the attic behind the final door did not reveal treasures for the imagination. Peering around the woman she saw no ancient dolls' houses or rocking horses, no seaman's chest or dressing-up trunk spilling clothes and hats from a bygone age. Instead there was just an ordinary attic like the one in the house she had grown up in, with a row of modern suitcases, a few mismatched wooden chairs and, surprisingly somehow, a cot.

Under the eaves were several large plastic crates, one of which Jacqui Moffat dragged closer.

'This is what she's after.'

Bryony took the photograph album, padded black leather and smelling of dust, and the battered, square short-bread tin, and retreated down the stairs feeling chivvied all the way.

'You've not got long,' Jacqui Moffat said as they sepa-rated in the hall. 'Tea's in twenty minutes.'

Not very gracious, but Bryony's strength was in affecting behaviour, not attitude.

The album covered a remarkable span in years, photographs pasted in from an age when cameras were uncommon and film processing cost good money. The captions were written in white ink on the black paper: *Shearing Trials 1936…Bowbeck Show 1951…Shepherds' Supper 1960.* Page after page was agricultural, with sheep and sheepdogs, and men in tweeds looking proud and shy. There were family pictures too, solemn toddlers on swings and tree stumps and high chairs, or older children, skinny and grinning and dressed in shorts or print frocks.

'They're absolutely all outdoors,' Bryony commented. 'Even the babies in the winter.' You knew it was winter from the bare branches and the layers of woollen clothing.

'Ordinary people didn't use flash in those days,' Rosalind said. She was trying to lever up the lid of the shortbread tin. 'I can't quite…oh!'

An avalanche of monochrome prints slithered over her lap and onto the floor.

'Oh dear.'

'Not to worry,' Dorrie said, leaning forward and stirring them with her finger. 'Now this is what you need. Most of these came from Bob's Mum. She never got around to mounting them. There!'

Bryony put the album down and picked up the snapshot. Two women in knee-length skirts and cloche hats stood with linked arms in front of a low stone wall.

'The names will be on the back.'

Bryony flipped the photograph. In faded ink, in a sloping hand, was written: *Lillian and Edith, March 1927.*

She turned it back again. 'What's that blurry bit?'

Dorrie peered. 'Oh that. Probably the photographer's finger in front of the lens. A lot of them are like that.'

Bryony picked up the next photo, this time of a woman

in a dress standing in a sunny garden. She was looking to the side and smiling, but whatever had pleased her was lost under the same foggy blur. Some photographer!

Edith, Hare Rigg, 1933, she read. Ten years after the murder scandal; ten years into the living-in-sin scandal. Where was John Day?

'Where's John Day?' Rosalind asked, gathering the heap together.

'Can't recall seeing any of him,' Dorrie said. 'I expect he was shy.'

'Perhaps it was him taking the pictures,' Bryony said, and Rosalind said, 'Perhaps. You'd think there'd be one or two though…'

'Was he shy?' Bryony asked Dorrie. 'You must have met him?'

'Not shy, no, but a quiet man. Quiet but strong. Quite a dream boat. Lucky old Aunty Edith, I always thought, although Bob was all right in his way.'

'Go on,' Bryony said. 'What was he like? Was he a local?'

'No, not local. Nobody seemed to know where he came from but he wasn't like us. Down south, probably – London or some such.' She sat back and folded her hands. 'Lovely manners. Old-fashioned. He used to bow when he came into the room and bow again when he left.'

'He *bowed?*'

'A little bow, you know. Lovely. Catch Bob doing that! But he never came up here. Aunt Ruth wouldn't have it.'

Ruth, the eldest sister.

'She didn't like being left back in Ravensburn by herself?' Bryony asked.

'No, no! Aunt Ruth was living here by then. She moved in with Mum and Dad Moffat soon after they were married; gave Mum and old Grandma Moffat a hand. Now she really was a piece. Told me off for cutting the fat off my bacon, she did. Old misery.'

Rosalind said slowly, 'So she didn't like John Day visiting? I wonder why.'

Dorrie shrugged. 'Who knows? Old biddy. Now let's see if there's one of us…'

THERE WASN'T NEARLY enough time, and when Jacqui announced that tea was ready they had looked at barely half the photographs.

'Come again,' Dorrie said, 'any time. Lovely to meet you.'

'We will,' Rosalind said.

Then, as they set off down the hall, Dorrie called after them, 'What happened to Aunty Edith's box?'

Bryony paused. She turned round. 'Edith's box?'

'She had a box full of stuff. I don't remember it coming to the farm after she died. Is it still at the bookshop, do you think?'

CHAPTER 33

Then

THE OVERCAST SKY HAD BECOME STILL DARKER IN THE PAST quarter hour and would surely spill its rain soon.

That was good, because fewer people would be in the street.

On the other hand, perhaps it was bad because her going out would be more noticeable. More memorable.

She ought to have a story. What story could she have?

She didn't need one at home. It was Lizzy's afternoon off; Lillian had already set out for Hare Rigg on their good bicycle, the one without the puncture, and Ruth was spending the morning with Margaret Eliot at the Forge. Edith wasn't the only one to find solace there.

Sarah Lynne would see her, of course; that went without saying. Sarah saw absolutely everything that went on outdoors. It was a mystery how she produced such beautiful embroidery when her eyes seemed to be everywhere but on her needle. But Sarah was discreet; if seen, Edith would be embarrassed but not tattled on.

But what if she were to meet someone in the street?

Um, um…

Edith pivoted, scanning her bedroom for inspiration amongst the mundane furnishings: cardigan over the bed rail, *Ivanhoe* lying open on the quilt, the asters dowdy now in the vase on the chest of drawers: nothing of use there; Sarah Lynne didn't read much and her garden, thanks to her husband, was considerably more fruitful than theirs.

Ah - fruit!

Lillian had been blackberrying yesterday and her bounty sat in a bowl in the kitchen, waiting to be washed. Taking produce as a gift was a time-honoured custom and a very useful device (take John Lucas and those eggs, for example). A cast-iron excuse.

It would mean foregoing the pie. Her sisters would string her up.

Oh well.

Edith poured the blackberries, gorgeous though they were, back into the basket and covered them with a cloth. There was still a chance she wouldn't meet anybody; one could only hope. It would be nice if she didn't have to give away the blackberries after all.

The first spots of rain were falling as she opened the door. Edith pulled her hat down and kept her eyes on the cobbles as she climbed the hill. She felt as if someone were watching her from every window. Oh to live in a village larger than Ravensburn, where anonymity had a chance.

Now that she had embarked on the venture her stomach was a shivery knot of tangled nerves. What if Alfred returned early? What if his ghastly mother was there? She shouldn't be; Sarah Lynne said Wednesdays and Sundays were the days she came by bus from Bowbeck to give the house a go-over, which doubtless it needed now Agnes had gone.

But even so, what if?

Edith bit her lip. But she needed to do this, take a look, see if there was anything, any little thing at all, that might point to Alfred's involvement with Primmy's drowning. She felt so sure…

And there was the other thing, that dreadful, creeping suspicion about Agnes, who had left so suddenly…

The Wintersgill house was set back from the street, the front yard larger than most. As Edith drew close she noticed the weeds pushing through the flagstones and the empty crates Alfred hadn't bothered to move. Not very prepossessing. Whatever had Ruth been thinking of? Being Surplus was infinitely preferable to this.

So far as she could tell she hadn't yet been seen but there was no excuse for hesitation. When she got to the house she must not dither…

Edith was level with the wall now. Her knees felt fluffy, her feet marching on as if they took orders from some other person, not her at all.

At this moment, she could still abort; she had not left the public street; she could simply walk on.

Edith felt sick.

Now.

She dived into the narrow alley between the wall of Alfred's house and his workshop next door. The gutter overhead was blocked and water spilled over the edge, bouncing on the stones and splashing her stockings. She slipped through the gate into the back yard and quickly, before her courage abandoned her, tried the door handle.

It turned.

Edith closed her eyes. In this respect at least Alfred was like most of Ravensburn's inhabitants, who seldom locked back doors except at night.

So now there was nothing to stop her.

CHAPTER 34

Now

BRYONY FETCHED DORRIE BECAUSE ROSALIND WASN'T insured to drive the Land Rover.

More than once Bryony had *almost* pointed out that it would have helped if Rosalind had brought her car when she came to Ravensburn, but so far she had stopped just in time; one really ought not berate a friend who is helping you for not being able to help you more.

She wondered why Rosalind had left her car behind. She realised there were a lot of gaps in what she knew about her friend, and that some of the gaps were suspicious.

Rosalind didn't seem like somebody on the run, though.

In any case, it was she who stayed behind to man the shop while Bryony drove out to Hare Rigg and helped Dorrie Moffat into the passenger seat of the Land Rover.

'This is very exciting,' Dorrie said, looking all ways as they bumped down the drive. She was wearing navy polyester trousers and a lightweight knit cardigan buttoned to the neck, and Bryony realised she had dressed up.

She felt her stomach give a little shiver. *I'll be old one day*.

'Good!' she said brightly. Then she said, 'Well, I hope you'll like what I've done with the shop.'

'I'm sure it will be marvellous. Cedric was a funny old bird. He had all these old books on the shelves instead of nice new ones. I don't know what he was thinking of.'

'I sell second-hand too,' Bryony said. 'As well as new. I sell both.'

'Well, I'm sure it will be marvellous.' Dorrie Moffat fell silent again, peering forward, backward, out of her side window and even craning to look behind Bryony as she drove.

Bryony went easy, taking the corners and blind summits slowly. She wondered whether she should be making conversation, but as the miles passed it became increasingly awkward to start; and anyway, Dorrie seemed perfectly happy sightseeing.

'Swindell's bull,' she said at one point.

'Pardon?'

'Swindell's old bull. Still there. A new one, must be.'

Bryony glanced in the mirror and saw the head and massive neck and shoulders of a dun-coloured bull in the field behind them.

How odd to have lived all one's life in this rural backwater. It was a far cry from Surrey.

At the bookshop Rosalind stood at the door to greet them. 'No customers at the moment,' she said. 'Shall I flip the sign?'

She gave Dorrie Moffat her arm to steady her climbing down from the Land Rover and ushered her indoors while Bryony parked at the pub. By the time she had walked back they were sitting on the second floor sofas waiting for the kettle to boil, so stairs clearly weren't a problem.

'Stairs aren't a problem for me,' Dorrie Moffat said, 'so long as I can take my time.'

'Good,' Bryony said. 'Now, do you know–' and at the same time Rosalind said, 'Dorrie's been telling me–'

But Dorrie Moffat spoke over the top of both.

'You know, seeing him again now after all these years… he really was dreamy, wasn't he? What we'd have called a real dish.'

THE YOUNG MAN in the portrait was John Day.

'Oh, definitely,' Dorrie Moffat said. 'A very good likeness, too. But not all that young, not really. They had it painted the year before the war broke out, in the spring. Nineteen thirty-eight. Easy to remember. That's what I was told.' Then she said, 'It's a treat to see it again.'

'You've seen it before?'

'Oh yes. Poor old Cedric. He never liked it but he had promised, you see.'

'Promised?'

'Mum Moffat and Aunt Ruth. When he bought the

house from them after Aunty Edith died. He was never to move the portrait, nor the quilt. Nor the clocks.'

'I wonder why,' Rosalind said, mildly.

'What quilt?' Bryony asked.

'The one at the foot of the stairs. It's not really a quilt, of course, just a quilt top she never finished. Grandmother's garden.'

'Grandmother's what? Whose grandmother?'

Rosalind said, 'It's the style of the patchwork. Hexagons arranged in rings.'

'That's right,' Dorrie said. 'Paper piecing, all done by hand. Some people love it but not me. Too slow. Dressmaking on my Singer, that's what I liked.'

Bryony felt she was being hopelessly distracted from the business in hand but couldn't quite resist asking, 'Paper piecing?'

'You cut out all these paper hexagons and then you cut out the fabric a little larger and fold the edges over the papers and tack them down. And then you slip-stitch the hexagons together, and then take the papers out and use them again.' Dorrie Moffat spoke with the complacency of someone who has been there, done it, and has no need ever to go back.

Bryony could understand that. It sounded hellish.

Rosalind made instant coffee and they drank it, looking at the painting.

'He's never in his forties,' Bryony said. 'Is he?'

Rosalind said, 'How old was John Day when he met your husband's aunt?' She had found no entry on Wikipedia for him, and no references anywhere on the internet apart from his illustrations of Edith's cat books.

'I don't know. A bit older than she was, I think.'

'Early forties by this time, then,' Rosalind said.

'He always was well preserved,' Dorrie said. 'People commented on it.'

Everyone looked at the painting again.

'I wish we had some photographs of him,' Bryony said.

'What about Aunty Edith's box?' Dorrie asked. 'Have you looked in there?'

'We can't find it,' Bryony said.

Rosalind cleared her throat.

'Oh all right,' Bryony said, 'we haven't actually looked for it, but I know it isn't here. I went through the whole place after I arrived' (*chucking out Cedric's junk*) 'and there was nothing remotely like that. I absolutely definitely did not get rid of anything I couldn't identify. No photos.'

'I wonder where that got to, then,' Dorrie said. 'There isn't anything at all left of the Waterfields?'

'Too much, frankly,' Bryony said. 'What you mentioned: the portrait and the clocks and the patchwork thing. Quilt. Quilt top. And there's an engraving of the shop front and a map, and the head of an angel out of some graveyard – I like the angel, actually – and the desk of course. But no box.'

'Oh dear. Well, then.'

'Right.' Rosalind broke the mood by springing up and collecting the mugs. 'Dorrie, is there anything you would like to do while you're here? Because Bryony wants you to choose some books. Her gift. The fiction is down on the first floor.'

They spent a good hour browsing, Dorrie seated on the stick-back chair Bryony carried upstairs – more supportive than the pouffe – and Rosalind ferrying armfuls of books to and fro. Bryony checked in now and then but got on with cataloguing her most recent house clearance. A niggly part of her wondered just how many books she was going to be making a gift of, but when they descended, step by careful step with Rosalind in front, there were only six paperbacks in her arm.

Although two of them were each the first of a series.

While she rang them up Dorrie said, 'Rosalind tells me you have put a notice in the parish newsletter. Asking for reminiscences.'

'That's right.'

'What fun! I wonder what will turn up. I hope you'll spill all when you next visit.'

Another visit was inevitable, Rosalind had made that plain already, quite independent of wanting to look closer at those photographs.

'But,' Dorrie added, as Rosalind packed the books in one of the latest carrier bags with the new logo, 'I'll tell you who won't respond. Lily. My sister-in-law.'

Lily! Still alive and living somewhere nearby! For some reason neither Bryony nor, she was sure, Rosalind had thought of that.

'Really?' Bryony asked. 'Why is that?'

'Well, I probably shouldn't be telling you this,' Dorrie Moffat said, evidently going to, 'but it was all tied up with the fact that they never married. Aunty Edith and Uncle

John. Scandalous, you see, back then. And it quite wrecked Lily's chances with Charles.'

'Charles?'

'Charles Rutherford-Hill. Lived in Hexham. Besotted with Lily and she with him, but his parents weren't having it, not with Lily's aunt living in sin. Nice boy but he wouldn't say Boo to a goose, let alone his father. Gave Lily up. She was broken-hearted. Such a sweet girl, Lily, the best sister-in-law you could wish for, and I never saw one jot of resentment from her towards her aunt. Far from it. She was quite sharp with anyone who made a remark, you know, about how they were carrying on. And all the time pining after Charles. But I say she was better off with Gussy. What good is a man who won't stand up for what he wants? For that matter, she was better off with Archie too.'

Gussy. Bryony narrowed her eyes, sensing a question forming in her brain even before she knew quite what it would be. What was Gussy short for?

'Augustus,' she said, thinking aloud. 'Lily married someone called Augustus?' It was not a common name, not even then.

'That's right. Augustus Heron. His family were printers. Just a little local firm but quite successful. And Gussy was pleased as punch to get Lily, although she made no bones about her heart belonging to Charles.' Dorrie Moffat shook her head. 'Lily and her men. She married again after Gussy died. Archie this time. Imagine one minute being married to an Augustus Heron and the next having to put up with an Archibald Pigg! Poor Lily.'

Dorrie Moffat shrugged her thin, cardigan-clad shoulders, fingering the handle of the carrier bag, apparently unaware that her companions were staring open-mouthed.

'Still, it was her choice,' she added, 'and Archie was a kind man. Though I'm glad I didn't have to live out my days as a Mrs Pigg.'

CHAPTER 35

Then

As she made her way cautiously through the rooms, Edith's stomach began to settle and her nosiness overcame her fear. Clearly Mrs Wintersgill wasn't around, and Alfred could hardly get to Hexham and back in less than two hours. She was all right; she was going to be all right. And in any case, her ears were on full alert for footsteps outside.

But there were no footsteps, only the rain drumming on the windows and porch tiles as she made her way through the house, treading carefully, touching nothing she did not have to, checking always that she left each door as she found it, closed or open or ajar. There must be no trace at all of her having been here. God forbid that Alfred should ever find out; the embarrassment would be mortifying.

Part-way up the stairs, Edith hesitated, struck suddenly

by the realisation that embarrassment, horrible as it was, might not be the only risk. That was precisely the point, wasn't it?

Her stomach gave a little, sick lurch.

Stop it! You're here now. Do what you came to do.

The sense of transgression was even stronger upstairs, where callers definitely do not venture. Her fear grew again, urging her to hurry, and she moved from room to room stepping quickly, treading lightly, her eyes constantly roving, searching for she knew not what.

It was a mad idea. She should drop it and go, now.

She stood in the doorway of the bedroom, Alfred's bedroom. It smelled of old cigarettes, like the rest of the house, but of something else too: an animal odour, faintly rank.

The bed was not made, a corner of the blanket trailed on the floor.

Not here, not here. She didn't have to go through this door, she could save herself that.

In the bathroom, a shaving brush and razor stood on the windowsill by the sink. How different from the all-female house she was used to now, with Charlie away in Edinburgh and all the others…all the others gone.

Men were very…different. Alien, really; unknowable. What must it be like, Edith wondered, to live your life knowing that if a crisis were to happen – a shipwreck, a burning building, and, yes, war – it was expected that you lay down your life if necessary. To know that you were required to sacrifice yourself if by doing so you could save women or children you might never have met. To live knowing you had to be heroic.

Women are not faced with that.

Edith thought *Thank God*, because her own courage was feeble and she knew it. Such a low threshold for pain; Ruth used to tell her off for squeaking when she was having the tangles combed out of her hair, and she desperately hated splinters.

It would be strange now to live with a man in the house, but, oh, so lovely…

The right man, that was. Not the likes of Alfred Wintersgill, heaven forbid, and not poor Billy Moffat either.

And so her thoughts trod their familiar circle: so many young men gone, so many Surplus Women, and only John, lovely John, filling her waking dreams and tormenting her with what she would never have.

The next door along was to Alfred's room of business, with a desk instead of a bed and rows of ledgers, account books, envelopes. There remained only the flight of stairs to the top floor and the box rooms, one of which had been used, no doubt, by Agnes.

What a horrible thought – keeping house for Alfred Wintersgill under the hawk-like scrutiny of his mother. Sleeping up here while he snored away down below. Ugh. No wonder she had run away.

Edith climbed the stairs quickly, conscious of time passing, aware of the futility of this whole adventure, sure she would find nothing up here that could help her make up her mind about Alfred Wintersgill and poor Primmy, but driven to be thorough. She had taken the risk this far; it would be stupid to leave the job incomplete.

Only two doors at the top. Junk behind the first: crates of old ledgers, a metal trunk, two battered wooden chairs and an ancient pram…a pram! How odd.

And behind the other door…

Edith stood on the threshold, gazing. Then, slowly, she stretched out one hand and touched, just touched, the corner of the fringed shawl that rested, bundled, on the chest of drawers beside the door.

Her lip trembled and tears gathered.

'Oh Agnes. Oh God. Oh Primmy.'

THEIR HOUSE WAS STILL empty when she returned; nobody home yet.

No-one to tell. No-one to share.

Edith roamed, picking things up, putting them down, her heart racing now worse than when she made the discovery. How could that be? Why?

Do something. Do *something*. But what?

Write. Go on. Think about Rose. Think about John. Make him do something, anything, so you can write about it and stop thinking about…about that room and what it must, surely must mean…

At her desk Edith dragged out her notebook and found the page, snatched up her pencil.

I'll send him somewhere. Don't know where yet, or why, just get going and see if I can think…

She wrote:

John walked.

CHAPTER 36

Now

'OH BRYONY.'

'Oh Rosalind, don't oh-Bryony me! How was I to know?'

She watched as Rosalind looked away, which meant the excuse was feeble. It must be common knowledge, then. The thing was she had never been good at common knowledge; *un*common knowledge was her forte.

Dorrie Moffat had stayed until five thirty and Rosalind had come with them to Hare Rigg, but she hadn't let Bryony drop her off at the Law House and when they got back to the bookshop she said, 'Let's find Edith's box.'

How telling. Not 'let's *look* for Edith's box', or 'let's *try* to find Edith's box'. How wonderful it must be, how cosily comfortable, how luxurious never to mislay the pencil you just put down, the screwdriver you almost never need, your car keys. Rosalind Cavanagh's experience of life was so different from everyone else's.

It was a quarter past six.

'All right,' Bryony said. 'Off you go then.'

Rosalind threw a dubious glance her way as if she detected sarcasm but wasn't quite sure. She cleared her throat. 'Well, you said you had searched the shop thoroughly?'

'I didn't exactly search. I didn't know anything was there to be found. But I've looked in every cupboard and corner since I've been here.'

'Well, even so…would you mind very much if we…'

'Not at all. Be my guest.' And then, because even to her ears that did sound sarcastic, Bryony added, 'Let's go round together. If you see anything I might have missed, just shout.'

So they began at the bottom with the stockroom, which had once been the kitchen, and the palatial downstairs toilet, which had once been the scullery, its door into the back yard now permanently locked.

There was no box in the stockroom or the toilet.

They worked their way up.

'Believe me, there's absolutely nowhere on the shop floors.'

'Could there be a concealed cupboard, though? In the panelling?'

So they looked. It took time. Cedric Stranger had kitted out most of the shop with racked shelving – mere skeletons with sides screwed to the wall but no back board. These were straightforward; they removed books a shelf at a time and knocked on the wall behind: dull but doable. Not so good was the room on the first floor where the books were housed on traditional mahogany shelves. Bryony thought they had been in the house before Cedric came along, and they looked immovable.

'Are they fixed?' Rosalind asked.

Bryony shrugged. 'No idea. Should they be?'

'It's generally advisable to screw a bookcase to the wall,' Rosalind said, 'to make sure it can't fall on someone. But they probably weren't so conscious of safety back then.'

Bryony frowned at the shelves, massive and crammed with books on the friendlier technologies: forestry, horticulture and animal husbandry. 'There are two of us. What do you reckon?'

They emptied one, piling the books in teetering stacks and dodging the fluff and three spiders.

'There is a lot of dust. Do you think it might be a good idea to…'

'Yes, yes,' Bryony said, 'I will, I will. Not now though.'

When the bookcase was empty of books, they joined forces at one end and leaned. After a couple of false starts due to their feet slipping on the dusty floorboards ('I know, I know') the mahogany base shifted an inch and a gap opened between it and the wall.

They shoved some more and widened the space enough for Bryony to squeeze in. She tapped and listened, tapped and listened.

'Nothing. Are we going to have to do this with every single bookcase?'

'It's worth it to be sure, don't you think?'

Bryony sighed. Rosalind was right, of course, and it was worth it, but oh so tedious. Very boring, this being methodical.

'Are you all right for time?' she asked, as they replaced the books.

'I'm all right if you are. It would be best to get it over with, wouldn't you say?'

By nine thirty they had cleared the mahogany room. By eleven they had searched behind every bookshelf, every table and every clock in the shop, including the grandfather clock, which had been scary to move partly because Bryony was afraid it would stop working and partly because a really *big* spider ran out from behind it.

'Bryony, it's only a spider.'

'I know. Sorry. Giant one, though.'

Rosalind scooped it gently up in her bare hands and dropped it out of the window. She might have guessed Rosalind would be a pro-arachnid kind of girl.

They took down the framed pictures too, even the ones in the stairwell, and Bryony stretched up to grab the bottom of the patchwork, which she now knew to be a Grandmother's Garden unfinished quilt top made by hand sewing using the paper piecing technique, but which still didn't look any better. It was less floppy than she expected, as if someone had stiffened it somehow to make it hang better. She flicked it aside to check the wall behind.

Nothing.

'The flat, then.' Bryony was totally bored by now, not to mention starving, but her flat was tiny so it couldn't take much longer. She trailed after while Rosalind peered behind furniture, knocked plaster walls, lifted rugs to examine floor-boards, and opened the airing cupboard.

'Not on the top shelf?' Rosalind asked, standing on tiptoe.

'No.' Then Bryony said, 'And the only thing I've ever found in here was behind the tank.'

She watched Rosalind's back for a reaction but there was none; she had forgotten. Bryony said, 'It was a desiccated cat.'

'*Bryony!*'

'It's all right. It wasn't yucky. It was completely dried out, shrunken, like a mummified cat.'

'Bryony—'

'I expect it died in its sleep and Cedric never knew where it had gone.'

Rosalind looked at her.

Bryony said, 'It was a tabby. Once.' Then she said, 'Anyway. What's left?'

'I think that's everywhere.' Rosalind sighed and looked about her. She was fingering the chain around her neck. 'I can't thing of anywhere else. If you have already looked in the loft.'

Bryony said, 'Loft? What loft?'

And that was when Rosalind said, 'Oh Bryony.'

BRYONY HAD GROWN up in a regency terraced house with an attic. The bookshop in Ravensburn did not have an attic, and she had assumed that was the end of the story.

'I've heard of a hay loft and a sail loft. I didn't know houses had them.'

'What did you think was above the hatch?'

They both looked up. Cedric's unpainted square of plywood was directly overhead.

'I don't know. Roof space, I suppose. Nothing.'

Rosalind sighed. 'Oh Bryony, that's what a loft *is*.' Then, because she was who she was, she added, 'I'm sorry.'

Bryony flapped her hand dismissively. 'It's all right, I'm the idiot. I'll fetch the steps.'

The hatch was lightweight and easy to move. Bryony took a deep breath and prepared herself for more spiders, but it lifted and slid aside without bringing anything down on her. She let out her breath and climbed another step.

Light from the room below showed a space that was bigger than she had imagined but still barely warranted the word *loft*, she thought, with no usable floor, just the ceiling rafters and some sad, limp lagging. No wonder the flat was cold.

'There's nothing– oh, hold on.' Bryony leaned across the beams and stretched towards the edge of something she could just see in the shadows. Her fingers met cold metal. She scrabbled about and found something rough but handle-shaped that she could grasp.

She tugged, and the trunk slid along the rafters.

'Got it,' she said. And then reality hit her. 'Oh Rosalind! I've got it! I've got Edith's box!'

CHAPTER 37

Once

JOHN WALKED.

The position of the sun, when it escaped the drifting clouds, and the smell of the chill air told him that he had started out early although he had no recollection of doing so, and he trod a road across the moors that was mostly straight and clearly led somewhere, but he did not know where and he did not know why he had taken it.

There was more. He had no recollection of deciding to do this today, nor of waking, rising, dressing or taking breakfast. He was simply walking, and he did not know why.

The heather was changing from purple to rust and the lambs in the fields were now as large as their mothers. It was autumn. In London the leaves from the great plane trees would be drying on the twigs, soon to let go their hold for the breezes to take them; drifts of leaves would blanket the graves in the cemetery and his marble angels would rise from them, shining white against the brown.

He loved the seasons, like most artists probably: the life-cycles, the changing colours, the endlessly varying light. The seasons were as rich in the city as in the country if you knew where to look: the garden squares, the graveyards, the great public parks offering their luxury of space, respite from the jostling streets.

Here all was open; here you didn't need respite.

Would he go back?

Abruptly, and so far as he knew without premeditation, John set off at an angle across the tussocks of heather and sedge. Sheep which had ignored him while he kept to the road lifted their heads and bustled away, affronted.

He would be late for whatever it was he had been going to; but since he had no idea what that was, he found himself untroubled. Puzzled, but untroubled. Taken all for all, being unable to remember where he was going seemed a minor thing.

He was, he had lately become aware, a man without a history. Try though he might, he could not put together an account of his life that did not leave vast gaps.

Father? Many people lacked memory of a father, but most had at least been told a story: *your father was a travelling man; your father was lost at sea; your father was a thieving scoundrel who beat me and without whom we are much better off.* He had one story: his father had taken him to the Master's workshop. But he could not remember him.

Mother? No, nor sister, nor aunt, nor any other matronly

figure. How could this be? Who had brought him up from a babe? What had happened that he should have emptied his mind so thoroughly of his childhood?

Home, playmates, occupations – all erased as if they had never existed. Except one: being handed a stick of charcoal and being allowed to make marks of thrilling blackness on a sheet of thick paper. That, he remembered, and later the ride on the coach, exhilarating and terrifying in equal parts.

Nothing else.

Yet he did not think himself ill. Surely such lapses in memory ought to disturb him, yet he was not disturbed, more…intrigued. *There is a mystery here*, he thought. It was, it seemed to him, as though the world had turned itself inside out; he, John Lucas, was as he should be, but everything around him was amiss.

Sometimes he felt himself to be in a dream, and the village and all the people in it conjured from his imagination. Even London, even the workshop and his fellow engravers and the towering form of Joseph Weatherstone: all unreal. The princess in the glass tower he had engraved before he travelled here seemed more convincing, more true, than the landlord of the Black Horse, or poor Burrows, Mr Stratford's maid-of-all-work whom he had not had the heart to dismiss, or even sweet Rose, who seemed so…dull.

He paused, brought up short by the word. He had not thought of the poor girl as – well, dull – before, but now that the description hung there, he had to acknowledge its truth. She was sweet, and serene, and clearly intelligent, but…flat. Simple. Not stupid, not that at all, but…

Perhaps 'straightforward' was a better description; *too*

straightforward. It was as if there were no more layers to her than the surface that everyone could see. He had met her a handful of times and conversed (although never very fluently) on a range of subjects and felt he now knew everything about her. There were no more qualities to discover, no surprises. She had no more depth – less, really – than his ghost.

Deep in the heather, John stopped.

His ghost.

His eyes softened.

He began walking again, but slower, easy in the morning sunshine, inclined now to smile.

She was…well, not beautiful, he could not say she was that. Her nose was too long and her hair so strange, chopped off before it reached her shoulders and falling loose in front of her ears. But it did not signify. She was wonderful! He had seen her writing, always writing, bent over her paper or pausing, tapping her chin with her pen – except that it did not look like a pen and he never saw an inkwell.

She had been misty at first, shifting and indistinct, like a woman seen through smoke, but in time he saw her more clearly, her figure slim and straight, her movements quick, her face so expressive of curiosity, irritation, puzzlement, humour…longing…

His ghost.

Perhaps she knew why he was on the moor this autumn morning. Perhaps he was on the moor on her account. Because since the ridiculous visit with the eggs, when he had first glimpsed her in the schoolmistress's mirror, she had haunted his sleeping dreams and his waking thoughts, seeming more real – how could that be? – more real than the real people around him.

Did that make him insane? It sounded insane.

'I do not think I am insane,' John spoke aloud to the heather and the sheep. 'I am not insane. But it is as if…

'It is as if I am bewitched.'

CHAPTER 38

Now

IT WAS A TRUNK, WITH LEATHER REINFORCING THE EDGES, tacked down with round-headed brass studs, and brass corner pieces and a large brass plate held in place by a sturdy-looking padlock.

The padlock was locked.

Ha!

The collection of keys lived in a plastic sandwich box now, the original cardboard one having given up, and was kept in the corner cupboard alongside the torch, two extension leads and a shoe-box of candles in case of power cuts. Bryony set it down on the coffee table and removed the lid.

'Goodness!' Rosalind said. Then she said, 'But aren't these clock keys?'

'Well, yes, some of them. Not all of them. There are a lot of clocks but not this many.'

'What are the others?'

'Who knows?'

They took turns, trying every key, even the tiny ones, to be thorough. The heap on the table grew larger, those in the sandwich box fewer.

Bryony frowned.

Rosalind said, 'I didn't know you had these. I thought perhaps they were lost.'

Bryony detected reproach.

'Rosalind. I don't keep the clocks wound because winding clocks is a pain.' Bryony scowled at the diminishing number of keys. She had been so sure.

'I suppose so.' Rosalind paused. 'But–'

'No. They're all different. Some of them are really fiddly. You'd break your nails getting the back plate off that domed one opposite the grandfather clock. And they all run on different schedules as well.'

'I see.'

'Nightmare.'

'Yes.'

'I'm not doing it.'

'All right, Bryony.' Then Rosalind said, 'But you do wind the grandfather clock.'

'Yes, well, it's a grandfather clock, isn't it!' Bryony dropped the last key on the pile and threw herself back against the cushions with a groan. Then she sat forward again and said, 'Where do you buy a hacksaw that'll cut through something like that?'

But Rosalind seemed unperturbed. She had the padlock in her hand and was stroking its cold brass face with her thumb. Bryony could see her concentration.

'The hardware store will have a hacksaw, I'm sure. But we might not need one.'

'Why?' Bryony asked. Rosalind's free hand had moved once again to the necklace. Bryony's pulse quickened and she held her breath.

Rosalind sighed. 'Well. I can…that is, I usually…I might be able to find the key.' She slipped the chain over her head and Bryony saw the pendant for the first time. 'If it is here to be found, that is.'

The chain was threaded through a ring. Bryony leaned forward. The ring was slender, a very pale gold, with no design or pattern: a simple wedding band. Rosalind's? From the little she had given away about her widowhood it seemed unlikely. Her mother's then? The original seventh-child?

The ring disappeared from view as Rosalind closed her fingers around it. The chain trickled out from her hand, catching the lamplight and winking.

'Bryony, this will probably look a bit silly.'

Rosalind's expression was apologetic. Bryony said, 'What, pendulum dowsing? No, not silly at all! Go ahead.'

'You know what it is?' Apology had morphed into surprise.

'Broadly, yes.'

No need to elaborate, at least not right now.

Bryony had tried dowsing of course, but without success - not from want of a reaction, far from it, but from want of a reaction that was moderate, useable. Whatever she chose for a pendulum, whatever mood she was in, whatever question she asked, the thing went crazy, swinging around in all directions, leaping up to rap her knuckles and practically taking flight around her head. Positively poltergeistical. She had learned very quickly to pick only soft objects for the pendulum.

It had not bothered her. Finding things, at least hitherto, had not featured much in her life, with the sole exception of any other first-edition copies of *The Holly and the Ivy*, and she had never felt the need to seek advice on what to do. But if Rosalind could really find this key…

'Rosalind, why didn't you use this to find the box?'

Rosalind had seated herself on the floor and rested her elbows on the top of Cedric's nasty coffee table. She did not meet Bryony's eyes.

'Something as large as a box we ought to be able to find by ourselves, don't you think?' She shifted, getting comfortable. 'I prefer not to – well, do this unless it's really necessary.'

Her thumb and forefinger held the chain lightly near its clasp, her remaining fingers open; no unintentional movement from them should influence the swing of the pendulum.

The ring trembled. Rosalind's left hand steadied it, then moved away. She said, 'Sorry if this seems crackpot.'

'It won't. Go ahead.'

'You must think I'm insane.'

'I don't.'

'But sometimes–'

'Rosalind, just do it.'

Bryony watched her give a little shake and straighten herself. Then she seemed to settle and her gaze went to the wall behind Bryony's left shoulder. She cleared her throat.

'Is my name Rosalind?'

The ring shivered and then took up a gentle elliptical swing anticlockwise. Rosalind glanced down, halted the ring with her left hand and looked back at the wall.

'Did this trunk belong to Edith Waterfield?'

The ring moved into its anticlockwise swing. Rosalind stilled it again.

'Is the key able to be found?'

Anticlockwise.

'Do I know where it is?'

Anticlockwise.

Rosalind took a breath, girding her loins, Bryony thought.

'Is it in this house?'

Anticlockwise.

'Is it in this room?'

Clockwise: *no*.

'Is it in Bryony's bedroom?'

Clockwise.

'Is it in Bryony's kitchen?'

Clockwise.

'Is it…'

'Is it in the ground floor sales area?'

The ring on its chain swung anticlockwise.

Bryony perked up. It had taken a long time to work

through all the rooms in the building and she had begun to drift off – it was nearly midnight and with nothing active to do it had been hard to stay alert; but now she met Rosalind's look and raised her eyebrows.

Rosalind said, 'Is it somewhere accessible?'

Good question, and not one Bryony would have thought to ask.

The ring swung anticlockwise.

Rosalind looked again at Bryony.

'Try the desk. It was here when I came.' Although she didn't believe it could have escaped her notice if it was there.

'Is it in the desk?'

The ring jittered a little, dithering, and did not take up a proper swing at all.

'What does that mean?'

Rosalind stilled the ring. 'It means my question wasn't specific enough.'

'How more specific can you get?'

Rosalind thought, then said, 'Is it *connected to* the desk?'

Anticlockwise.

Connected to…What could that mean?

Rosalind closed her hand over the ring and slipped the chain over her head. 'I think now we look.'

They looked. Despite the pendulum's reluctance to describe the key as being in the desk, Bryony tipped out the first drawer and scrabbled through the contents. Rosalind, though, sank onto her knees and peered underneath, her hands stroking the wood.

'Ah.'

'Ah?'

Bryony stopped rifling through the pencils and coins and paperclips and cotton reels (cotton reels?) and bent down. Rosalind was tapping the underside of the desk.

'There's a slot…do you have a bodkin?'

'A what?'

'No, sorry…a knife? Something very thin?'

Bryony kept a paper knife in the drawer as well as, apparently, cotton reels, and handed it across. Rosalind scraped at something unseen.

'There's a sort of box,' she said as she worked. 'On the base. Very shallow. Open-ended. If I can just…ah,' she said again, and something clattered on the wooden floor.

It was, of course, a key.

Bryony picked it up, the cold brass weight of it, and looked at Rosalind.

'That was lucky,' Rosalind said.

'No.'

It was past midnight, the locked trunk was waiting and she had yet to drive Rosalind back to her flat, but Bryony knew the time had come.

She closed her hand over the key and said, 'No, Rosalind, not lucky. And not insane either.' She stood up, and Rosalind stood too. 'We will open the box, of course we will. But before we do, I want to talk to you.

'It is time,' Bryony said, 'for you to know what you are.'

CHAPTER 39

Then

'You will be all right?' Lillian asked.

'Yes. Yes, of course I will.'

'Because I don't have to go.'

Her sister was so sweet. Edith smiled. 'Oh Lillian, of course you must!'

Billy's birthday, and Lillian was to be the only outsider at Hare Rigg to celebrate an event Mr and Mrs Moffat had hardly dared hope to see. *I thought he would end himself,* Mrs Moffat told Edith when they met at the cobbler's, *until your Lillian took him up. Depressed and shell-shocked and in pain so much of the time.*

Oh, Lillian! What kind of a husband was that?

It would be dark early. Lillian was going to stay the night, in the room that once belonged to Billy's brother, Joe.

Ruth was in Hexham, visiting an old friend for Christmas shopping. It was her annual treat; she had been looking forward to it and would not be put off by the dreadful weather. But it was also Lizzy's monthly weekend visit home, which meant that Edith would be alone overnight.

The ridiculous thing was that she had been excited about this for days – a childish glee at having the house to herself after the lamps were lit, free to eat toasted cheese for supper, to sit and read with her feet tucked under her in comfortable solitude, to lift her head and hear only the clocks and the crackle of logs in the grate, and perhaps the rain on the windows.

She had rather hoped it would rain and she had got her wish; the wind had been rising since breakfast and rain had started after lunch, driven in horizontal gusts to hurl itself at the windows and walls all afternoon and evening without any discernible let up.

And now, because of her stupid adventure and because of damned Alfred Wintersgill, it was spoiled.

I am not nervous at all. Definitely not. Why would I be?

Except that she was.

When she told them, Ruth's reaction had been predictable. 'Really, Edith, don't be silly.'

'I–'

'Ruth, she's not being silly. If she saw it, she saw it.' Lillian, in her defence.

'But it's ridiculous! A girl like that? To leave anything behind? She never would.'

'I know,' Edith had said. 'Of course she wouldn't. That's the point.'

And it wasn't 'anything'; it was *everything*. Edith had shivered then as she did still when she thought of the room at the end of the landing, sparsely furnished and cold but full, absolutely full of Agnes White's belongings: her hair brush on the chest of drawers, and the fringed paisley shawl, which surely had been a treasure; a tin of sewing thread and needles, and her prayer book by the bed; in the wardrobe, three faded dresses and her coat, a surprisingly nice camel wool with a moth hole near the bottom button – Edith remembered it well, both the niceness and the hole – and her shoes, both pairs, the tough workaday ones and the Sunday best.

Shoes, for heaven's sake! Had she gone barefoot? And then never sent for her possessions? Where would she have she run away *to?*

Alfred Wintersgill had said she'd *gone off*. Those were the words he had used that day when he was talking to Ruth in the parlour while Edith lurked, eavesdropping, on the landing: *The girl's gone off without a word*. Complaining because he was left in the lurch and had to do his own cooking *until I get another*. But he hadn't got another and for the first time the Waterfield sisters wondered why. It wasn't as if there were not girls to be had; it had been barely three weeks between Primmy's death and Lizzy coming to work for them. Why could Alfred Wintersgill not find a maid in nine months?

*The girl's gone off without a word…*He never said she had gone without her belongings too.

'But,' Ruth said, but had no words to follow.

But what? What explanation could there be? Nothing any of them could think of, and knowing Ruth she would have been wrestling with the problem all evening, desperate to come up with a plausible reason that would exculpate Alfred. But she couldn't, and the next step was unavoidable.

Edith went to the police station in Hexham. She didn't want to; she wished Ruth or Lillian could go instead, but although Ruth accompanied her it had to be Edith who spoke. It was only Edith who had seen.

And in the event, the police were scarcely interested.

'I expect she was homesick,' the duty sergeant said. 'Fed up being on her own, wanted her mum. That'll be it. But we'll take a look, if you like.'

And they did, two of them arriving in a car, according to Sarah Lynne, and staying all of ten minutes.

Ten minutes, after which they left with cheery smiles and a wave, Sarah said, 'So whatever it was it all ended happily.'

That was last week. And now, as the evening closed in and the lamps were lit, and the street outside became dark as a cave and the last of her neighbours had closed their curtains, Edith knew she would not be answering any knock at the door unless she recognised the voice accompanying it.

And then the back door wheezed open. There was a moment of suspended time, three seconds perhaps, perhaps four, and then footsteps sounded on the stairs.

.   .   .

'ALL ALONE ARE WE? Ready for a spot of company?'

Edith was already running.

It was about time; she should have got moving at once, at the first hint of sound from downstairs, but like an idiot she had lifted her head to listen, puzzling over what she was hearing as if it were not instantly obvious.

The scullery door. How completely we know the speech of our own homes; a thousand doors might open in a thousand stone-flagged rooms without matching that precise combination of rasp and scrape that means *mine*. Edith knew at once what she was hearing, knew too that it could not be Ruth or Lillian returning unexpectedly because they would use the front door, would call up to her: *Edith! It's me! I'm back!*

Yet she sat, frozen, straining to listen as someone moved in the house below. Did she think that by refusing to react she might make it unreal? That only when she acknowledged to herself that Alfred Wintersgill had entered the house he would truly have done so?

Because it was him, no doubt about that, the voice calling up the stairs the one she had heard so often in the past, on and on about himself and his dealings, while Ruth attended and Lillian sewed and Edith herself sat tight and twitching and desperate to run away.

Run away. Like Agnes.

It was that, the crossing of the boundary between the public rooms and the private family part of the house that galvanised her. Somewhere inside her a switch was thrown and she convulsed into action, launched upwards from the cushions and ejected from the sitting room as if by a force that was external, nothing to do with her muscles at all.

Up, up!

She took the stairs two at a time, holding her breath for extra speed, her arm outstretched, yearning for the newel post. She would swing herself around and dash for the bathroom, because there was a bolt on the inside – the only lockable door in the house. Her brain must have decided this even as she reacted, hurling her on her way as if by instinct, not thought. A bolt would be enough; Alfred Wintersgill would not break down the door, surely?

'Now, now, Lady Edith, all airs and graces, so full of yourself, so ready with the lies and stories.' He was behind and below her on the stairs. 'I've a word or two to say to you.' Panting a little now and oh, too close, too close.

Edith reached for the wood and her fingers found it, but her legs could not keep up and suddenly her ankle was grasped and jerked back, throwing her onto elbows and knees.

The shock was great. Edith had probably not fallen over since she was a child. Her trapped breath escaped with a rush and she gasped for more, twisting and kicking but on her back now, her hands behind her, fighting still but scarcely hoping to get free.

Alfred Wintersgill stood over her.

'Little bitch,' he said, and smiled.

. . .

He took his ease now, no need to hurry. He must have planned this, known that her sisters and Lizzy were far away and that she would be defenceless.

Alfred dropped his coat, sodden and dark from the rain. His hair was dripping, the water shining on his face, and his boots either side of Edith were muddy and wet.

He unbuckled his belt. 'So, you little bitch, you broke into my house and thought you'd tell about my sister's bedroom, did you?'

From somewhere Edith found a voice. 'You don't have a sister.'

'Of course I do. Little Annie. Doesn't visit me often, Annie, but I like to keep her room ready for when she does.'

It was nonsense. Everyone knew, the whole village knew, that Alfred was Flora Wintersgill's only child, the apple of her eye, nothing ever too good for him.

He loosened his tie and pulled it over his head. What was he doing? Edith realised she was shaking and heard it in her voice, which was off again, speaking words without her permission.

'Her coat. Agnes's coat.'

'Annie's got one just like it. Funny, isn't it? Moth hole in the same place and all. We used to laugh about that.'

So he noticed moth holes. Edith shivered, imagining the man's eyes following his maid as she left his house, watching her when she returned.

He unfastened the top button of his shirt, and then the next one, his fingers leisurely, no haste, no hurry. She wanted to scramble and kick but knew that at the first sign of movement he would catch her. It was so easy for him; she was frozen in the present, untouched at *this* moment, and *this*, but with no hope of remaining so.

He could take her any time he chose.

So what are you going to do, then? Lie here and let him? She could feel her breath tight at the top of her lungs, her muscles taut but inactive: a hopeless state.

Breathe!

Edith forced her ribs to open, her shoulders to drop. With her weight on her hands behind her she was unbalanced and without strength, but if she even thought of moving, bringing her legs under her, gathering herself, Alfred would stop her and she would be finished.

'You stupid little cow.'

It seemed any animal would do. Edith stared as he shook his head, bemused at her naivety, so relaxed, so easy, and his hands at his waist now, unfastening the buttons there. He was smiling, the way you might smile and shake your head at a small child's antics, and in that instant Edith knew.

Before, it had been conjecture, but not any more. Alfred Wintersgill – the leather worker who made and repaired harness and saddlery and boots for the inhabitants of Ravensburn and Bowbeck, who helped the cricket team to victory last season, whom her sister Ruth had served tea and scones to over and over again in the hope that one day he would become her brother-in-law – Alfred Wintersgill had raped and then murdered Agnes White, raped and then murdered Primmy, and would now rape and then murder her. And she could think of nothing, nothing that she could do to prevent him.

Grief and terror rose in her together, side by side. As

Alfred knelt astride her, ridiculous images galloped through her mind: her father, climbing the stairs with his candle and a book, peering over his spectacles and wondering what the fuss was; Eddie, not dead but in the room behind her, levelling his army pistol; Samuel Eliot, bursting in with his forge hammer raised; poor Billy Moffat even, for as Lillian said, he was still a man, was he not?

And John Lucas, lovely John, with his quiet strength and his clever hands and his steadfast heart, for all the world as if she thought he could rise out of the pages of manuscript lying on the desk through the open door behind her and take form, become flesh, come to life and save her.

How could it be that her brothers had died and John Lucas not exist and yet the likes of Alfred Wintersgill should be here, lumpen and foul, to use the world as he liked?

Whimpering, Edith retreated from the hot, heavy weight lowering onto her, pressed onto the floor with her wrists pinioned by his hands while his knee forced her own knees apart – and then all came to a halt.

Alfred lifted his head. 'What the—'

The floor creaked in the bedroom behind her, the spot between the door and her desk where the boards dipped.

'No. No.' Alfred's voice was suddenly breathless, panting, panicking even, as he shuffled off her, crawling backwards.

Her hands were free. She twisted and pushed herself onto all fours, scrambling to her feet with the help of the banister, and heard something else, something beyond the noises she was making and Alfred was making: the air being stirred, wood whispering, a groan in the structure of the old house as it responded to someone, someone else, a third person where there should be only two.

She swung round, her back to the rail, staring, and behind her now, in a voice from which all the substance had gone, Alfred Wintersgill found a new name to call her.

'You...you witch!'

Edith spun back to see – what? Something impossible: Alfred Wintersgill, built of bone and flesh, clothed in wool and leather, becoming as smoke even where he stood.

I'm going to faint.

She couldn't be fainting. She never fainted. But something was happening to her vision and her hearing and her legs, and with a sense of despair, Edith began to slip.

EDITH SLIPPED, but she did not fall. Before she reached the floor she was caught by quick, strong arms and laid down with care.

CHAPTER 40

Now

THEY DID OPEN THE TRUNK, AND IT DID NOT DISAPPOINT, although by mutual agreement they decided not to deal with its contents that night. Rosalind had rather feared Bryony would want to dive in there and then, and was relieved when she agreed to wait.

But it was not the contents of the trunk that occupied Rosalind's mind while she prepared for bed.

'It is time for you to know what you are,' Bryony had said to her, and said it in a voice so uncharacteristically gentle that Rosalind's blood had slowed in her veins. 'Come and sit down.'

They returned to the flat and she had sat down on the sofa. Bryony took the chair and they faced each other across the coffee table, the locked trunk on the floor and its key presumably in Bryony's pocket. Rosalind had not noticed her put it away but it could not be in her hands now for they were clasped together in her lap, the fingers interlaced.

Rosalind was not sure whether the pause was for Bryony to choose words or to give her, Rosalind, time to prepare. Something momentous was coming and she had no idea what.

Bryony was looking at her in a considering kind of way, and when she spoke it was apparent she had decided on the direct approach.

'Rosalind,' she said, 'You are a witch. But it's all right, I'm a witch too.'

...

WITCHES

CHAPTER 41

Now

SHE OUGHT TO HAVE LAUGHED, BUT SOMEHOW SHE DIDN'T.

'When did you last get caught in the rain?' Bryony asked her, which felt jarringly like a change of subject although of course it wasn't.

'I…don't think I have ever…'

'No. On wet days I can tell exactly where you are by looking at the sky. Where there's a chink in the clouds, that's where you'll be. I can even track you. I know when you're coming.'

She felt herself flush, as if caught in a lie.

Bryony flapped her hand. 'Don't worry, nobody else will have noticed. It must be lovely I should think.'

'Well, it is quite useful…'

'And pretty nice for the people you're with, too.'

'Well…'

'Can I ask you something? Does it work the other way as well? Can you bring rain when you want it, for your garden for instance?'

Could she? Rosalind cast her mind back. 'I…no, I don't think I do that. I've never thought about it…the garden just…grows by itself with whatever rain we get.'

It did, it always had done, despite summer droughts and hosepipe bans. She had thought it was good fortune, a chance quality of water retention in the soil. It was true there had been long, dry summers when the grass had lost its greenness but if she watered by hand, just a little, with the old galvanised steel watering can she so much preferred to modern plastic ones, it seemed to revive overnight.

'And cut flowers?'

'What about cut flowers?'

'You must be aware that every time you shuffle them they rejuvenate by at least two weeks?'

'Oh Bryony, that's just changing the water! Of course they last longer if you give them fresh water.'

Bryony shook her head. 'Nope. Has to be you that changes it. Believe me, I've tried everything to keep them going longer, made my own flower food from bleach and sugar, everything. But Rosalind, you only have to walk past them and they perk up. You can make chrysanthemums last for months, you know you can, and the geraniums have exploded!'

'Oh, well, geraniums are always easy.'

But Bryony had changed tack again.

'Your cooking is divine. In fact it's magical.'

Rosalind felt the floor firm up beneath her feet. 'Oh no, really, that's just being able to cook.'

'Mm. Maybe.'

'Grace Eliot can match me easily.'

'Mm,' Bryony said again. 'That's another thing, though. They say wives grow to be like their husbands, don't they?'

Rosalind was mystified but Bryony was moving on.

'Why do you think I get you to make the coffee? What do you think of this stuff?' She held her mug aloft.

Bryony had made coffee for them, and as usual it tasted less than delightful.

'I thought you were using a different brand from the one in the shop?'

'Nope. Same brand. Same water. It's just that you make it taste like filter coffee. *And* you stir it widdershins.'

'Pardon?'

'Widdershins.' Bryony demonstrated, circling her finger in the air.

'Oh no, not that again! Is it significant?'

'Yes. It's an indicator. As is the fact that your younger sister is called Octavia and you told me you have a lot of aunts and uncles. You said you had to be very organised with birthday cards.'

'But why–'

'You're the seventh child in the family, aren't you? And so was your mother. You're the seventh of a seventh. Like me. And that's why you saw John Day on the second floor when even I've only ever heard him and smelled that lovely woody smell.'

'Boxwood.'

'Yes, boxwood. But I've never seen him, not ever, and you just waltzed in and did it! On your first visit! *My* ghost, *my* bookshop's resident spirit! After all the hours and hours I've spent sitting up there meditating in front of his stupid portrait, *willing* him to materialise, show himself, come up and shake my hand. I wanted to hit you!'

Rosalind said, 'Oh dear.'

'Yes. Well. Anyway, there it is. You're a witch, Rosalind, just like me, and I thought it was time you knew it.'

Extraordinary. And the most extraordinary thing of all, Rosalind thought, getting into bed an hour later, was that it didn't really seem incredible. It was almost, she thought, as if she had known all along.

Bryony's experience was rather different. She began by voicing the question Rosalind had so often wanted to ask.

'Why do you think I don't have a mobile phone? Why do you think I don't use computers? Why do you think I ring everything up on that ridiculous old till, like something Noah would have used to stock up the Ark?'

'Ahh...'

'That's right. I'm death to everything electronic. Everything tiny enough. I can use basic electricity. I can use a hair dryer.'

'It isn't just that you can't use them,' Rosalind said, realising. 'No-one else can either when they're in your – well, when you...'

'In my proximity,' Bryony filled in for her. 'Dead right. Computers crash, mobile phones lose their signal, calculators give up the ghost. I'm very good at mental arithmetic, you know. Lots of practice.'

But she had other talents.

'I can influence people. At least, I'm pretty sure I can, when I need to. I get my own way a lot.'

Rosalind had wanted to laugh. Bryony faced her across the table, small, dark and fierce, and so utterly, so supremely self-confident. You would just bet she got her own way a lot!

'Although,' she went on, 'I very nearly didn't get my own way in London last year.' She stared hard at Rosalind. 'On the South Bank. At the book stall.'

'Oh.'

'Yes, oh. I was really shocked, Rosalind, having to work so hard to beat you that day. And even more shocked when you turned up here a few months later. That got me thinking, I can tell you. And look, just look at how quickly you've mastered this computer stuff – email, the internet, everything. Robby's really impressed.'

Goodness, she had impressed Robby!

'Although I grant you that might be just brains, not witchcraft.'

Bryony had paused – at last – and slumped back, gazing blankly at the scratched table top. Rosalind watched her warily, too stunned to think about what she had been told and anxious that there might yet be more to come.

And she was right, although it was not directed at her this time. Bryony took a gulp of the horrible coffee and waved the mug in the air.

'And that's not all. I've been wondering a lot about our Edith recently. *How* many brothers did you say she lost in the War?'

CHAPTER 42

Then

EDITH OPENED HER EYES. THE ROOM WAS DIM, LIT ONLY BY the candle on the chest of drawers, and the figure of the person sitting in the corner by the curtains was just a shape in the shadows.

A man's shape, though. He sat with his feet apart and his elbows on his knees, unmistakably masculine. When Edith stirred, pushing herself up, he rose at once but stayed by the chair, not stepping forward but granting her space.

He was not Eddie. Quite why she had thought he might be, she could not now explain. He was no ghost but breathed and possessed substance; the floorboards creaked under his feet.

And he could speak.

'You are my ghost,' he said, and the words sounded to

Edith as if they were only partly directed at her, mostly spoken aloud to himself.

You are my ghost. That wasn't right; it should be the other way round.

Edith shuffled herself into sitting, feeling the bedstead knobbly against her spine but unable at the moment to organise pillows. The wind thumped and moaned outside. She stared into the gloom, thirsty for detail, gripped by the need to see his features. 'Who…' Her throat was so dry. She swallowed. 'Who are you?'

'Forgive me.'

Now he stepped forward, and in the candle's wavering light Edith saw a form she almost knew: the structure of his bones; the dark eyes, puzzled now and intent; the hair framing his face longer than was usual and softly curling. 'Who…' she said again, her question scarcely more than a breath.

'Allow me to introduce myself.'

In the candlelight he bowed his head briefly.

'My name is John Lucas.'

CHAPTER 43

Now

ONCE AGAIN BRYONY SAT ACROSS A TABLE FROM ROSALIND, keeping quiet, trying not to hold her breath, watching the slender, pale circle swinging on its fine chain.

Clockwise; always, after those two initial questions – *Am I Rosalind? Do I know?* – clockwise.

It should have been riveting but in actual fact it had become dull. Bryony's thoughts began to drift as her eyes were distracted from the dangling pendulum to wander around the room.

They were in the coachman's flat at the Law House. When they drew a blank in the bookshop, Rosalind said she had never tried dowsing outside her own home before and suggested they try again here. Bryony hoped a temporary, rented flat weighed as much in the balance as a permanent home, owned outright and in which you had raised your family.

The living room of the old coachman's flat was neat and vacuumed and smelled of roses and of lemon cleaning products, tempered slightly by perhaps less than perfectly clean carpet. That must irk Rosalind, but Bryony supposed it probably wasn't possible to bring in professional carpet cleaners to a rented flat. Not tactful, anyway. But the roses were apricot and white and sat graciously in a tapered glass vase, breathing their summer-garden scent into the room.

How could even Rosalind make roses last months?

'Is it at Hare Rigg?' Rosalind was asking.

Clockwise.

Oh well, at least they didn't need to tangle with Jacqui Moffat again. Not a pleasant woman. Poor old Dorrie, stuck with her for company.

Dorrie Moffat and Lily Pigg. You couldn't make up names like that, Bryony thought. She realised her impression of Mrs Pigg had changed now she knew her Christian name. Lily – such a pretty name; it was those Ls, Bryony thought: any girl's name beginning with L is beguiling: Laura, Lorna, Lucy…lovely, languid, liquid L, and lucky little Lily had two of them.

'Is it, oh I don't know, in the Handsome Jack?'

Clockwise.

Rosalind was running out of questions. She had an L too. How much nicer was Rosalind than Rosamund, for example? But she was getting nowhere with the search.

Bryony leaned forward and placed her hands palm down

on the polished table to interrupt. Rosalind stilled the ring and looked at her.

'It's time to be systematic,' Bryony said. 'Start at the bottom and go all the way up to the top on one side, and then go back to the bottom and start again with the other side, and then go along the side roads. It will take forever, but I think that's what we have to do.'

We, as if she was contributing anything here. Apart from guidance, perhaps.

So Rosalind began at the foot of the village where the bridge crossed the river and, prompted by Bryony when she went adrift, named every house or shop on the street, sometimes having to resort to descriptions: *'the house next to the bakery; the house next to the house next to the bakery; the house after that'*, while Bryony, restless, abandoned her chair and roamed the room, staring out of the windows, wishing there were bookshelves to be nosy about, wondering whether the missing diaries really existed. The pendulum insisted they did, but was it right?

They had opened Edith's trunk, the key turning in the old lock with only a little difficulty and the lid stiff but not heavy.

What had they expected? For her own part, Bryony had thought there would probably be more photographs, hopefully nicely mounted in albums with proper labels identifying the people and places depicted, and perhaps a few personal items: school certificates, book prizes, maybe even some letters. Could they be that lucky?

But there were no letters and very few photographs, only

a handful slipped down the side of what the trunk did contain, which was diaries. Lots of them.

'Goodness!' Rosalind had said, reaching out to touch.

The books were leather-bound and packed vertically, spines uppermost. They were in series: a number of chestnut brown covers, followed by a number of dusty blue, then brown again and then pale grey. The dates were stamped in gold leaf and covered the years immediately after the First World War right up to the late fifties; the last diary in the trunk was 1957.

How excited she and Rosalind had been, greedily pulling out a volume each and flipping through the pages. And then how disappointed.

They were not journals. They were appointment diaries, no more, and the entries were sparse: *12 February – Dentist…25 July – Church flowers…4 September – Winifred arriving.*

'Not exactly riveting,' Bryony had said.

'No. And an author, too.'

'Perhaps that's it. She was putting it all into her books. No need to keep a journal. What a pity.'

They worked their way through the volumes, flipping through and setting aside just to make sure nothing was being missed, although Bryony wasn't sure what. Edith had lived her whole life in this village, being first a daughter, then a sister, then a…paramour…and finally dying here. What had her life ever held that was exciting, apart from having books published? Although admittedly that was pretty exciting.

'Oh well.'

Bryony put the last book on the stack and reached for the photographs, but Rosalind said, 'That's odd.'

'What's odd?'

Rosalind shuffled through the diaries on the floor. 'There's one missing. No, two.'

'Really?'

'Nineteen twenty-one and nineteen twenty-two. Not here. How peculiar.'

'Lost,' Bryony said, dismissively.

'I wouldn't have thought so. Someone meticulous enough to keep appointment diaries like this wouldn't just lose two, surely? And consecutive years.'

Their eyes met.

'Secrets!' Bryony whispered.

Which was why she had persuaded Rosalind to dowse for the missing volumes, with absolute zero success. She had drawn a blank. It was frustrating and a waste of time, and tantalising too, because the more Bryony thought about it, the more she agreed with Rosalind. Edith would not have carefully preserved so many diaries yet thrown away two, unless there was something different about those two.

What is different from a list of appointments?

Accounts of what has happened.

Why would accounts of what has happened need to be hidden?

Because they are personal, embarrassing, awkward, or even, perhaps, incriminating.

What *did* happen to Alfred Wintersgill that night of November 1921? And just *how* did John Day arrive unseen in Ravensburn?

CHAPTER 44

Then

LATER, WHEN EDITH LOOKED BACK, SHE OFTEN THOUGHT that *that* was when she should have fainted.

But she didn't.

'John…' She sought for words. 'But you…it can't be… I'm not…John *Lucas? Really?*'

'Yes. Where are we?'

Later, also, Edith would love that use of the plural pronoun. *Where are we?* he asked her, not *where am I?* She would remember how he stood, warm and solid, his feet planted, staring round the shadowy room as if it were the walls and ceiling that were strange and she herself not part of the strangeness but subject to it, with him.

You are my ghost.

He had seen her before.

'I am Edith Waterfield,' Edith said, working hard to steady her voice. 'And we are in my house.'

EDITH DRAGGED up a pillow to lean against and tried not to tremble. Her insides felt fluttery, as if white mice were doing back flips in there, and she was cold. She tugged the quilt over her legs – they were in Lilian's bedroom, the closest to the stairs – and shifted to get comfortable, all the time trying not to think about Alfred Wintersgill.

Not possible, of course. Not possible to stop remembering her terror as she fled upstairs, nor how her terror turned to horror as she realised what was going to happen.

What she had thought was going to happen.

But not possible either to stop thinking about his breathless, panicking cry as…as what? As he began to fade, like smoke in a chimney, thinning and spreading and losing its form. That was all she had seen before she passed out, which she assumed was what had happened. How stupid and useless; how weak.

But John – was he really John? – must have seen more, surely?

'What happened to Alfred Wintersgill? What happened to that man?'

John Lucas shook his head. 'I don't know. He seemed to vanish.' He hesitated, then added, 'Slowly,' which made Edith shiver.

'He didn't just…go away?'

'No. He…dissolved.'

He dissolved. Edith shut her eyes momentarily, and then

thought, *But he killed Agnes and he killed Primmy and he was going to kill me*, and she opened them again.

The man standing at the foot of the bed was watching her with an expression, she thought, of wary compassion and curiosity, and she felt a wave of energy and resolve wash over her. Alfred Wintersgill, wherever he had gone, was in the past. A man who had every appearance of being real and yet claimed to be John Lucas was in the present.

The present is what you deal with.

Edith swung her legs over the edge of the bed and stood up.

Good. A bit rocky, but that was mostly the mice in her stomach. She was aware of her face being unable to decide what to do – smile? gape? laugh? – and took a deep breath in an attempt to stabilise everything.

Everything, which now apparently included the impossible.

'Let's go downstairs. More light.'

She blew out the candle and led the way. There was a hiccuppy moment as her feet trod the runner where minutes before Alfred Wintersgill had been standing, but she pushed on through and walked down the stairs to the parlour, where the lamps were still burning as if nothing had happened.

Gas had not come to Ravensburn; all the lamps were oil. Nothing to alarm him there, then.

In fact the furniture was old, and a man, Edith thought, would be unlikely to take much notice of patterns and colours.

Even an artist? Possibly not…

So the house should not present too much that was strange.

Just me, then.

Just herself, with her straight-cut shift dress and what must seem an awful lot of leg. But when they sat down, Edith on the sofa and John Lucas in the wing chair opposite, it was her eyes that he watched, not her ankles.

'Miss Waterfield, do you know how I find myself here? Because it is a fact that I do not.'

His voice was lovely, a light baritone, steady and measured, just as she had imagined.

Well, of course.

'I don't know either,' Edith said, which was nothing but the truth. 'But you said I was your ghost.'

He smiled a little crookedly, which caused Edith's internal organs to lurch. 'Forgive me. I thought…you looked so like someone I have seen. You still do.'

This was intriguing.

'Someone you have seen where?'

Where could he have been that she had not sent him? Where could he have seen her, flesh and bone and blood that she was?

'In mirrors. And in my dreams.'

But I never gave him dreams.

Edith said slowly, 'Tell me who you are.'

CHAPTER 45

Now

THE FIRST LETTER TO ARRIVE WAS TYPED ON A4 AND POSTED in a long window envelope. Bryony opened it expecting business: a request for an out-of-print book, an invoice, advertising. Instead, she read:

Dear Ms Bower,

I never saw Edith Waterfield, who died before I was born, but I am writing at the request of my 96-year-old mother, who lived most of her life in Ravensburn and remembers the Days very well.

My mother says that Edith wrote the best stories she ever read, although she admits she might have been influenced by the knowledge that the author was a local girl. In any case, we still possess the first editions she collected as a child, all of them signed by both the author and the illustrator, which I imagine to be unusual in the world of books.

I regret that my mother is too frail to leave her home, near Prudhoe, but if you have any particular questions for her I should be happy to relay them.

Perhaps you would care to comment on the value of a complete set of signed Waterfield first editions?

Yours sincerely,

S P Whitbread

S P Whitbread, eh? Cagey kind of signature. Bryony made a private bet that he was a man, based mostly on what seemed like a greedy nature that he wanted to disguise as public spiritedness.

If the books had been bought by his mother when she was a child, it was unlikely they included a first edition *The Holly and the Ivy*. And S P said they were signed by the illustrator as well, and there were no illustrations in the novel.

She laid the letter aside.

The following day two more arrived, one badly typewritten on what had to be a manual typewriter, peppered with spelling errors overtyped by Xs *('I later found out that they had never married, although we were always told to call her Mrs Day')* and one handwritten in very loopy script inside a note card with a watercolour painting of a tortoiseshell cat on a window sill *('There was something magical about Mrs Day, as she called herself, and the way she collected cats. They all adored her! And she used to let me help pour the milk').*

Bryony thought, *mm, magical, I wonder.*

Then she thought, *tch, milk, how ignorant.*

She stretched for the shelves behind the desk and tugged out a fresh card folder, wrote *Waterfield Responses* on it, and put both letters inside. Then she shuffled through the papers on the desk until she found yesterday's letter and put that inside too. She dropped the folder into the middle drawer.

When Rosalind arrived from a morning of baking at the Forge, bringing a break in the rain and a divinely spicy, juicy, aromatic fruit cake that was not yet quite cool, Bryony retrieved the folder and showed her the letters.

'They're beginning to come in,' Rosalind said. 'How exciting!'

'Not that exciting.' Bryony paused, her next mouthful on hold. 'I'm hoping for more than the fact that people were embarrassed and told their children to call her Mrs Day. We could have guessed that much. Likewise that the children were besotted with her cats.'

'Well, yes, I suppose so. But it is interesting to learn that she had so many, isn't it? I mean…twenty!'

Bryony paused again, and this time put her slice of cake down. 'Ah.'

Rosalind looked up.

Bryony said, 'I forgot you don't know about the cats.'

She hadn't wanted to broach the matter with the old Rosalind who believed two and two always make four and thought she never got rained on because she was lucky. And since breaking it to her that the rules by which the world runs can sometimes be bent, there had been other things on her mind.

But now it was probably time.

Rosalind's response suggested the rules were still pretty firm.

'Oh Bryony, that's ridiculous!'

'Says the woman who saw John Day.'

Rosalind looked discomforted. 'Well…but–'

'But nothing. You saw him, Rosalind, you told me you did at the time. So why not cats?'

It did strike Bryony as perverse that Rosalind should be so perceptive, so sensitive, so open to influence as to see the spirit of John Day as a living man, albeit fleetingly and out of the corner of her eye, and yet never to have had so much as a whiff of the wretched cats that swarmed all over the shop, while she, despite all her efforts, had never seen John and yet was forever glimpsing little furry forms at ankle height and almost, *almost* tripping over them and tumbling to her death on the wooden stairs. It didn't seem fair.

'Gabriel sees them too,' she added, realising even as the words left her mouth that they were hardly likely to inspire trust.

But she was mistaken. Rosalind looked thoughtful.

'Yes, I think he probably does.'

Bryony brightened. 'There you are then. Although why you should trust a cat more than me I'm not sure. I might take offence.'

She noticed Rosalind did not fly to apologise but ignored her, and was pleased. Perhaps she was toughening up. Perhaps knowing she was a witch was doing her some good.

Bryony said, 'What I don't understand is why Edith's cats all left ghosts behind to haunt the place when every other cat in the world seems happy just to turn up its little furry toes and go in peace to the great duvet in the sky. Edith obviously took good care of them – apart from the milk–'

'Everyone fed milk to cats in those days, Bryony.'

'– so why are they Unquiet?'

'Is every ghost really Unquiet?' Rosalind asked. 'Perhaps some just can't bring themselves to let go.'

'They feel Unquiet when they nearly trip me up.'

The problem was that they materialised, or almost materialised, right by her feet, without warning. It is very hard, Bryony had found, to step on something furry even if it is only partly there, even if you know it can't be harmed. She had learned to tread extremely slowly on and around staircases, and indeed everywhere else in the shop if she was carrying something that could be spilled or would break if dropped.

'Anyway, it doesn't surprise me that Edith had tons of cats but it is peculiar that no-one seemed to know where she got them from.'

The loopy writing had been emphatic about that: *Every year a new one, and they didn't come from local litters like everyone else's. Claudio was a Siamese of all things, and Mrs Day kept it very secret where she obtained him.*

Edith's stories were all based on her own cats. Claudio made his first appearance in a book called *Calpurnia and Claudio*, in which Calpurnia, the svelte tortoiseshell queen, went a-wandering as far as the coast and met up with a debonair cat with exotic features who caused her all kinds of trouble on their way back. Bryony especially liked that the female lead was able to retain her independence and strength despite falling hopelessly in love.

Rosalind said, 'Perhaps people brought them to her.

When people know you will give animals a good home they will bring all sorts to you.'

'Mm. Maybe.' But a Siamese in the middle of the Northumbrian moors?

'I think Mercutio was her favourite,' Rosalind continued. 'Did you notice that he's the only one to have been photographed? I thought that was rather odd.'

Bryony also found it surprising. He was a big, handsome black cat, not unlike Gabriel although more sleek and lacking Gabriel's fluff. Among the photographs in Edith's trunk had been one of Mercutio alone, sitting loftily on a wide stone gate post – this at a time when photographs were expensive – and he cropped up in several family groups. None of the other cats made a showing, not even exotic Claudio, not even sweet little Cobweb with her kittens.

'Do you think she acquired cats specifically with a view to writing about them?' Bryony wondered. It seemed somewhat callous. It seemed somewhat pointless too; surely that was what imagination was for? 'Do you think she had book jackets in mind when she named them?'

Rosalind shrugged. 'Who knows? The problem we have is that it was such a long time ago. There can't be many people still around who were adults when Edith was writing and really knew her. What a pity Dorrie Moffat lived so far out of the village. What a pity Lily Pigg won't talk to us.'

'Ah.'

Rosalind shot her a look. 'Bryony, what?'

'It's just that I've been thinking about that. And I might, just might have an idea.'

CHAPTER 46

Then

HIS GHOST SAID, 'TELL ME WHO YOU ARE,' BUT BEFORE HE could answer a gust of wind thumped against a window hidden behind curtains and something somewhere crashed.

Without knowing why, he felt quite certainly that they were alone in this house, even to there being no servant indoors.

'It sounds as though a window or door is open. With your permission I shall—'

'No. I mean, yes, but I'll come too.'

His ghost rose, and once again he found himself marvelling at her extraordinary clothes, so loose, like infants' clothing, and the hem so very short.

She seemed vulnerable. 'Are you certain you are well enough?'

'Yes, yes, I'm fine now. Thank you,' she added, like a child remembering her manners, and despite the strangeness of his situation – the strangeness of everything really – he smiled.

She saw.

'What is it?'

'I…you…ah.' Impossible to put into words. He opened his hands, shrugged, shook his head, but could not stop his smile, although he turned it into a rueful upside-down smile.

And his ghost woman smiled too. 'Come on, then. It'll be the scullery door I expect.'

They descended more stairs, the ghost woman leading the way and giving every appearance of having recovered from her faint. Two steps behind, watching her by the light of the candle he held, he could not but notice how the collar of her gown had twisted, turning inwards against the smooth skin of her neck.

As if his thought had been transferred, she put up her right hand and folded it back, tugging the cloth straight.

The kitchen was in darkness, a cold draft flowing into it. In the scullery, the yard door was wide open, letting rain into the room; hail stones too. Shards of pottery were strewn across the flagstones.

He moved past his ghost to push the door to, pressing against the wind. The noise of the storm lessened as it thumped into place, and he bolted it, top and bottom.

The ghost woman – except that she had felt warm and full of substance in his arms, so could she truly be a ghost? – had knelt and was collecting the broken pottery, dropping sharp fragments into her cupped hand, so he joined her and they cleared the floor together. When they had done, they placed the broken pieces in a bowl on the table.

'I should think that will do.'

She was looking around, considering what else needed repair. He retrieved a cloth from the floor and folded it and laid it on the table next to the bowl.

'Thank you.' She had turned her gaze on him now, and he saw that a smile was twitching at her mouth.

And now it was his turn to ask, 'What is it?'

She shook her head. 'Just…us, here, together, tidying up. You and me. As if…as if it were normal!' She laughed and bit her lip, and he thought, *How easy it is to be with her; how comfortable!*

How unlike Rose.

'Um…would you like a cup of tea?' she asked, raising her eyebrows as if the invitation were ridiculous.

And perhaps it was; but he said, 'Indeed, yes, thank you,' and for some reason both of them laughed again.

LATER HE WOULD HEAR Edith's theory: *It was because we sorted out the scullery together. Once you have worked alongside someone, the barriers are broken down.*

It might be true. Certainly it did seem easy to let go of formalities, to relax and to converse as if they were already friends of some standing. It was strange to find himself feeling this way in so short a time; but in truth there was so much about his situation that was strange it seemed unreasonable to fix on this one thing.

Even the house was strange: as they passed back

through the kitchen he found his eyes falling on a head broken from a statue, life-size or nearly, its marble eyes hooded and unfocused, its curling hair bound by a circlet of ivy.

'Oh yes, my angel,' Edith had said airily. 'I draw her sometimes.'

'Truly? I draw angels too. Statues, in churchyards.' He felt a small thrill of excitement at this thing that they shared.

'I know.'

'You know?'

'At least, that is…um…oh, look, the door's swung shut! Could you…?'

He reached past and pushed open the door, and flattened himself against the wall to allow her through. Even so, her hand holding the tray nudged his sleeve.

She seemed less ghostlike to him with every minute that passed.

They sat in the drawing room and Edith poured the tea, and he remembered her question, spoken in the candle-lit bedroom, and answered it.

'I am a wood engraver,' he said, because that felt like the base of him, his grounding, his rootstock. 'But I have to tell you that my own life is a puzzle to me.'

And he talked. He told her about the charcoal and the Master and about the swaying, bumping coach ride to London, and then he described the Weatherstones' workshop – the benches and the quiet and the dust in the sunbeams. He talked about drawing the angels in the cemetery, and about the excitement and satisfaction of making an image, from the initial conception through designing with pencil and pen to the painstaking process of engraving on boxwood.

'But I cannot tell you anything about my family,' he said, 'or of my lodgings in London or my friends – if I have any – because I cannot remember them. It is as if they never existed. And how that can be, I do not know.'

She grew serious then, concern in her face as he told her about his unexpected fortune and his indecision as to what to do with it.

Casting down her eyes, lacing her fingers together, she said, 'And did you…were you…was there anybody special to you in Castlehope?'

Rose.

He sighed. 'I thought at one time that perhaps there was. But I was mistaken. I have been mistaken about many things, I think.'

He looked at her bent head, comparing it with the image of her he had seen over and over in mirrors and window reflections and in waking and night-time dreams. She was, he realised, less perfect in the flesh and also more entrancing; she was not an idealised image of a woman frozen in time, like the mermaid by the shore or the princess in her glass tower, but a living, changing creature, uncertain and prone to errors. And funny.

'Do you know,' he said, 'I have no idea where I am. I have been here less than two hours – I think – and do not know how I came. But this house – that lamp, this tea, *you* – feel more real to me than anything I have ever known before.

'Now how on earth can that be?'

CHAPTER 47

Now

ROSALIND WAS OUT OF CREDITS. SHE HOVERED THE CURSOR over the buttons on the screen and tried to make up her mind. She had intended to buy another batch of credits with which she could view the results of her record searches, but was tempted now to go the whole hog and pay for a subscription.

How much more research into genealogy was she going to do?

Technically, Bryony ought to be paying for this; researching the background of Edith Waterfield was a marketing tactic of the Stranger Bookshop. On the other hand, Rosalind knew Bryony was struggling and she would feel mean to let her pay.

Bryony had offered…sort of. 'Does this cost a lot?' she

had asked one day. 'Let me know how much and I'll reimburse you.'

Rosalind had not wanted to lie (*No, nothing, it's all available free*) so she had fluffed something vague and allowed Bryony to forget the matter.

In any case, it was fun. She might look up her own ancestors next.

She clicked on *Full Subscription* and entered her card details.

Bryony wanted to know how many siblings Edith had. The short cut to that was to view the 1911 Census return for the Waterfields' home and Rosalind had already done this. Up onto the screen once again came a list of everyone living in the house, including their age, birth year and occupation.

Rosalind folded her hands to read.

WATERFIELD, Frederick Charles

Relation: Head

Condition: Widowed

Age: 52

Birth Year: 1859

Occupation: Physician

Where born: Prudhoe Northumberland

And then his family:

WATERFIELD, Ruth Elizabeth – aged twenty-two and single; WATERFIELD, George Frederick – aged twenty and also single; William George, seventeen; Lillian May, sixteen; Francis John, fourteen; Edward James and Edith Susan, both born in 1899 and both twelve years old at the time of the Census; and finally Charles Arthur, aged seven.

Edith was a twin. Rosalind had forgotten that.

Her eyes roved over the list. There was no mother. When had she died, and what had been the effect of her loss on the girl Edith?

She liked how the children were each listed as *Scholar* rather than simply *At school*. She noted, too, that no marital condition was listed until maturity – if you could call seventeen mature.

There were household staff on the list as well: two, both women, their occupation stated as *General Domestic Servant*. All of them in that tall house, Rosalind thought, where now there was only Bryony, surrounded by thousands of books.

Next, she needed to search the records of births and deaths for all these Waterfields.

IT WAS extraordinary how using the internet hijacked your sense of time. When Rosalind clicked to send off the request for all the Death Certificates (*all the Death Certificates* – what a terrible phrase) she saw to her amazement that it was early afternoon and she had worked straight through lunch.

Admittedly she had allowed herself to become sidetracked along the way, hunting for more information on the two domestic servants, which was quite unnecessary, looking up other premises in Ravensburn at that time, and using Google to search for really quite random ideas, most of which came to nothing.

She also found, read synopses and reviews for, and

ordered several books on social history in the nineteen-twenties, particularly women's social history, about which she realised she knew very little. She thought it would help them to get a handle on Edith Waterfield if they knew more about the world in which she had matured and become an author.

She made herself a quick salad and then donned boots and coat to walk to the village. The roads were wet from the morning's rain, and Rosalind reached for her collapsible umbrella. But then she paused.

Small, lightweight and compact, it lay on the shelf by the door, waiting. It had never, not ever, been opened. And she had owned it for years.

Was it really true, what Bryony had said?

Slowly, Rosalind withdrew her hand, leaving the umbrella on its shelf. It felt like an outrageous temptation of fate. On the other hand, the worst that could happen was that she would get wet.

She let her wool coat stay in the wardrobe and instead put on the washable micro-fibre jacket she had bought in Hexham. It was only sensible, she thought. Silly to risk more than she had to.

At the bookshop Bryony was eating a sandwich and trying to keep it secret; her plate was hidden on her lap under the desk. 'It doesn't look professional to be eating on duty,' she explained.

'Isn't it a bit late for lunch?' Rosalind asked, instinctively glancing at the clock on the mantelpiece, which was ormolu and rather hideous but probably valuable, although of course Bryony was not at liberty to sell it. The clock claimed it was eight fifteen, as she knew it would. Once she had assumed its key was lost; now she knew better.

'Not lunch. Had that. Half-past-threeses.'

Oh yes – she had forgotten that Bryony ate very early in order to keep the shop open during the lunch period.

'What have you got for me?'

'Well.' Rosalind opened her bag and drew out the folder. 'Edith had a large family.'

'How many?'

'Eight in all.' *Like me. Like us.*

'But what number was she?'

'I'm not sure. She was a twin, so either sixth or seventh.'

Bryony took the print-out. 'Her father put her down as seventh and he would have known. And the twins are not entered in alphabetical order.' Rosalind watched her musing. 'Edward. Edward and Edith. Twins make people do that kind of thing, don't they? My parents were the same – Holly and Hazel.'

Rosalind said, 'And look at all the deaths.' It was dreadfully sad.

Bryony looked, for once her expression sombre. 'How ghastly. Edward too – that must have been grim for Edith, losing her twin. Do we know for sure that they died in the war?'

'Not until I get the Death Certificates, but if you look at the dates…'

'Mm.' Bryony shuddered. 'We are so lucky.'

Rosalind thought of her sons. 'Yes, we are.'

Bryony popped the last inch of her sandwich into her

mouth, dusted her hands and set the plate on the floor under the desk. 'Got some more responses.'

She pulled out the folder and handed it to Rosalind. There had been a steady trickle for over a week, and slowly they were building a picture of Edith.

She liked to wear green. She had learned to drive and had an MG Midget, which was rather dashing at the time. She was fond of children and was good at talking to them, but never had any of her own. Her cats seemed to live for ever, although the only one to have a litter of kittens was Cobweb. She went into the local schools to give readings, and John Day gave lessons in drawing and, to the older children, lino-cutting.

John Day had set up his own engraving studio in the house and each year there were new designs for Christmas cards based on local rural life: a farm labourer in shirtsleeves gathering holly; a robin perched on an old plough entwined with bindweed; a wreath of twisted willow and rosehips; starlight over rolling hills and sleeping sheep; an angel with hooded eyes and ivy in her hair.

When World War Two broke out, John Day did not enlist but instead went to work on the farm adjoining the village, while Edith dug up the back garden to grow vegetables, and knitted socks and balaclavas for the troops. And when rationing came to an end and petrol was available again, Edith often visited her sisters at Hare Rigg, and Lillian Waterfield, now Moffat, sometimes came to Ravensburn, but not the elder sister, Ruth.

Ruth Waterfield never came, one correspondent wrote. *My*

Mam said that Ruth said they were uncanny and that she never could bear things being uncanny.

'I wonder what was uncanny,' Rosalind said.

Bryony said, 'Mm,' and looked thoughtful but said no more.

Edith stopped writing for publication in the 1950s and then, sometime in the 1970s, she fell ill with cancer and died in 1978.

'I have ordered a copy of her Death Certificate too,' Rosalind said. 'But the odd thing is that I can't find any record of John Day's death. Not his death, nor his birth. Of course, it's difficult when we don't know how old he was or where he was born, or died.'

'I thought the Census gave you ages?'

'It does, but he wasn't here in 1911.'

'And 1921?'

Rosalind said, 'That's not available yet. A hundred years has to pass before the information is made public.'

'Oh.' *A hundred years has to pass…*very forests-and-fairy-tales; very Grimm.

'I searched for a long time,' Rosalind was saying. 'I'm sure his records will be somewhere, but still…it is strange.'

'Mm.'

Rosalind glanced up from the letters and caught the expression on Bryony's face. 'What? What are you thinking?'

'Oh, just…something. Rosalind, could you do some more looking up?'

Rosalind reached for her notebook. 'Who now? Edith's mother?'

'Yes. I'd like to know how many siblings she had. And the other one is Charles Rutherford-Hill.'

The name was familiar; Rosalind searched her memory.

'Isn't that the person Lily Pigg wanted to marry? Lily Moffat then, of course.'

'That's right. Double-barrelled name, oughtn't be too many of them, and we know he lived near Hexham in the fifties.'

She was buoyant and bubbly, full of confidence, just like when she first thought of telephoning the Moffats at Hare Rigg. Rosalind suspected trouble.

'Bryony, why do you want to know about this man?'

Bryony said, 'Oh, just curious.'

And she smiled.

CHAPTER 48

Then

LILLIAN WAS THE FIRST TO ARRIVE.

It was just before half past three. They were in the library, working their way through all the volumes that had engravings in them: botanical encyclopaedias, travel journals, poetry collections, Tennyson, Longfellow, Robert Burns. Edith pulled out books and John sat at her father's desk, hitched on the edge of the mahogany swivel chair, leaning forward as he turned page after page and drank in the illustrations, so many of a style unknown to him.

He was rapt, and Edith watching him was rapt also.

The rasp of the front door as it opened made them both jump. Edith laid her hand briefly on the man's shoulder as she moved behind him – so quickly had they become that intimate – and left the library, closing the door softly.

They had agreed this. Edith would greet her sisters alone and explain what had happened…what was happening. She was dreading it. She crossed her fingers and prayed that Ruth would not be the first to return, and rounded the corner of the stairs to find her prayer had been answered.

'Lillian!'

'Hello.' Her sister was unwinding her scarf, her umbrella leaning sodden against the front door. 'Had a nice time all alone?'

Suddenly Edith was engulfed by the gigantic impossibility of all she had to tell; it sucked away her breath as if she had been plunged into icy water and left her weak-legged and faint. She clutched the banister. 'Oh Lillian…'

'Edith? What is it?' Her sister paused, her coat half unbuttoned.

Edith drew herself together. 'It's all right. Take off your coat and come into the parlour. I have to…I have something to tell you.'

She led the way, conscious of Lillian's curiosity, dreading the scepticism that would surely follow.

They sat. Edith leaned forward, her elbows on her knees, looking at the rug because she could not quite make eye contact.

'You know…you know I used to, sort of, *do* things sometimes. Make things happen. Make things happen that, well, shouldn't really.'

'Your magic,' Lillian said.

'Yes.'

They had rarely used the word, partly because it seemed so ridiculous, and partly in deference to Ruth, to whom the word, the notion, the very principle of tampering with reality in that way was anathema.

It had only ever been little things, accidents really, brought about by wishing for something too strongly: more barley twists in the jar; Father to take them all to the pantomime in Newcastle; for Sarah Lynne's Snowball to have a litter despite her age – which she duly had, but which did Edith no good at all as Ruth's allergy put paid to any idea of having a kitten.

As Edith grew she learned not to upset the apple cart and refrained from wishing for things so hard, and gradually the magic faded out of their lives.

When the time came that wishes were great, desperate, wrenching things born out of longing and despair, it seemed she had no power left. God knew she had tried and tried to protect her beloved brothers, and Eddie, oh how she had strained to wish Eddie back from the grave, but all in vain. Rags and cinders and memories were all they remained, and she had resigned herself to the bitter truth that any magic she had once possessed had fled.

Until last night.

Edith said, 'I've done something. Last night. I…made something. Or at least, I made something happen.'

She didn't like the thought of having *made* John, although that seemed to be not far from the truth.

Lillian said quietly, 'What did you make happen?'

Edith licked her lips. 'John Lucas. My John Lucas, from my book. He…well, he's in the library.'

There was no reply. Edith risked looking up and found her sister's face turned sideways, her eyes on the mantelpiece where their mother's treasured ormolu clock reigned over the ornaments and bits and pieces that had collected around it. But Edith did not think Lillian was seeing it.

'Lillian?'

Her sister sighed. 'Edith, I'm sure there is a man in the library, or you wouldn't be telling me so. In which case, either he is someone we don't know but who you have let into our home, or, I suppose, he really is imaginary and you really have brought him to life.'

'Yes.' Edith felt her heart flutter. She had expected this to be harder.

'But in that case…oh Edith, why not George? Or Will, or Frank, or Eddie?'

There was water standing in Lillian's eyes. She jerked into motion, searching her pockets for her handkerchief, and Edith watched helplessly as her beloved sister mopped her tears before they spilled.

Lillian blew her nose. 'All right.' She stood up. 'Introduce us, then.'

Edith had never loved her more.

RUTH WAS MUCH HARDER. She began to cough before she had crossed the hall.

'Good grief, Edith, what have you done? If you've brought a cat in here—'

'There's no cat,' Lillian said, helping her out of her coat. 'Let me take your bags. Come and sit down.'

'Then what has she done?' Ruth was wheezing, her hand pressed against her chest. Edith, at the top of the stairs, caught Lillian's glance as she chivvied their sister into the parlour. Two hours ago she had delivered information to Lillian that surely must have altered her very understanding of the world in which they lived their lives. Like a trooper, like the angel she was, Lillian had accepted it, allowed her understanding to shift and rebalance, and soldiered sternly on.

Edith feared it would not be so with Ruth.

'She won't be able to stand your presence,' she said now to John, waiting out of sight in the library. 'Physically, I mean. She is allergic to anything that is…' Edith sought a word that would not sound like an insult. '…odd. Strange.'

'Uncanny.'

His eyes smiled. Edith felt relief and adoration wash through her.

'Uncanny – yes!'

She forced herself down the stairs and found that Lillian, tactful as always, had done the hardest bit for her. Ruth was seated, one hand clutching her balled up handkerchief, the other alternately pressing her breastbone or fanning her face, which was blotchy, red and white. She did not look well.

'Ruth.'

'Edith.' Her sister's voice sounded hoarse and breathless. 'What have you done this time.' The words were not inflected to suggest a question; it was more like the pronouncement of a judge.

'Ruth, I am so sorry. I really didn't mean to. I don't know how I did. But I have and I don't think there's anything to be done.'

Ruth flapped her hand. 'But I can't...I can't even breathe here! If he cannot leave, what is to happen to me?'

She has not even seen him, Edith thought, *and yet she doesn't question that he exists!* How extraordinary her sisters were, how much more extraordinary than she had guessed!

And now Lillian, sweet Lillian, rescued them all yet again. Edith watched as she straightened up.

'You will come to Hare Rigg with me,' she said, decisiveness in every syllable. 'Billy's mother will love to have your company. We will live together and leave this house to Edith.' And, being Lillian, she quickly corrected herself before anyone else even registered a mistake.

'To Edith and John,' Lillian said.

CHAPTER 49

Now

ON MONDAY BRYONY SLIT OPEN A MINIATURE ENVELOPE and found inside it a note card barely larger than a credit card, the message handwritten in tiny script that made her think of the Brontës' childhood writings.

Lucky she had good eyesight, she thought, as she squinted her way through the lines to read yet again that Edith Waterfield had dozens of cats and that her favourite was the big, bold Mercutio.

She dropped the card into the folder.

On Wednesday there was a typewritten letter telling about Edith's MG and the dash that she cut therein.

The stream of memories was down to a trickle; they had garnered just about all there was to garner, Bryony thought as she added the letter to the file.

Then on Friday came an A4 manila envelope addressed by hand in hasty, careless ballpoint. The envelope was thick and promisingly weighty, and the sender had reinforced the flap with sticky tape. Bryony slit the stiff brown paper and drew out pages stapled together at the top left corner. They were typed (good) using well-spaced lines and a justified right margin, and there was a yellow note stuck to the first sheet.

The note read: *Post to Stranger Bookshop, Ravensburn, North'd, pref 1st class.*

What kind of person doesn't bother to remove the reminder note? Bryony checked the envelope and saw the second-class stamp. She shook her head and peeled the note off.

The first page was headed: *What I Know About Edith Waterfield at Ravensburn.* Bryony began to read.

Mrs Barker is going to type this up for me, which is very kind of her, and I've said she must include this part as well so that she knows how grateful I am.

My daughter Amy told me about Miss Bower asking for memories of Edith Waterfield and I decided straight away that I would respond, but Amy is too busy at work to help with typing it out so Mrs Barker said she would do it for me instead. I am speaking into a little voice recorder so that she can play it back while she is typing.

Bryony flipped over the page and scanned the next sheet. How long did this explanation and vote of thanks go on for? Her eye caught several capital E's for Edith and resumed reading.

My grandmother lived all her life in Ravensburn, and my mother was born there. My mother moved to Wylam when she married, and then later we all moved to Twickenham near London, but I remember visiting Granny at Ravensburn when I was a child.

My grandmother was called Sarah Lynne, and she had a terrible accident when she was a young woman that left her in a wheelchair. Imagine that, with two small children! One moment she was an ordinary housewife and mother just like everyone else, and the next she had been run over by a cow and couldn't move her legs, and she never moved them again. Having that in your family can make you very timid, I think, and my mother was always terribly cautious. She never let me have a bicycle.

My grandfather was a wonderful man and he brought up my mother and my two uncles with the help of their maid-of-all-work, and Granny supervised.

Most of what I have to tell was what my mother told me that Granny had told her. That sounds a bit of a muddle. What I mean is that my grandmother took a lot of interest in the neighbours because she was stuck in the wheelchair, and there was something about the Waterfields that stayed in her mind for years so that she talked to my mother about it often when my mother was grown up. There was a bit of a mystery, and it weighed on her mind, Mum said.

Bryony, who had started to get bored, perked up.

The thing is that my grandmother watched. She was never much of a reader, Mum said, and so she used to sit at the window and watch everything that went on outside. She used to sew as well – patchwork and quilts and cross stitch and crewel work, so many things all beautifully hand-made – but she did it in her wheelchair in the front window. It was a bay window, which meant she could see up the street and down as well as straight across. She stayed there after dark, too, watching by the lights from the windows. People said she was like a sentry, keeping guard. Nobody could get into Ravensburn or leave without Sarah Lynne seeing them. And that's just it, you see.

What's just it? What? Bryony thought.

I don't want to disturb the past…

Oh do, do!

…but how did he arrive in the village without Granny seeing him? She was adamant that the only way he could have done so would have been by night, after everyone was in bed, and yet that night was so wild and windy and wet surely no sensible person would have crossed the moors on foot. It puzzled her all her life and she could never let it rest, no matter what anyone said. "How did he get here?" she used to say. "How did he get past me?"

Of course they all told her she must have blinked and missed him, but she wouldn't have it. And it was the same with the man called Alfred Wintersgill. They all told her she must have missed him, just turned away for a minute and missed him, but she was so certain that she hadn't. My mother said she used to say, "I was watching because I thought he was up to no good".

Well, he might have been up to no good, but no-one ever saw him again so we'll never know.

Anyway, that's what I want to tell. I want to pass on what my mother said my grandmother always wondered about, and then my mind will be at rest and hopefully hers will be too, if she's up there still watching us down here, and she probably is.

So here it is: the business of the Waterfields and John Day and Alfred Wintersgill.

Bryony reached the end of the paragraph and slapped her hand over the next, so that she could tear her eyes away.

Wow! Gold!

Unfortunately, though, she had customers to attend to.

Perhaps 'unfortunate' was not the right word. However, she was sufficiently self-aware to know that she would struggle not to snap if one of them interrupted her when she was reading what looked like it just might be the facts at last behind the famous Waterfield Murder Rumour. So she slid the pages back into their envelope.

Five minutes later she put the envelope on her chair and sat on it.

Ten minutes after that she abandoned the till and bolted up three flights of stairs to throw the envelope into the flat and run down again. Definitely out of temptation now.

Rosalind arrived mid-afternoon. Bryony almost told her the news but realised in time that if she did then she would have to invite her to go upstairs and read the account straight away, and she didn't want to.

Selfish, undeniably; on the other hand, Bryony already knew she was selfish so that was no great shock.

She can read it tomorrow. In her lunch break.

Rosalind now helped all day on Saturdays, the busiest day of the week for the shop.

So the afternoon wore on. Rosalind went home and an hour later the rain arrived. At a quarter to six Bryony opened the door and looked both ways along the cobbled street, found it utterly deserted, and decided to lock up early.

Ten minutes later she was curled up on the sofa with a mug of hot chocolate in one hand – it was hot chocolate weather – and the pages on her lap.

My grandmother said that there had been bad feeling between the Waterfield girls and Alfred Wintersgill since the Waterfield's maid-of-all-work, Primmy, drowned…

CHAPTER 50

Then

THE WEATHER REMAINED SEVERE. WIND BEAT AGAINST THE
windows and rain streamed down, overflowing from gutters
clogged by autumn leaves, and the back yard turned into one
great puddle. Lizzy sent a telegram asking permission to stay
away a few days longer because her family's home was
flooded. Lillian took over the cooking and discovered the
milk had turned sour overnight, and Ruth, red-faced and
wheezing, kept to her bedroom and ate invalid food. But for
Edith, December had turned into midsummer.

It was accepted that John needed a new name, and
needed it quickly. 'I can't keep indoors all day. I must walk
out.'

'Yes, and I will need to introduce you.'

Everyone thought.

'Lucas is too...rare,' Edith said. 'I'm not sure anyone actually has Lucas for a surname. People will ask questions. It would be best if you had a commonplace name.'

'But not a local name,' Lillian said, 'or there will be questions.'

They chose Day. John liked it for its brevity and simplicity. *John Day.* You could speak it swiftly and move on.

Edith liked it for its connotations. 'As bright as day,' she said, grinning ridiculously as she so often did now. 'As clear as day. As new as day.' *As beautiful*, she thought, *as the day is long*.

She could not believe he was real, and at the same time she could not believe he had ever not been. In the space of one day, just hours really, everything had changed. Perhaps for the first time since George walked out of the house to join the regiment, definitely since the arrival of the first, terrible telegram, she was happy, and hopeful, and joyful — oh, yes, full of joy! She barely felt the floor she walked on and laughter quivered beneath the surface of every waking moment.

Astonishment too, and wonder, and a delicious sense of exploration, because John Lucas, John Day, was not a creature of her imagining alone. He was no poor, hollow character formed from the fancy of a girl, but a man complete and whole, with thoughts and intentions she had no notion of. She never knew what he would say next, or do, or what occupied his mind when he fell silent.

And he was funny. She had not realised he was funny. And he was considerate, much more considerate than Edith herself, so that it was touch and go whether he would stay.

'Your sister is distressed,' he said. 'This is her home. Of course I shall leave.'

Panicked, Edith sought for arguments that sounded even half reasonable, but it was Lillian who rescued her.

'There's no need for you to leave, John. Ruth is going to Hare Rigg as soon as the weather lets up. Mrs Moffat will love to have her company and Ruth is happy to go. It is decided.'

Home with no Ruth. It was a sobering prospect.

'You will have to learn to cook,' Lillian said solemnly.

'Oh yes, so I will. Well, Lizzy can teach me!' Buoyant spirits could keep one's head above water even faced with learning to cook, and Edith's spirits were extremely buoyant.

This would be the best Christmas ever.

So Ruth packed, including her books and some china and the clock that meant most to her, and rode in Dixon Blyth's dog cart to Hare Rigg, her cough improving with every mile. At the farm, Mary Moffat welcomed her with the heartfelt warmth of a lonely woman in a household of men, and their first project together was to repaint the room that would be Ruth's and to make new curtains for it using Mrs Moffat's Singer sewing machine.

Their second was to plan the wedding of Billy to Lillian, who left them to their pleasure and instead began working quietly on a patchwork coverlet for her marital bed.

'How you have the patience I'll never understand,' Edith commented, watching her sister cut hexagons of cloth and fold them over the papers.

'I know. That's why I'm making this instead of expecting you to make one for me.' It sounded caustic but Lillian glanced up and smiled. 'Don't worry. If you were to make a quilt your stitches would be huge and you'd probably forget to take the papers out!'

'True. But what *can* I do for you, Lillian?'

Lillian snipped off her thread and made a fresh knot in the tail. 'Finish your book. That's what I'm looking forward to: holding in my hand *The Holly and the Ivy* by Edith Waterfield!'

Yes. Two weeks had gone by without Edith writing a word. She thought it was forgivable under the circumstances. But John was drawing, using Lillian's paper and pencils, and had placed an order for tools and engraving blocks, so she too must face real life and stop pretending she was on a holiday that would never end.

She went to her room and closed the door. She sat at her desk and skimmed the last dozen or so pages of manuscript to find her bearings.

Poor Rose, Edith thought: you have lost your lovely John. And it was strange and inhibiting to write about John Lucas in Castlehope when she could hear him moving about in the room above her head.

But it had to be done. Sighing, Edith took up her pen and formed the next words of her story.

By lunch time she had managed her personal daily quota of pages, and flipped back to the beginning to read over the morning's work. And as she did so, she noticed something that made her shiver.

CHAPTER 51

Now

M<small>Y</small> <small>GRANDMOTHER SAID THAT THERE HAD BEEN BAD FEELING</small> between the Waterfield girls and Alfred Wintersgill since the Waterfield's maid-of-all-work, Primmy, drowned although she never knew why. For a while, she said, Wintersgill had been a regular visitor at the Doctor's house and Granny suspected he was courting Edith, and then all of a sudden he didn't go there any more.

But what bothered Granny a lot was that Edith Waterfield called at Alfred Wintersgill's house one afternoon when he was away in town on business. Regular business, so that everyone in the village including Edith would have known he wasn't at home. Now why would she have done that?

Granny could just see the Wintersgill house if she craned her neck, and she said she saw Edith Waterfield go down the side alley. She was there for twenty minutes or so, and then came back out and practically ran all the way home.

Well, Granny always thought that was peculiar. Edith later told her she had been returning Wintersgill's cigarettes that he had forgotten when he last visited them, but she never believed that. It didn't ring true at all. How could it take twenty minutes to pop a packet of cigarettes on the table? And why didn't she push it through the letter slit in the front door anyway? And she was carrying a basket, so what was that for?

Then a week or so after this, two policemen turned up and went inside the Wintersgill house, stayed there for ten minutes and then went away again. Wintersgill let it be known that they had wanted help with something or other he had seen happening in Hexham – Granny knew what it was, she knew everything, but I can't remember now. He was a witness, that was the point. But in the days that followed he never spoke to the Waterfields, not even a nod of the head in passing, and my grandmother said there was an Atmosphere with a capital A. She said you could have walked into it and knocked yourself out. Not very nice in a village at all.

IN BRYONY'S FLAT, Rosalind turned the page, folded it behind the others, and reached for her cup. 'Don't hurry down,' Bryony had said. 'I'll hold the fort until you've finished.'

Rosalind read on.

.   .   .

Now, that autumn was a wet one, a right bad'un apparently, and as November turned to December they had some terrible storms. Ravensburn was in the middle of nowhere, still is really, and in those days not many people had cars. People were still using horse transport, and you wouldn't want to take a horse and cart out across the moors on a wild night, not unless you had a life to save.

So this is what plagued my grandmother for the rest of her life: how did John Day get to Ravensburn?

He wasn't there on Tuesday. Both Ruth Waterfield and Lillian, they were Edith's two big sisters, called to see Granny on Tuesday before they went away. Lillian was going to the home of her fiancé to celebrate his birthday with his family, and Ruth was doing her Christmas shopping in Hexham and staying over. She did that every year. Granny said it was her Christmas treat. My mother said she thought Ruth Waterfield led a rather dismal life.

Anyway, no mention was made of any visitors, and it was unthinkable, in those days, not to tell people if you had someone staying. Much less coming and going than nowadays, you see, and visitors were a bit of an event even in the nineteen-twenties. Yet the next day, there he was! Battling against the wind and rain with Edith to buy milk because it had all gone off overnight, apparently! And Edith pink cheeked and suddenly shy and telling everyone he was "my friend, Mr John Day, from London".

Surely, if he had come all the way from London then he would have stayed overnight in Newcastle or Hexham and come on to Ravensburn in daylight?

So that's one half of the mystery.

Now the second half.

Storms didn't stop my grandmother from watching out. My mother said nothing did that. So come half past ten that same night, when the storm was rattling about and everyone was safely tucked indoors and all the curtains drawn, save my grandmother's of course, out comes Alfred Wintersgill and off down the hill, leaning into the wind and holding tight to his hat. Granny wondered about that straight away. The public house would have been closed by then, and what else was there to take a man out of his house on such a night at such a time? So she watched him very closely, following him by the light of his battery torch as there were no street lamps in Ravensburn then, and saw him go into the alley leading round the back of the Doctor's house. Like Edith but in reverse, she always said.

And he never came out.

I mean, really – never-ever. He was never seen again. My grandmother, Sarah Lynne, was the very last person to see Alfred Wintersgill alive. Or dead, come to that.

Perhaps I should say she was the last person to admit to seeing Alfred Wintersgill alive. Who knows what happened in the Doctor's house? Edith was there, by herself, unless John Day had already arrived, and that begs the question what Alfred Wintersgill thought he was up to, calling on a young lady at that hour when she was alone.

The thing is, Wintersgill was not well liked. People didn't care for the way he had dodged enlisting. My grandmother certainly didn't think much of him.

There was never a proper enquiry. His mother, poor woman, tried to get the police involved but there was nothing for them to investigate. He had simply gone. They told her he probably decided to cut off and try his luck elsewhere, somewhere nobody knew he had shirked his duty in the war, and that was that really. She reckoned he had been done away with, but there was no body ever found. No disturbance at the Doctor's house, nothing ever thrown up by the river.

That wasn't all, though. The police did go so far as to search Wintersgill's house, and they found a whole room full of the personal effects of his last housekeeper, the one he said had run away. They traced her family, who said they had lost all contact with her, and then started digging about and found her, all dead and decomposing – I'm sorry, but that's how Granny told it – under the slabs in Wintersgill's back yard. Isn't that terrible? Poor girl.

So there you have it. Everything pointed to Alfred Wintersgill having murdered his housekeeper and buried her, and to Edith having suspected something like that – although why she did, my grandmother never knew – and gone to have a look. Wintersgill wriggled out of the matter when the police came, but took his first opportunity to have it out with Edith and found himself facing her friend from London.

Did they kill him? It doesn't seem very likely to me, but if they didn't, what happened to him? That's what bothered my grandmother, and that's what she told my mother, and that's what my mum told me.

So now I've passed it on, and I won't think about it any more, not any of it.

. . .

AND THERE THE TYPING STOPPED. Rosalind put down her mug and straightened the papers.

Goodness!

She placed the pages neatly on the table and went downstairs. Bryony was ringing up a satisfyingly large total for a woman in a sheepskin coat who was loading books into a canvas grocery bag as Bryony took the prices. Rosalind withdrew between the shelves until the transaction was finished and the customer had left, the door bell jangling joyously behind her.

Bryony peered round the corner. 'That was Mrs Beaton. She comes in twice a year, before Christmas and before the summer holidays, and loads up. One hundred and seventy three pounds that lot came to.' She perched on the edge of the desk. 'So what do you think?'

'Astonishing. When did you get this?'

'Yesterday morning. I read it last night.'

'Ah. Christmas Morning Syndrome.'

'Christmas what?'

Rosalind waved her hand. 'Nothing. But how extraordinary to come out with all that now, after so long.'

'Mm. Well, yes and no. I am,' Bryony said, 'extremely good at persuading people.'

'You've met her!' Rosalind was startled.

'No. I didn't even know she existed, not as such. But I can do it at a distance, you know – get my tentacles out there, niggling away. I have heard of this Sarah Lynne before, from the oldest residents, and I thought it was just possible she had descendants. Worth a bit of effort anyway. And bingo!'

Rosalind's face must have been registering scepticism, for Bryony continued, 'And don't look like that. It's no more astounding than you being able to locate your son's house key across the Atlantic.'

Rosalind had told her the story – Christopher locked out of his rented apartment in Chicago in the early hours, gang members cruising with knives at the ready, or so Rosalind imagined. She had surprised even herself when she suggested he look under debris in the gutter but there it was, where he must have dropped it six hours earlier.

So Bryony could truly influence a total stranger at several miles' distance?

'Have you thought how you could use your…gifts?' she asked. 'You are clearly very…potent.'

Bryony raised an eyebrow. 'Talking jumpers off roofs?' she asked. 'Persuading runaways to phone home? Doesn't work. Can you find lost property? Missing murder weapons? Missing children?'

Rosalind shuddered and shook her head. 'No. I did once try, but I have to–'

'–to have a personal connection. Be personally, deeply interested. Yup, me too. Although it is possible, it seems to me, that we might aspire to that level of, shall we say, competence.'

'Might we?'

'Musicians practise scales, don't they? Painters paint. Writers write. Engineers engine. I'm twenty-three and I'm sure I'm getting better at it all the time. I intend to be unstoppable by the time I'm seventy.'

'I'm forty-eight, Bryony.'

'Yes, but you've only just realised what you've got. Why do you think witches in stories are always ancient crones with warts and whiskers?'

'Not absolutely all. Snow White's stepmother was beautiful.'

'Young, beautiful witches are old, ugly witches using Glamour. Besides,' Bryony said, 'we can't possibly own up. Can you imagine? They'd have us hog-tied and in a window-less van in seconds. We'd be investigated – researched into. Why do you think,' she asked, 'I took so long to talk to you about it?'

'Ah. Yes, I see.'

'Yes, you'd better, Rosalind, because we witches have to stick together. That's you and me, and our girl Edith.'

'Edith?'

Bryony gave her a clear, steady look. 'Don't you know yet who John Day was? Haven't you worked it out? Rosalind my friend, *think!*'

CHAPTER 52

Then

In the room on the second floor that had once been Ruth's, John Day, no longer John Lucas, took up his stance at the bench and pulled his eye shield down to block out all but the detailed work before him. He picked up his graver and settled it in his right hand, his forefinger along the top, his thumb steadying the block; his left hand held the sand-filled cushion firm. He positioned the point of the cutter with care and began the quiet curve of a stem.

The point moved through the surface of the boxwood and the delicate thread of wood lifted in a curl above it in the manner he found so pleasing. It was good to engrave again, to mark with Chinese white a fresh block, pungent and inviting, and to feel the familiar fit of the tools in his hands. It grounded him. And by heaven he needed grounding.

He lived each day amid a battery of experiences and sensations, most of them new, some of them bizarre. He could, any time he chose, turn a tap in the scullery and cause a steady stream of pure cold water to flow into the sink below. Any time at all. And next to the sink, on a shelf, lay a lantern which needed neither spark nor fuel but produced light at the press of a thumb! While outside men and women – the women all clothed as strangely as Edith – rode on inge- nious machines called *bicycles*.

And then there was the food. For supper tonight, Edith had said, there would be a dish she called *pork cheese*, and when he went to the kitchen to fetch a cup of water it already smelled good in preparation.

In some ways it could be said that the cooking, the food, was what most marked this new life as the real one. Pork cheese tonight, roasted chicken and potatoes last night, and a pie of fish and cream the day before that; and he could remember all of it: the smells, the tastes, the textures, the talk. They held conversations, he and Edith and anyone else who happened by, about the village, the people, farming, weather, or sometimes about nothing at all, and he remembered them, all of them.

They fixed him in time, his new memories, this morning and yesterday and last week and the week before that, all of them stretching out behind him, supporting him like a following wind, telling him where he had been and who he was. No longer did he feel himself drift, living in the moment and isolated there.

And the physical world was a wonder to him – the pressure of the floor beneath his soles; the chill of the window pane when he raised the sash of a morning; the irritation of sleeves too short and collars too tight on the shirts lent him so kindly by Mrs Moffat before new clothes could be got for him from Hexham. The warm, stable smell of horses, the sourness of milk left too long, the bitter, savoury tang each morning of last night's wood fire.

There was no doubt in his mind that Edith was correct: it was not she but he who had been the wraith and had become flesh.

Sometimes he smiled for sheer wonder and delight.

The carriage clock above the fireplace sounded the hour; they had brought it there to replace the mantel clock Ruth had taken. From the street below drifted muffled voices: Edith talking to a tradesman, perhaps. Rain spattered on the windowpane and afternoon turned to dusk as, slowly and painstakingly, he transformed his artist's vision into printable reality.

John remembered a moment such as this when he felt he could have been in it for ever, but those times were gone because today it was Thursday, and it would be Friday tomorrow.

He finished his stroke, pinched away the curl of wood, and repositioned his graver for the next.

IN THE KITCHEN, Edith scraped potato peelings into a basin and ran the water away. One job the less. The chore of cooking didn't get any better, although she supposed she was getting better at it. If tonight's pork cheese was half decent – somewhere approaching poor Primmy's, say – she would feel justified in awarding herself a pat on the back. A month ago, on Lizzy's day off she had settled for toast. Pork cheese was a definite step up.

The potatoes sitting in water in one saucepan and the carrots in another, Edith went up to her room. She still preferred to write there, despite the parlour being free these days.

Apart from tinkering, it was finished: her magnus opus, her novel, her first ever proper, real, full-length book. She had absolutely no idea whether it was any good.

The stack of notebooks lay in the middle of the desk, the dictionaries and thesaurus tidied away, the pen in the drawer. Edith drummed her fingers on the top page and pondered.

Who could she ask to read it? Not John, obviously – how appalling would it be to read about your fictional self? Edith shuddered.

Not Ruth, who always claimed to be too busy to read novels. In any case, she had already told Edith: *Give me a copy when it's published. I'll read it when it's in nice print.* She always had disapproved of Edith's scribbly handwriting.

Lillian would find it hard to be critical, she knew, and in any case she too was busy in her new role of farmer's wife.

Winifred Platt? Too scary. Edith would feel shy asking.

Sarah Lynne? Not a great reader.

The ideal person, Edith thought, was Margaret Eliot at the Forge, who was educated, moderate, thoughtful, generous of her time, considerate of others' feelings, truthful, balanced and just. She had good taste as well. But

Margaret was on a prolonged stay down south, visiting distant relations in Devon and Cornwall, and would not be back for weeks. Edith couldn't wait that long.

She wanted to publish, quick. If forced to be truthful, she was a little bit afraid of what she had made.

It was, she knew, a peculiar book. John Lucas – oh, John! – was as good as she knew how to write in the first half of the book, but dwindled sadly in the second half. She could forgive herself for that; it seemed understandable.

But Herbert Douthwaite, built so firmly on Alfred Wintersgill when she was inventing him, had grown in strength and credibility beyond all expectation, frightening her because she thought she knew why.

You could rationalise it, sort of. Physical laws can be bent only so far. When the universe made that subtle adjustment, easing itself aside, molecules squeezing, making space for someone new taking form where before there had been nothing, it could be only moments before balance had to be restored. Molecules cannot remain squeezed. If one man emerged from her imagination, another had to be absorbed into it.

There was no doubt in Edith's mind that Alfred Wintersgill had in some way become one with Herbert Douthwaite. Her fear was that her fragile pages were not stout enough; she felt hard covers and print were needed to keep him contained in her sentences and paragraphs.

Edith stroked the top notebook. It was, she knew now, not only her debut novel but her sole novel. It was unique. Never again would she – could she – invent people and write stories about them because somehow, some day, they might burst out of their literary lives and spring forth into the real world. The responsibility was gigantic and terrible and she could not risk it. *The Holly and the Ivy* must stand alone.

But she would publish it, and she would do it under her own steam. If she wanted test readers, then the whole village could do the job. Tomorrow she would take the notebooks to Mr Heron and ask for a small print run, just fifty or so in time for Christmas, and the book could sink or swim on its own merits.

Decision made, Edith went downstairs to start the vegetables.

CHAPTER 53

Now

Rosalind watched the customer button up her mackintosh, tie her hood under her chin and shake out her umbrella. There was a swoosh of rain as she opened the door.

When she had gone Rosalind said, 'Why do you call her Mrs Bobble-hat? She wasn't wearing a hat at all.'

'She usually does. She would have been if there was room under that hood.'

'But why–'

'It's how I remember them, Rosalind: Mrs Bobble-hat, Mrs Dangly-earrings, Mr Bald. If they always use cash I don't find out their names.' Bryony saw Rosalind's face and sighed. 'Don't worry, I never say them aloud. Or only to you.' She added, to change the subject, 'You could have offered to escort her home, you know. Keep her nice and dry.'

'That would be…very strange.'

'Yes.' Bryony swivelled in her chair. 'Christmas soon! What are you going to do?'

Rosalind sighed, and immediately regretted it. She injected some energy into her voice. 'I'll be going home. To Monk's Walk, I mean. For a couple of weeks.'

It was expected. Everyone would want to come for their turkey and Christmas pudding, not to mention cooked breakfasts and hot suppers. And in any case she wanted to see them, her sons and their families, the children…It was children that made Christmas, not presents or decorations: children and carols. But it did seem like a step backwards, somehow.

Bryony had said there would be carol singing in the village. 'Every year, I'm told. *God Rest You Merry Gentlemen* in aid of the children's ward at the hospital.'

'Will you join in?'

'Not likely. I sing like a frog. I'll put some money in the pot, though.'

Rosalind would have enjoyed carol singing but nobody organised any at home; not proper carol singing, outdoors in the dark and cold, with your breath smoking in the lantern light. She gazed through the glass at the Ravensburn high street, darkening now, and thought of wrapping up warm in scarves and gloves, and the pale, clear sound of voices in open air; *Hark! The Herald Angels* had long been her favourite.

Christmas was in the air because she had been Christmas baking; two cakes were finished and safely wrapped in baking parchment and foil, each snug inside its own decorative tin: one for Monk's Walk, and one as a gift to the Sopers, which she would take round before the taxi arrived. Food gifts were an important part of any festivity, Rosalind felt.

She had wanted to bake one for Bryony too but had been headed off when her friend commented that she had never cared for the dark, boozy, fruit-laden kind of cake and preferred something with chocolate. So a chocolate and cream roulade was secretly scheduled for presenting just before Rosalind left the village.

She would make mince pies too, for sharing in the shop.

Bryony was staying open until the day before Christmas Eve and then abandoning Ravensburn until the New Year. She was spending Christmas week with her eldest sister Clover's family in York. 'Quite close, really. Compared with Surrey, anyway. They had twins at Easter, and I think I'm wanted for child-care duties.'

'Oh Bryony, don't say that. They want you for yourself, I'm sure.'

Bryony grinned and Rosalind realised she must have missed a joke…again. She never quite knew what Bryony would come out with next, and sometimes struggled to keep up.

This business with Lily Pigg, for instance.

Bryony had visited the old woman armed with the information Rosalind had collected and had somehow persuaded her to visit the shop. 'Come with me when I get them,' Bryony had said. 'I'll need you for crowd control if things get ugly.'

'Them?'

'Lily Pigg and Dorrie Moffat. We're going to bring them back together again at last. Light the blue touch paper and retire.'

'Bryony,' Rosalind had said, 'please tell me you did not coerce this poor lady.'

'Nope. No coercion at all. I just told her – very gently and kindly, Rosalind – that Mr and Mrs Charles Rutherford-Hill both passed away years ago, and I asked her if in view of that she would feel able to talk about her family, and about Edith and John. And she said yes.'

Rosalind remained doubtful. How long had it taken Mrs Pigg to 'say yes'? She hoped Bryony had not bullied her.

'And Dorrie?' she asked.

'It's all right, I got permission from her too. If you ask me they'd both have liked to get together long ago, but neither of them have transport and Hare Rigg is awfully cut off. We're doing them a service, Rosalind.'

Perhaps. In any case, it was arranged now. As well as the two Christmas cakes Rosalind had made a batch of short-bread to offer the two old ladies, impressed with a pattern of scrolling ivy tendrils from Grace Eliot's lovely ceramic dish.

Grace had made her Christmas cake that day too, but had been distracted by the rain running down the windows. She had never worried about flooding before, she told Rosalind, the Forge having stood for at least three hundred years, but she could not shake off the thought that the mobile phone mast might upset the natural drainage of the land – the platform they had built and the road leading to it. 'Not that you can help, I know,' she added.

Which wasn't quite true, although Rosalind thought at first she'd have to camp outside the door of the Forge if she was to have any effect.

But Bryony had said they could become more effective with practice. Rosalind decided to start practising immediately, beginning with keeping rain away from the Forge.

Perhaps, she thought, it might be possible to lend the Eliots' home her immunity on a temporary basis. After all, she had an umbrella.

WHEREAS DORRIE MOFFAT had once again dressed up for her trip to the bookshop, Lily Pigg had decidedly dressed down, or so Rosalind deduced from her faintly grubby green beret and black wellington boots. Although, hadn't Bryony mentioned once that she always wore wellingtons?

Rosalind glanced over her shoulder and saw Lily Pigg sitting at one end of the back seat of the Land Rover and Dorrie Moffat, trim and tidy in slacks and a quilted windcheater, at the other.

She said, 'We'll have a cup of tea when we get to the shop. I hope you like shortbread.'

Dorrie Moffat said, 'Oh, shortbread! How lovely! My favourite!'

Lily Pigg said, 'I'm just coming to look at the stuff. I told that one. So don't go buttering me up with your biscuits.'

Bryony just drove.

But after they had climbed down from the Land Rover and been ushered into the bookshop, Mrs Pigg seemed to stall. She stood on the door mat, staring at the shelves with her whiskery jaw slack.

Her whiskery jaw? Where had that sprung from? *I'm turning into Bryony*, Rosalind thought, and said guiltily, 'May I take your coat, Mrs Pigg?'

'No.' The old woman clutched the gabardine and glared.

Rosalind took a breath. 'Well…shall we go upstairs?'

Dorrie led the way with a confidence Rosalind read as just a little smug, and Lily Pigg trailed several steps behind.

At the foot of the stairs, Dorrie said, 'Is that one of your mum's quilt tops?'

Lily Pigg said, 'No chance. Great, ugly stitches. Very poor.'

As they turned the dog leg between the ground floor and the first floor, Dorrie called back, 'Lovely old map!'

Lily Pigg said, 'Why have a map when you know where you are?'

When they reached the second floor, Dorrie laid claim to one end of the sofa and said, 'This is very nice!' and Lily Pigg, lowering herself, gabardine and all, onto the other end, said, 'Hurry up with the tea, then.'

And Rosalind gratefully withdrew to put the kettle on. *Come quick, Bryony*, she thought. *You're needed!*

CHAPTER 54

Then

EDITH HAD TURNED THE BOOK AROUND, SO THAT WHEN SHE held it out the title and author's name could be read by the person standing in front of her.

Which was Lillian.

Lillian put out her hands, both of them, and took the book carefully. She read the title and raised her face, and her expression shone.

'Oh Edith! How wonderful! Well done!'

Edith tingled with excitement and pleasure but she felt obliged to say, 'It's only vanity publishing, Lillian. I've paid for a small print run. Just to see how it goes.'

'But you finished it! A complete novel! I could no more do that than fly to the moon.' She lifted the cover – they had chosen soft green as being suitable – and Edith watched her eyes flicker over the title page and come to the frontispiece. John had made a beautiful, intricate little engraving of holly entwined by ivy and set within a frame of rough hewn oak: rustic and appropriate. He would have done something larger but Edith was in a hurry and engraving was a slow process.

'Edith, I'm so looking forward to reading it at last. Have you given Ruth a copy?'

Lillian had been to Newcastle again, accompanied to everyone's surprise by Billy. They had been to have his mask adjusted. Apparently Mrs Moffat had wept with relief and joy when Billy agreed to go, and to travel by public transport what's more.

Edith said, 'I gave it to her yesterday.' She hesitated. 'Lillian, I might have been a bit…reckless in chapter twenty-three. Try and get there before Ruth does, and let me know what you think.'

She kissed her sister and watched her climb up beside Billy on the dog cart. It still felt strange, this saying goodbye each time Lillian left to go to Hare Rigg; how odd that Ravensburn was no longer her home.

Any goodbyes to Ruth had to be said at Hare Rigg. Ruth had visited the village only twice since she moved, and both times became very flushed and complained of her chest. Ruth and magic, as they had always known, just did not mix.

Edith was very anxious about chapter twenty-three.

It was the usual problem: her imagination was too powerful to be contained. Nobody really believed how helpless she was to control it. Lillian looked as blankly at her as the rest, although she was at least sympathetic.

'Just don't do it!' was Ruth's contribution, which simply proved how alone Edith was in the matter. *Not doing it* was not an option; if she did not write her imaginings out, either at once or retrospectively, she was convinced they would tear her mind apart. Something deep within her that she could not even reach, let alone influence, drove her to put them into words, and once those words were out on paper all she could do was to pray that would be the end of it.

Usually it was. All her life she had been trying to tame this… this power, and in all those years only Eddie, dear Eddie, had ever really understood.

And now John.

'Ruth will murder me,' she told him.

'Not while I am here,' he said.

SHE CAME CLOSE, though.

'Edith! How *could* you? What were you thinking of?'

Ruth steamed across the hall like a locomotive, a mass of momentum impossible to deflect.

Edith backed up until her shoulder blades hit the wall. How could Ruth have reached chapter twenty-three before Lillian? And in three days? She had been skimming, must have been.

'Oh, Ruth,' Edith sighed, saddened though hardly surprised that her sister had not been able to read the story properly, even though written by her own flesh and blood.

Ruth misinterpreted her. 'Now don't you start with

your excuses! "Ruth, I can't help it, Ruth, you don't know what it's like"…You *can* help it! You could have not published it!'

Edith had nothing to say. She had no argument against that because it was true: she had not needed to publish. She could have written the novel, stuffed the notebooks on top of her wardrobe or under the bed and never let them see the light of day again. But how cruel would that have been? She had spent months and months and months of her life writing *The Holly and the Ivy* in the hope that one day people, all sorts of people, people she didn't even know, would read her sentences and follow her story and fall in love with her characters.

But how could she explain this to Ruth? Edith wilted before the relentless energy of her sister's anger.

Ruth was brandishing the book like a Zulu warrior shaking his shield. 'How many copies? How many copies did you have printed?'

'Fifty.'

'*Fifty!* And how many have gone out, apart from Lillian's and mine? The Eliots, I suppose. The Dixons. Madge Howard. Your friend Wilma.'

'Winifred.'

'Yes, her. Who else? Sarah Lynne?'

Edith said, 'I was going to give it to Winifred next time she visits. I haven't seen Sarah yet.'

How telling was that use of the past tense: *I was going to*, no longer *I am*.

'Well you must go round and get them all back.'

'But what can I tell them? What can I say?' Edith tried

hard not to whine. 'It's so peculiar! They'll think I'm so rude!'

'Better rude than mad. Just do it, Edith. We'll burn them.'

'*What?*'

'Don't shout. Why do you think I want them back? We have to get rid of them. If you want to publish this story of yours you'll have to change that chapter. The rest of it's all right, I expect.' Edith saw doubt cloud her sister's face. 'Or is it? You didn't put in anything else that I've missed, did you?'

'No. Although I do think you might have read it properly.'

Edith, becoming resigned to her fate, saw that Ruth was beginning to calm down too.

'Well, I'm sorry Edith, but you know how I am about reading. It isn't that I don't think your stories are good, but I don't have a lot of time.'

The creak of the staircase above their heads drew Ruth's attention. She took a step backwards and her face lost some of its colour.

'Look, I need to be going. Make sure you get all those books back and let me know. All of them, mind – don't go keeping one for yourself!'

As John turned the corner and spoke: 'Good morning, Ruth!' Edith watched her sister grope for the door handle. She drew a wheezy breath.

'Good morning, John. I'm just leaving. Remember, Edith!'

And she was gone.

Edith turned around. 'Exactly how were you going to

stop her murdering me from two flights up in your workroom?'

'I had second thoughts about that. She is very formidable.'

How she loved him when he laughed.

CHAPTER 55

Now

It was still raining. Sometimes the rain was hard and heavy, the water hitting the window panes as loud as hailstones, sometimes so soft and misty you almost didn't realise rain was falling at all until you stepped outside. But all of it was wet.

'Yuck!' Bryony said. She had made the dash from parking the Land Rover without a coat and was now regretting it.

Rosalind looked up and said, 'You should have put your coat on,' which was the kind of thing Rosalind did say from time to time. On occasion she could be annoyingly mother-ish.

'Sometimes one just cannot be bothered to go to all the

hassle of putting a coat on,' Bryony told her. 'But then, that is something you know nothing about.'

She took the groceries up to the flat. On the way she glanced at the patchwork on the wall, still not really able to see that the stitches were uneven or too big – they looked pretty neat to her eye – and then, on the next floor, poked her head round the door to catch a glimpse of John Day's portrait, the existence of which made much more sense now.

As always, the painted eyes seemed to meet hers.

'I wish you'd let me see you,' she said grumpily.

'Pardon?' A young couple Bryony realised too late were enjoying a kiss and a cuddle looked up in surprise.

'Sorry! Nothing!'

Bryony scurried on past.

Must not talk to myself during open hours!

He might reveal himself to her, though. One day. Since Lily Moffat had spilled all those lovely beans, he had been visiting (was that the word?) more often. Twice in the last week Rosalind had caught a glimpse of his heel disappearing round a corner, just as she had on her very first day at the shop, and it was not uncommon to hear his tread on the floorboards or even, if all was quiet, a distant, tuneful whistle.

If one were a ghost, Bryony mused, would it be better if people knew about you, or worse?

She reached the flat and began putting away the packets and jars.

Her idea about Lily Pigg had worked like a dream. She hadn't had to *coerce* her, as Rosalind unkindly put it, or not really. Or at least, not much. Realising that her youthful sweetheart was not even living, no more than her two husbands or her brothers or her aunts, had enabled Lily Pigg, once Lily Heron and before that Moffat, to take stock of where she was in time; one by one the barriers shutting off the past began to come down.

And bringing her sister-in-law Dorrie into the equation released the final lock. If Bryony were not the hard-headed little witch she was, she might have become quite emotional when the two old women got together after so many years. She was touched.

The first revelation to emerge was that for all Lily's aggressive-defensive attitude she had a complete lack of resentment towards her aunt Edith, even though it was Edith's chosen lifestyle that had prevented her from marrying delectable young Charles Rutherford-Hill.

'It wasn't her fault,' Lily Pigg said, affronted. 'What else could she do?'

'Marry him?' Dorrie suggested.

One of the problems with old people, Bryony thought, was that you had to tell them everything three times.

'They couldn't marry,' kind Rosalind explained yet again. 'There was no record of John's birth, no proof of who he was.'

'Because he sprang out of Aunty Edith's book?' Dorrie said, seeking confirmation.

'Yes,' Lily said, emphatic.

'Yes,' Bryony said, impatient.

'Well…we think so,' Rosalind said.

'My goodness. No wonder people talked.'

'People *didn't* talk,' Lily said. 'Nobody knew. Even you didn't know, did you? Only family. Blood family. Poor Aunty Edith had to live the rest of her life as a loose woman, unable to explain why. And poor Uncle John too, everyone thinking he was a bounder.'

'He didn't act like a bounder,' Dorrie said.

'Of course not. He was charming. Everybody liked him even though they thought he was a bounder.'

'Not Aunt Ruth,' Dorrie said.

'Except Aunt Ruth. But she was allergic.'

Once again everyone looked at the portrait.

'Such a handsome man,' Lily Pigg said.

Edith had commissioned the portrait because the camera was no use.

'At first we thought it must be someone's thumb getting in the way,' Lily said.

'That's what I said,' Dorrie chipped in. 'Someone's thumb!'

'But it was Uncle John. Photography couldn't cope. He was just a blur, like a column of mist. Useless.'

Bryony felt her brain scrambling to grab hold of this information. She said, 'But lots of the photos have blurry patches. *Little* blurry patches, low down.'

And Lily said with impressive cool, 'Yes, those are the cats.'

Edith's cats. Edith's storybook cats. The stories were not written about her cats at all; her cats sprang forth out of the stories. No absconding sailor from the orient had traipsed across the Northumbrian moors to bring her a Siamese cat named Claudio; Claudio had been invented by Edith's fertile mind and only then came into existence.

'So Mercutio…'

'Mercutio was the real cat,' Lily said. 'The first cat. Aunt Ruth was allergic, you see. Aunty Edith could never have one while Aunt Ruth was at home, but as soon as she left she got herself the biggest, boldest, most conceited cat she could find.'

'And wrote stories about him,' Rosalind said.

'And wrote stories about him. That's why she didn't realise it was going to happen again, not until she needed a new cat for a new set of stories and made up Calpurnia.'

Bryony mulled this over.

Rosalind was mulling too. 'So', she said, 'all of them – Titus, Cobweb, the kittens – they were all the product of her storytelling!'

'Yes. And that,' Lily Pigg added, 'is why she stopped writing in the end. Too many. They wouldn't grow old and die, you see, just carried on and on. Even the kittens – kittens forever. Sooner or later someone would have noticed. And in any case, she was frightened what else might happen.'

'You mean, what else might arrive?' Bryony said.

'Exactly. She would never write specifically about people but she could hardly avoid the occasional fleeting mention. Eventually she decided the whole thing was too risky.'

Another pause while everyone pondered. Goodness knew what Dorrie was making of it all; perhaps being eighty-something makes you more receptive to the prospect of the paranormal.

'So what happened to all the cats after your aunt died?'

Rosalind asked, with a flicker of a glance in Bryony's direction.

'Oh, they all vanished. Poof. Just like that.'

'I see.' Rosalind glanced at Bryony again.

Bryony gave her a severe look and said brightly, 'Well, fancy that.'

'And John Day?' Rosalind asked, gently.

'Well. He must have gone the same way. He was here for Aunty Edith's funeral, but that was the last anyone ever saw of him. I don't,' Lily Pigg said firmly, 'like to dwell on it.'

Upstairs, a floorboard creaked.

'I DO WISH we had Edith's missing diaries,' Rosalind said.

Bryony, concentrating on watching the road between sweeps of the windscreen wipers, said, 'Me too. I've been working on it, believe me.'

'Working on it?'

How to explain? Rosalind was undoubtedly a witch but she was a very innocent one. 'Thinking about it. Wishing for it. Willing for it. Hard.' The rain was appalling.

'And does that work?'

'Can do. It did with Lily Pigg.'

The old woman, formerly so angry and now suddenly mild of manner, had become chattier by the moment. On the way down she paused at the patchwork facing the stairs and said, just as Dorrie had once before, 'Grandmother's Garden'.

'Yes,' Bryony said, not stopping. 'We know.'

'One of your mum's?' Dorrie asked again. The lack of a

short-term memory must be crippling; or perhaps, quite nice: everything a surprise.

'Never.' Lily snorted. 'Look at those stitches! All over the place, and the size of them! And Mum never left anything unfinished, either. If that was one of hers,' Lily said, 'it would be properly finished and lying on a bed somewhere, not dangling off a wall with the papers still in like as not!'

They had driven the two old girls home through what had become a deluge, Bryony bringing the Land Rover right to the doorstep of the shop to load them up and parking as close as possible to their front doors to drop them off. She couldn't get as close for Rosalind, who was faced with dashing under an arch and up a flight of steps to reach her front door.

Rosalind pulled up her hood. 'Drive carefully.'

'Of course.'

'I suppose the shop is quite safe from flooding?'

Bryony said, 'Always has been. The whole village is okay, everyone tells me. Not even the bottom houses seem to get in trouble. There's a flood plain just beyond the bend and that takes care of what the river can't handle.'

'Good.' Rosalind had tucked her bag under her arm and was holding her front door key, ready for swift and economical entry. She opened the passenger door, a gust of wet air blew in, and Bryony said sharply, 'Hang on! You're getting wet!'

'I know.'

'But—'

'I know.'

Rosalind slammed the door and Bryony watched her pelt

across the gravel and disappear under the arch. Rosalind Cavanagh running through the rain. Amazing.

Suddenly she felt uneasy about Ravensburn's reputation for survival.

DRIVING through rain this heavy with only the headlamps for light was uncomfortable – Bryony refused to admit to scary – and it was with relief that she turned in at the Handsome Jack and parked.

The whole village was awash, water streaming downhill over the cobbles, but the doorsteps were well above the flow. Shoulders hunched and hands deep in her pockets, Bryony splashed up the street towards the projecting sign of the Stranger Bookshop, looking forward to shedding her wet things and drying her face – rain on eyelashes was horrible. She would do her level best not to be surprised by any ghost cats on the stairs, and – who knew? – tonight might be the night John Day, who was really John Lucas (or should that be the other way about?), would finally let her see him.

Bryony was two doors away when she registered the sound of voices in the distance and, with them, the sense of something wrong.

She peered behind her down the hill. The lights by the bridge were not the steady, stable glow from windows but were swooping about, and were white, not yellow.

Torches.

Bryony hesitated fractionally, then turned her back on home and hurried down the street. As she drew nearer to the bridge it became ever more clear that trouble lay ahead.

The river had not overrun its banks. It was flowing fast and high and Bryony had no doubt the water would be spreading across the flood meadow, but here the river was contained. Yet as she set foot on the bridge she could see quite clearly the cause of the disturbance.

The Forge was flooded.

CHAPTER 56

Then

EDITH PINCHED THE NEEDLE BETWEEN HER LIPS WHILE SHE reached for the scissors. They were Lillian's dainty silver ones, shaped like a stork. She snipped the cotton thread close to the double stitch, and then cut off a fresh length from the reel. She retrieved the needle, licked her fingers, smoothed the cut end of cotton, held everything up level with her nose and threaded up.

So far, so good.

She picked up the next hexagon, put it right sides together with the one on her lap, and stabbed herself.

'*Ow!*'

Again!

'Oh dear.' John, mild, from the other side of the hearth. He had a stack of books beside him and was slowly turning pages: more engravings. It was as if he sensed the decades between his previous experience (she chose the word with care) and current trends. As if he needed to live through the changes even if only in his mind. What must that feel like? The Arts and Crafts Movement, the pre-Raphaelites and Impressionism, William Blake and Millais and all the dazzling painters to be tasted and analysed and appreciated.

Practical advances as well. She had shown him Muybridge's photographic studies proving the sequence of footfalls of animals in gallop, but despite this he still drew animals running in the old-fashioned stylised way, leaping tidily with their front legs and hind legs in pairs.

'It's wonderful,' he said, 'but I can't draw them like that. It doesn't look right.'

How odd, Edith thought. But it didn't seem to hinder him. This year everyone in the village wanted his Christmas cards, and Mr Heron was keen for John to illustrate a collection of children's poetry to be published next summer. It seemed his style struck a chord: a hark-back to a previous age.

At this rate they would have enough money for Edith's ill-judged vanity publishing not to matter.

Everyone seemed to like John himself too, except for Sarah Lynne, who for some reason always looked away when they walked past her window and seemed most uncomfortable whenever Edith visited.

One of life's mysteries. Perhaps, Edith thought, Sarah felt his strangeness even if she was quite devoid of witchcraft herself. Like Ruth, in fact, who was still wheezing and sneezing every time she came near, which was not often.

Edith sucked her finger, checked for blood, found none and returned to sewing. Why on earth would anyone choose to do this? How on earth could Lillian sew for fun? It seemed never ending. The hexagons in the basket, all with their edges folded and tacked over their papers, seemed as many as ever, and the completed circles – six hexagons around a centre patch – numbered only five. And she felt as if she had been sewing them for *ever*.

Lillian had been astonished. 'Patchwork?' she repeated. 'You?'

Edith did her best to brush away the questions. 'I have to start being a home-maker somewhere. I can't be baking cakes in the evenings!'

She might have added *and I don't have the book to write any more* but she did not want to draw attention to that, not yet, and quite possibly not ever.

It had been horrible, so horrible that even now, months later, she didn't like to dwell on it.

She had collected all the copies, including the one Madge Howard had sent to her mother in Newcastle, and thanks to Ruth's skimming ahead nobody else had yet reached chapter twenty-three. Everyone was very nice about having the books she had only just given them whipped away again, but if people doubted her story about having noticed a major plot flaw they kept their doubts to themselves. So far as she knew, her reputation for sanity remained intact.

Soon, when she could face it, she would rejig the book. She would take out that offending chapter, with its too-thinly described account of what had happened to Alfred that night, and knit the story together over the gap. Then she would submit it to a publishing house, a proper one, and see what happened. One never knew, after all, and surely her publishing career couldn't end here, before it had properly begun, in a pile of ashes?

Ruth had built a bonfire in the back yard, coughing fit to burst despite John having shut himself up on the top floor, and they had stood and watched all the lovely pages burn.

Almost all the lovely pages.

That had, of course, been the nastiest part, and Edith thought she would never forget the dread of thinking she would have to lie to her sister. It was awful, evil and wicked, and she had felt sick while Ruth was outside, stacking books and logs all in a heap for burning. But in the end she had not needed to lie.

'Forty-nine,' Ruth had said, counting the pile.

'You said I could keep one, just for myself.'

'With the pages removed,' Ruth said, unnecessarily grim, Edith thought, but she too was probably unhappy.

Edith opened the book and showed the closely cut stubs and how the page numbers jumped. She tried not to hold her breath.

But Ruth nodded. 'Very well.' Then she softened a little. 'I am sorry, Edith, but you know I'm right. Don't you?'

'I suppose so,' Edith said; so there was a lie in there after all.

But not a big one, because Ruth never asked where the cut pages had gone.

CHAPTER 57

Now

THE WATER WAS OVER BRYONY'S ANKLES. IT SLOSHED ABOUT and spread upwards through her jeans, reaching icily for her knees. She wished she had stopped for wellies.

'Where has it come from?' she asked, bemused.

'Mast workings. Must've diverted the run off.' Dan from the pub, and he had no time for her silly questions.

Bryony stood in the kitchen of the Forge surrounded by people all of whom had found themselves jobs to do and were doing them. Pete Bragg was squatting by the dresser, hoicking out china dishes and plates from the bottom cupboards and handing them to his wife, Jenny, to stack on the huge kitchen table. Karen Bradford was emptying the fridge and an elderly man Bryony didn't recognise was clearing the larder.

Ben Bradford and Aaron splashed into the kitchen to seize the bookcase (a bookcase in the kitchen! Bryony approved of that) and lug it upstairs, books and all. Aaron called over his shoulder, 'Empty the box and we'll take that next', and Grace, wearing the expression of a woman who simply did not have time to cry, lifted the lid of a mighty chest against the wall, its edges smooth and polished as if by centuries of use, and let out a sob.

'The water's got in!'

Bryony splashed across and looked. At the base of the chest she could see the creeping dark of water soaking the wood.

'Oh no!'

Grace started snatching out the contents and Bryony took them from her, stacking them on the table at the far end from the china. She found herself interested in what she was handling.

A couple of old albums first, one of stamps and one of pressed flowers, followed by a tissue paper parcel of something soft, like cloth. That was quite dry. But next came a cardboard box heavy with old pennies, and the cardboard was damp. Bryony set it aside.

Water didn't matter on the pewter dishes and vast china serving plates that followed, but a package of folded linen was very damp and after that came paper that squelched, which was serious.

'Oh no! Oh no!' Grace said again.

'It's not too bad,' Bryony said, hoping it was the truth. 'You got to them quickly.'

'I don't even know what all this is!' Grace bundled a

jumble of books into Bryony's arms and leaned down for more. 'It's all old Eliot stuff. I don't think Aaron's ever got down this far.'

'Well then it probably isn't vital,' Bryony said. 'Is that all of it?'

Grace straightened up. 'Yes. But they're ruined.'

'Maybe not. I'll take all this, the books and papers, and dry them for you. I can do it properly. Yes?'

'Oh Bryony, would you?'

'Of course. It will take a few days but I'll start right away.'

And that was how Bryony found herself walking – paddling – back up the hill with her coat wrapped around an armful of sodden books, wondering how exactly you do dry books properly.

She was a bookseller, and she sold second-hand books as well as new ones, so she ought to know. Grace had not doubted her. But no flood-damaged books had yet come her way, neither here nor at Circe's shop, and Bryony realised she was going to have to learn on the job.

And quickly, too.

SOME OF IT was just common sense. Bryony spread the books out on the floor, brought down the two rolls of kitchen paper she possessed, and interleaved every page with a nice, clean, absorbent square until they ran out. Then she rang Rosalind.

'There's been a flood at the Forge,' she said, 'and you will never, ever guess what I've got.'

Rosalind wanted to come immediately, on foot if necessary.

'No, no, you've got to help me with the internet first. See what you can find out about drying wet books.'

While Rosalind set about finding what information was available on-line, Bryony crossed the street to hammer on the door of the grocer's shop. She didn't bother with a coat as she had got soaked anyway on the way back from the Forge, using her coat to protect the books.

'There's been a flood,' Bryony said, when Barbara Coleman came down from the flat above. 'I need kitchen roll. Loads. Sorry.'

Armed with as many multi-packs as she could fit between her hands and her chin, Bryony returned to the bookshop. She overrode the timer on the boiler first, to get the heating in the shop going, and then interleaved the remaining pages and loose sheets of paper. After that she went up to the flat to change out of her wet clothes, and she was just beginning the slow procedure of replacing each damp sheet of kitchen paper with a fresh one, right the way through all the books including the tantalising ones, when Rosalind phoned.

'You need to interleave the pages in batches with absorbent paper, something like kitchen paper. Then you have to keep changing it until all the pages are dry.'

'In batches? Why not individually?'

'Too many paper towels would distort the spine. Why? Is that what you've done?'

'I'll whip them out. Not a problem.' *I hope.* 'Anything else?'

'Keep turning the books over and keep changing the towels they're lying on. I've printed out some instructions. I'll bring them over.'

Bryony, the phone tucked between her jaw and her shoulder, began removing sheets and said, 'Rosalind, you'll get drenched, and I have to do this first. I'll come and get you in an hour or so.'

'No need. Geoffrey Soper is kindly going to drive me. I told him it was an emergency.'

Bryony was impressed. 'Brilliant! This'll be a lot quicker with two of us!'

'Not you! The Eliots!'

However, an hour later Rosalind walked in after all.

'There are plenty of helpers down there, and it's muscle they need now, really. I was just in the way.' She put a carrier bag on the desk. 'May I put these in your freezer? I know you don't have much space but every little helps.'

The Eliots' perishable goods were being distributed around the local kitchens.

Then Rosalind looked at Bryony on hands and knees and said, 'Is the floor the best place to be doing that?'

'It's the only surface I've got that's big enough. We don't all have a kitchen table the size of a tennis court!'

'Let me help, then.'

Bryony, bored and with sore knees to boot, rocked back on her heels and allowed Rosalind to take her place.

'Like this?'

'Yup.'

Bryony watched her opening books and swapping fresh sheets of kitchen paper for damp ones. After a few minutes she said, 'Have you noticed what those are?'

'Not really. Why, what are they?'

'Oh, this and that from the Eliot family's past. Bits and bobs. Stuff. And…'

Rosalind was barely listening, busy with the kitchen roll, being careful and efficient. Bryony watched her face closely.

'Edith's missing diaries.'

CHAPTER 58

Then

THE DEATH OF MERCUTIO WAS THE TRIGGER.

Not Romeo's friend, or at least, not Romeo's friend in the play. Not a friend of Romeo the cat either, so far as Edith had ever seen.

But no, it was the death of her lovely, beloved cat, whom she had always suspected of being a naughty by-blow of the splendid graveyard sentinel, her original Midnight Cat; Mercutio, the feline prince, all twelve pounds of him, sleek and muscular and oh so self-assured.

He lived to a good age – nineteen is a good age for a cat – and never knew a day's illness. But one night he did not come in, which he had begun to do that winter, and in the morning Edith found him cold and stiff and spangled with frost in the long grass bordering the vegetable patch.

Oddly, it was that more than the loss of her brothers that caused Edith to confront her own mortality. Perhaps it was because she watched John dig the grave and fill it back in. Perhaps simply being forty instead of twenty made death more imaginable.

Whatever the reason, Mercutio's passing away sparked questions in Edith's mind about what would happen when she and John were no longer there. There were too many secrets.

'What can we do with the diaries?' she asked Lillian.

'I don't think I can help. Nothing stays buried for long here. Bob and Lily can't promise to keep them hidden.'

So Hare Rigg was out.

'What can we do with the diaries?' Edith asked Winifred Platt, who had no idea of their contents but had been a wise and experienced friend for more than twenty years.

'If they must not be read, then destroy them. If you don't wish to do that, then bequeath them to someone you trust and who will never move house. That last bit is important, I think.'

Someone who would never move house. Someone with roots in Ravensburn and ties to their home. Someone she could absolutely trust. And preferably someone who already knew what the diaries contained.

There was really no other choice.

CHAPTER 59

Now

SLOWLY, THE PAGES DRIED. ROSALIND COULD TELL BRYONY was itching to read the diaries, as indeed she was herself, but they restrained themselves and limited contact with the vulnerable paper to replacing the towels and turning the volumes until at last Rosalind said, 'I think this one is only a little damp now. I'm sure we could let the air finish it off.'

The shop had to open so they had moved the operation to the sitting room in the flat. The individual papers had dried quickly and there was enough room on the sofa for the books.

Leaving aside Edith's diaries, there were some unexpected items.

'Grace told me that chest held the Eliot family history,'

Rosalind said. 'She didn't think Aaron had ever looked through it.'

There were accounts books and recipe books and journals written in sloping handwriting using permanent ink (fortunately), sometimes illustrated by sketches dashed down in the margins. There were picture postcards from between the wars, and school certificates from a hundred years ago, and a Victorian Valentine's card, unsigned but with a handwritten message: *Marry me*.

Between the pages of a manuscript book written in German, which neither Rosalind nor Bryony knew, was a watercolour, a picture of a tower in a forest, wound about with briars and vines. At the foot of the tower a young man stood, gazing up at the girl who leaned towards him from the crenulated top. The artist had made the tower transparent, as if built from blocks of glass, and had painted a border of roses and bindweed. It was beautiful.

'Hans Andersen?' Bryony asked. 'Grimm?'

'I don't know. I don't recall any stories about glass towers.' Rosalind examined the picture. 'Her hair isn't long enough to be Rapunzel.'

Surprisingly, the watercolour had been unaffected by its soaking.

A strange collection, but everything else – saving perhaps the watercolour – pertained to the Eliots in some way. Why were Edith Waterfield's diaries there?

'She wanted to keep them private,' Rosalind suggested, 'and this was the safest place she knew. That must be it.'

She could sympathise. She had known Grace and Aaron

for barely half a year but already could imagine herself entrusting something very personal, very special, to their stewardship. There was something timeless about the Forge; something enduring. It seemed a much better bet than her sons and their wives.

At first Rosalind had doubts as to whether they should read the diaries, but then she saw the first page of the earlier volume. Above the date, in a different ink and slightly different handwriting, Edith had written:

I cannot destroy these diaries because I cannot bear the thought that nobody will ever know. Someone must know, one day, but not yet. Not while we are alive, and not while anyone is alive who might be hurt by knowing the truth.

That seemed to be only Lily Pigg, who no longer cared.

So they read, one evening after the bookshop had closed. Bryony went first because it was she who had rescued the diaries, and while she read in the armchair, Rosalind prepared a hearty, winter casserole of lamb and root vegetables and barley, a triple quantity so that there would be leftovers to freeze. Then, after they had eaten, Bryony cleared away and washed up while Rosalind read.

Rosalind could feel Bryony's energy fizzing out from the tiny kitchen.

When she had finished, Bryony said, 'Well?'

'Extraordinary. It certainly corroborates everything Lily said.'

'I knew she was a witch!'

'Yes. Well.'

Bryony pounced.

'What's that supposed to mean? You can't not believe her? You said yourself it's exactly what Lily Pigg told us.'

'Yes, but Lily only told us what Edith and Lillian told her. It's still just one person's account of things. Edith's account.'

'And you don't think we should believe Edith?'

Rosalind sighed. 'I didn't say that. But it's so…incredible, Bryony. You have to admit it is incredible.'

Bryony sat back. 'I believe it. It certainly explains how this place manages to stagger on in the middle of nowhere. I reckon Edith put a protective spell on it.'

'Bryony!'

'Well, I do. Don't you?'

'I don't know. I would need to think about it.'

There was a pause, for which Rosalind was grateful, and then, happily more mildly, Bryony said, 'So if you could make real a fictional character – a guy – a hero – who would it be?'

'Jem Merlyn.'

Goodness – I didn't even have to think about that!

Then she said, 'Or…no. Flan Callaway.'

Bryony perked up. 'Who?'

'Flanders Callaway,' Rosalind amended.

'Flanders!'

Bryony was all but spluttering, her face lit up with astonished delight. Rosalind felt defensive.

'He was a real person. He married the daughter of Daniel Boone, the pioneer. But he was also in a novel, an old one of my mother's.' An old book with faded boards and spine missing, with the story told in heavy print on thick, spongy pages full of the romance of great forests and native Americans and living off the land…and absolutely no need to be politically correct.

Rosalind smiled. 'Flan Callaway was my first literary crush. I was twelve and he was seventeen and I remember thinking he really was The Business.' Then she said, 'What about you?'

'Piglet. Sorry, I jest. Calvin O'Keefe from A Wrinkle in Time. You know – Madeleine L'Engle? Brilliant, kind, and a little hard done by. His sleeves were too short because they couldn't afford to buy him new shirts as he grew. I've never forgotten him.'

'Oh, Calvin – yes, he was lovely too…'

Another pause. Rosalind thought, here we are, two women a generation apart, brought together by books we read as children and by our girlhood yearnings.

It was strange. Although stranger still was their shared belief – because she did believe, didn't she? – in the physical existence of magic.

It was wonderful, she now acknowledged, to influence the weather so that she was never rained upon, although she was disappointed that her very deliberate, heart-felt attempts to transfer her protection to the Forge and keep it free from flooding had failed.

As if her thoughts had been read, Bryony said, 'I'm sorry the Forge got flooded. I didn't mean that to happen. But I'm so glad we found the diaries.'

It took Rosalind a moment to catch up. 'You say that as if you caused it.'

Bryony pulled a face, a kind of shrug. 'I did, I think. I've been trying to draw these diaries out of hiding for a while. That kind of thing usually works, but I never know how it's going to pan out. To tell the truth, I'm surprised it took so long.'

'Bryony! I've been trying to protect the Forge!'

'Oh. Whoops.'

Whoops indeed. Was this the sort of thing that happened when two witches got together? Three, if you included Edith?

Does this mean I accept that witches exist?

'We can never let this become public.' She was thinking aloud.

Bryony said, 'I know. Gruesome fuss and nobody'd believe us anyway.' She picked up one of the volumes and flipped pages. 'She was quite careful, actually. It seems obvious to us because of what we know, but a real dyed-in-the-wool sceptic would probably be able to argue it away. *Can this really have happened?* she says here. *Is John really real?* You could claim she was some bonkers, hysterical spinster having hallucinations.'

'I don't think she was, though,' Rosalind said.

'No, I don't think so either.' Bryony put the book down. 'What a good thing she bit the bullet and reworked the novel around that missing sequence. And what a good thing she submitted it to Maxwell Harvey.'

'Very true.'

'But,' Bryony continued, 'you know what I would really love to find? What I want most of all to find? What I have wanted to find for absolutely years, ever since I discovered that first edition of The Holly and the Ivy – which, by the way, Circe never explained how she had?'

'The missing pages,' Rosalind said.

'The missing pages,' Bryony said. 'But if they're not here and they're not at the Forge, where on the planet are they, and how will we ever find them?

EPILOGUE

Next Year

PAUL BELL LEFT HIS WIFE AND GRANDCHILDREN ENJOYING ICE creams at one of the round ironwork tables outside the tea shop and walked up the cobbled hill towards the signboard he recognised from the website, projecting out over the pavement like a pub sign. There was the sort of early evening sunshine that washed everything in gold, and made you want to bask.

They'd had moans from the kids earlier, excited to be on their way to Ullswater with Nanna and Granddad and longing to get there and put the tent up, but Ravensburn wasn't much of a detour and even kids couldn't whinge for long in this weather. The ice creams helped too.

The village was more compact than he had anticipated, but these days small, idiosyncratic bookshops were managing to survive in even remote places thanks to internet trade. This one in particular had an ace in the hand with its Edith Waterfield connection, and it did not surprise Paul to find the place apparently thriving. Even this late in the day there were three customers on the ground floor and from the creaking joists above his head he guessed there were more upstairs.

Then the assistant on the till looked up and all thoughts of business fled.

'Good afternoon,' she said, and then, because he was tongue-tied in his confusion, 'Can I help you?'

Less vulnerable, he thought, and less timid; less like a hart in the chase. But she was still lovely, still very feminine, flowers on her dress and a fine gold necklace. He recognised her instantly.

He found his voice. 'Well, yes, I hope so. Are you the proprietor? Miss Bower?'

'Oh no, I just help out. Let me fetch her for you.'

She slipped away, and Paul set down his rucksack to wait.

The glorious sunshine streamed through the open door. A black cat strolled past, casting a sardonic glance in his direction. Half a dozen walkers in shorts and wrap-round sunglasses passed by outside.

'Here's Miss Bower.'

Paul turned round and took the second shock in two minutes as he recognised this woman too.

In fairness, despite his good memory for faces, he would probably not have remembered her had he not already seen the other woman, the gentle one. But now, as she looked him squarely in the eye and thrust her hand forward to shake, he saw again her square look across the table of paperbacks under the arches, her hand thrusting the Waterfield novel at him.

'How do you do,' she was saying. 'How can I help you?'

And these two were in business together?

They had coffee, which they told him was instant but which tasted like freshly ground, and Paul pitched his deal. Good for trade; good for the customers; a way for us both to win. Twenty minutes later they had an agreement: any Edith Waterfield books that came his way he would post to Ravensburn, and in return the Stranger Bookshop would send him surplus Enid Blytons. 'The Waterfields don't do particularly well for us,' he said, 'but Enid Blyton flies off the tables. Very retro; very cool.'

After shaking on it, he was offered a tour of the shop. 'It was the house Edith lived in all her life,' he was told by the little spiky one, and he was quietly pleased to be able to say, 'I know'.

He did. He had read it on her website.

'Who's the chap over the fireplace?' he asked.

'John Day.'

'The engraver?'

'The same.'

And at the foot of the stairs: 'Why the tapestry?'

'It's not tapestry! Tapestry is woven. This is patchwork.'

Did she speak to customers that way?

The gentle one, Rosalind Cavanagh, said mildly, 'It is an easy mistake to make,' and Paul caught the look she directed at Bryony Bower. 'We think it was sewn by Edith herself,' she added.

'Funny kind of thing to put on a wall,' he said, bruised from being corrected.

'It would have been part of a quilt for a bed,' Rosalind said. 'But it was never finished.'

'Why not?'

She paused. 'Erm…I don't know.' She paused again. 'I don't think we've asked that question. Have we?'

A different sort of look passed between them. Little dark Bryony Bower said, 'No, I don't believe we have. But we might do. Soon.' And she waggled her little dark eyebrows at her friend.

'As soon as possible, I think,' Rosalind said.

'Or even sooner.'

Paul had the feeling now that he was being hurried, but there was not much more to see. Some massive Victorian mahogany bookcases in one room; bizarrely, the broken off head of a stone angel in another. Then he was shaking hands again and heading off to collect his family.

'I lo-o-ove ice cream,' Keira was crooning over her spoon. 'I'm going to *marry* ice cream.'

Alfie ate with silent concentration.

Penny said, 'Did they agree?'

And he realised why he felt so unencumbered. His rucksack was on the floor in the shop, still full of his contribution of cat stories to cement the deal.

That woman had turned his head.

Better not mention that.

So back up the hill, gone six now, and sure enough the shop was closed. Paul was about to ring the bell, his hand raised, his finger reaching to press the button, when he realised he could see Bryony Bower sitting at the table between the shelves.

He moved along to peer through the main window, catch her attention.

She was seated with her back to him, and Rosalind Cavanagh was sitting opposite, facing the window. She should have seen him staring in, but her attention was elsewhere.

Conscious that he was spying but somehow unable to stop, Paul watched.

Rosalind held something, a cord or a chain perhaps, so that it dangled above the table, and even at a few feet distance, even through the glass, Paul sensed something of the moment. It was important, he felt, what they were doing, although he had no idea what it was.

He drew back a fraction, unwilling now to break their concentration, for concentration it undoubtedly was. He saw Rosalind Cavanagh's lips move, and the chain moved too. He watched her still the movement, then speak again, and again the chain swung.

Once more she stilled it, once more she spoke, and once more the chain moved, but this time both women started. Through the window Paul saw them stare at each other, and then, in perfect symmetry, swivel in their chairs, one to the right and one to the left, to face the patchwork that hung on the wall.

ON THEIR WAY back to the car park, Penny said, 'Really? You're sure they're the same two?'

'Definitely.'

'And now they're friends?'

'Seems so.'

A more mismatched pair it was hard to imagine. But perhaps their shared appreciation of Edith Waterfield had done it, or maybe the rural idyll in which they lived.

Or perhaps you might put it down to the sunshine.

AUTHOR'S NOTE

I hope you liked this book. If you did, please leave a review online, as this will help other readers find it – just a few words will be a huge help to me and very much appreciated!

A free book is available exclusively to members of my Reader's Group, who have signed up to my monthly newsletter. To receive your free copy of Emily's Story, read about the inspiration and personal stories behind my books, and hear advance notification of new releases, sign up to my newsletter at www.joanna-oneill.com. You can unsubscribe at any time.

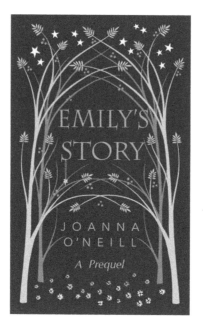

"I went through the woods that day…"

In 1839, thirteen-year-old Emily sets out to visit her grandmother and meets a dark and intriguing stranger in the woods.

Twelve years later and a hundred miles away, she meets him again, and this time he will take her on a magical journey that will alter the course of her life and the lives of generations to come.

Visit here to get started: <u>joanna-oneill.com</u>

Emily's Story stands alone but is connected to my World trilogy: A World Invisible, A World Denied and A World Possessed.

A World Invisible was my first published book, but of course it was not the first book I ever wrote, and there is a very old typescript of a rather poor story buried in a drawer somewhere here!

Having been intensely secret about everything else I had written over the years, sending A World Invisible out into the world was one of the bravest things I have ever done. There is nowhere for an author to hide, and it matters so much that people like it, or at least don't think it's ridiculous. Positive feedback is tremendously morale-boosting, but more than that, it enables other people to discover the book.

With millions of titles now available, it is only reviews that can lift a book to where it can be seen on Amazon and other on-line stores. Reviews from readers are not the same as reviews in newspapers and magazines; no analysis or summary is needed, just a line or two about whether you l liked it. I do hope you will leave a review.

Thanks!

Joanna

ALSO BY JOANNA O'NEILL

THE UNTHANK BIBLE

My name is Lenka Midnight and this is my story…

Out of work and bordering broke, city girl Maddy's life is turned around when she unexpectedly inherits a minor castle on the edge of the Northumbrian moors.

So far, so good.

But unguessed forces are at work, and Maddy's plans to measure rooms and audition estate agents are derailed when she becomes enmeshed in a trail of riddles planted by her reclusive uncle.

Struggling to keep afloat amidst the debts and decay, Maddy gradually becomes obsessed by two questions, and two questions only: just who was Lenka Midnight, and what is the significance of the Unthank Bible?

Paperback: ISBN 978-1-8384387-0-8

ebook: ISBN 978-1-8384387-2-2

ALSO BY JOANNA O'NEILL

A WORLD INVISIBLE

(Book 1 of The World trilogy)

You're telling me the Victoria and Albert Museum only exists because seven Victorians needed to hide a handful of objects for a hundred years?

Finding she can draw nothing but vines, Rebecca reluctantly puts her ambitions as an illustrator on hold when she is drawn into the machinations of a Victorian secret society founded to make safe an interface between parallel worlds.

But first she has to grow up.

Dragged into helping a cause in which she barely believes, Rebecca finds herself playing Hunt-the-Thimble amongst England's oldest institutions. Over one summer she will break a code, discover her astonishing ancestry, and half fall in love – twice.

But what begins as a game will shake her to the core.

Hardback: ISBN 978-1-9163476-4-9

Paperback: ISBN 978-0-9564432-8-1

ebook: ISBN 978-1-9163476-1-8

ALSO BY JOANNA O'NEILL

A WORLD DENIED

(Book 2 of The World trilogy)

'Stand on the island of glass and look toward the great circle.'

Three years ago Rebecca was drawn into hunting for a doorway to another world, and cannot forget the terrible consequences of finding it. And it seems she is still involved.

When the heating in her flat breaks down, Rebecca pays a visit to her friend in Oxford – good company, a change of scene, and warmth; what could be better? But by Sunday the university boathouse has burned down, there are reports of a strange animal loose on the streets, and three old Oxford professors are showing far too much interest in her.

What is being built amid the ashes on the riverbank? Who is the mysterious tramp in outlandish clothes? And what is the significance of the Queen of Clubs?

Soon Rebecca has embarked on a quest for another rift between the worlds, and this time she fears she is alone. But the World Invisible stretches wide, and there is a stranger in Vermont who is trying to reach England…

Hardback: ISBN 978-1-9163476-5-6

Paperback: ISBN 978-0-9564432-9-8

ebook: ISBN 978-1-9163476-2-5

ALSO BY JOANNA O'NEILL

A WORLD POSSESSED

(Book 3 of The World trilogy)

I always said I'd never do this. Why am I doing this?

On New Year's Day, outside the Royal Festival Hall where she is enjoying an innocent holiday among the buskers and street performers, Rebecca receives the first message, slipped into her pocket by sleight of hand while she is unaware.

And so the riddle begins. From London's South Bank to the Colleges of Oxford, from a hotel in the Peak District to her beautiful home on the Isle of Skye, Rebecca cannot evade the questions that hurtle at her thick and fast.

How many ways can you use a knife? Where did Shakespeare meet his Dark Lady? What is the point of a telescope with polarised lenses? Are foxes heroes or villains? And above all who, or what, is the Jack of Hearts?

As the significance of the messages emerges, Rebecca comes to realise that her path was laid long ago and the time is coming when she must tread it.

Hardback: ISBN 978-1-9163476-6-3

Paperback: ISBN 978-1-9163476-0-1

ebook: ISBN 978-1-9163476-3-2